DECEIVED

A Green Bayou Novel
Book Five

RHONDA R. DENNIS

Copyright © 2013 RHONDA R. DENNIS

ISBN: 1482326248
ISBN-13: 978-1482326246

DEDICATION

For you, Auntie Pat.

ACKNOWLEDGMENTS

To the people of St. Mary Parish, thank you for embracing
the series! Thank you to the Shrimp and Petroleum Festival
Board for allowing me to use their festival as a setting and to
Lee Delaune, for all you did to help that along. Brandi
Money and Ramona Clement—again two of the most
wonderful people to work with for the cover. Thank you for
helping to bring Green Bayou and Emily to life. To my
Preview Squad: You should all know how much you mean
to me by now! To my editor—thank you for helping to
make my dreams come true.

DECEIVED

RHONDA R. DENNIS

1

Being recently married to one of the most amazing men *ever* should have me basking in wedded bliss—right? Holden Dautry is damn sexy and incredible in nearly every way. He fathered my nearly three month old daughter and held the respectable position of Sheriff of Atchafalaya Parish. Wasn't I supposed to be lazily lying in bed and relishing the feel of my husband's strong embrace? Nope! Not Emily Boudreaux Dautry! All I felt was panic. Pure, heart-pounding, nausea inducing panic!

The sound of urgent pounding on the door startled us very early the morning after our wedding. My good friend, Chief Deputy Bert Hebert, came to deliver some devastating news—there were two bodies in the boat shed of my family home, Greenleaf Plantation.

Holden and I were rushing upstairs to change, but I stopped mid-step, turned, and demanded answers. "Who?" I inquired, stomach acid suddenly scorching my throat.

"Maybe we should wait to discuss this once you're dressed," Bert suggested.

"No, I want to know now!" I ran back down the stairs to confront him. "Tell me!"

Bert looked at Holden, who gave him a slight nod suggesting that he answer. Bert's gaze fell to the floor.

I sat on the bottom step before my knees buckled. "Oh, God! It's them! It's Mom and Dad!" I cried.

Bert grasped my shoulders so I'd look at him. "No, Em! No! Your parents are fine—shaken up, but fine. It's Colin and Miranda Richardson. I'm sorry. I know you were close to them."

In that instant, I understood the true meaning of the word conflicted. While I was unbelievably relieved to discover my parents were safe; I was heartbroken to hear of Colin's death.

My hands shook uncontrollably while tears welled in the corners of my eyes. "This is so tragic," I whispered. "He only just found happiness with Miranda. Colin had no enemies. I don't understand. Who would do such a thing to them? And why in our boat shed?"

"Maybe you should go upstairs while Bert and I talk this over," Holden suggested.

I sucked up my tears. "No, I want to know what's going on. I'm okay. What else do you know, Bert?" I asked after blowing out a shaky breath.

"I'd like to give you more information, but I rushed right over as soon as I found the bodies. All I can tell you is that it's Colin and Miranda and they're dead. I only went in for a second. The scene is being secured by some of the road deputies until we get there," Bert explained.

"Let's get moving," Holden said, taking my hand and practically pulling me up the stairs.

"But, I just want to know…"

"We'll get answers once we get there," he said, tossing me a t-shirt and a pair of jeans. I quickly threw them on.

Dressed in black tactical pants and a departmental polo shirt, Holden quickly fastened his gun belt around his waist. Noticing my forlorn look, he pulled me tightly into his chest. "This is a terrible way to spend our first full day as husband and wife. Are you okay, baby?"

"I hate this so much. I really thought my luck had changed."

"Ah, Em." He sighed. "I know how rough this is on you. Do you want to stay here?"

I jerked free from his embrace and stooped to put on my shoes. "No way! I'd go insane sitting here waiting for reports. I need to check on my family and I want to know what happened just as much as you do. I've managed to get through every other catastrophic incident these past years. Just add one more tic mark to the post."

"That's my girl," he said, quickly ushering me out of the door.

Greenleaf's backyard still bore signs of the prior night's festivities. The sky was pink and purple as the sun began its ascent—not yet warm enough to pull the moisture from the dew-kissed tables and chairs that were scattered under the majestic oaks. Extinguished tiki torches lined the walkways and the large, flower covered arch where Holden and I exchanged vows framed the calm Bayou Assumption. Everything was still, peaceful, and quiet—save for the occasional singing bird that flew overhead. That would all end really soon.

Dad met us on the back patio. "Do I get to know what's going on yet?" he directed to Bert.

"You don't know?" I asked Dad.

"No, Bert mumbled something about some deputies coming to secure the boathouse and that we should stay inside."

"Oh, Dad," I said, hugging him.

"What is it, Doodlebug?" he asked, his voice laden with concern.

"There was a murder, Dad," I answered.

He tightened the embrace. "A murder? In there? In our boatshed? Who? Why?"

"Colin, the ER doctor and his wife, Miranda," I answered.

Holden and Bert started to the boat shed so Dad and I followed them.

"How did they die? Was it an accident?" he asked.

"We're not sure. You want to explain, Bert?" I questioned.

"I couldn't tell you, Don. I opened the door, saw the bodies, and after checking for a pulse, called it in. Holden needed to be here. No one answered the phone, so I told the responding deputy to stand guard while I gave Holden the news. That's why I needed you to make sure no one came outdoors," Bert explained.

"I'm at a loss for words." Dad looked in deep thought as he slowly rubbed the stubble on his jaw. "What should I do?"

"We'll handle everything out here. You should warn the others that it's about to get pretty chaotic around here. Remind them to stay inside and we'll update you guys just as soon as we know something." Holden stopped at the doorway of the boathouse, nodded to the deputy standing guard, then tossed Bert a roll of yellow and black crime scene tape. "Good job, Deputy Landry. Bert, why don't you two finish tying off the perimeter?"

They silently went to work securing the area and I quickly caught up to Holden.

He stopped walking to softly palm my cheek. "You shouldn't be here. Why don't you go inside with your dad?"

"I appreciate your concern, but we both know that's not going to happen," I challenged.

His tone changed. "Don't push it, Emily. This is a

crime scene and I'm in charge. I'll handcuff you to a pillar if need be, but there's no way you're going in," he warned.

I softened my approach. "I don't doubt that for a second, but Holden, I *need* to know what happened. Yes, it's a crime scene, but I've been to crime scenes before. I know what I can and can't do. I promise not to touch anything and to stay out of the way. Please, Holden? I have to know."

He mulled it over for a bit. "I suppose you'll counter every reason I have for not wanting you in there, right?"

I slowly nodded. He shook his head.

"Fine, put these on," he said, passing me a pair of shoe covers.

After we suited up, Holden entered first and was followed closely by Bert. As soon as I crossed the threshold, my senses overloaded. Stagnant, humid air and the metallic scent of blood assailed my nostrils. My eyes worked to adjust to the dim light emanating from a single overhead bulb. Still dressed in her formal attire, Miranda was slumped against the far wall of the shed. Her discolored skin and glassy eyes left no doubt that she had been dead for some time. Colin, his back to us, lay next to her, his head in her lap. My stomach wrenched at the sight.

"Can you tell what happened?" I asked Holden once he moved to get a closer look.

"No, nothing obvious with Miranda…"

I interrupted Holden. "Wait! Bert, you said you checked for pulses, right?"

"I felt her neck and his wrist; there was nothing. Why do you ask?"

"I swear Colin just moved his finger." No one so much as breathed as we anxiously watched his hand. I was so disappointed that there was no movement. "Oh, just forget it. It was probably the lighting messing with my eyes," I said, rubbing them.

I gasped when I was once again able to focus. Though the motion was barely detectible, his little finger definitely twitched. Forgetting all about my promise to not touch anything, I dropped to my knees to feel for a carotid pulse.

"Oh, my God! He's still alive!" I yelled, quickly turning him over. "Get an ambulance here, now!"

Holden immediately keyed up his radio to summon medical assistance while Bert squatted next to me.

"Emily, I swear that I felt for a pulse," he insisted, nervously running his fingers through his hair.

"You checked his wrist. If the blood pressure's too low, you won't feel it there," I explained, lowering my face to check Colin's breathing. "Run to the house and get Connie. I'll need her help. There's a medic bag in the closet under the stairs. Hurry!"

I rolled Colin to his back. Dark crimson blood soiled the lower half of his white dress shirt; a bullet hole tore through the middle of the large stain. Buttons flew when I ripped open his shirt to expose the injury. Holden anxiously looked on.

"I need your help. Let's roll him so I can check for an exit wound." An intense feeling of déjà vu consumed me. *Don't be like Jacob. Have an exit wound. Please don't be like Jacob.*

Holden didn't hesitate. I exhaled when I discovered the hole in Colin's upper back.

"How can I help?" Connie, Bert's wife asked, quickly taking in the scene. Holden moved away so she could take the spot next to me.

Since she was a nurse, I pulled a blood pressure cuff and stethoscope from the bag she set down between us.

"Would you get vitals while I set up the IV's?"

"No problem." She quickly cut away what remained of Colin's shirt and slid the cuff into place. I was just inserting the second catheter into Colin's arm when my coworkers, Carter Melancon and Joe Naquin, entered the shed.

"What's going on Em? Whoa! Shit! Is that Dr. Richardson?" Carter asked in disbelief.

"It is and he needs to get to the hospital yesterday. Where's the stretcher?"

All Carter had to do was nod and Joe took off, quickly reappearing with the stretcher before I could finish giving a report.

"Are you riding in with us? I could use the extra hands," Carter asked.

I looked at Holden. "Go. We've got this. Connie, would you mind following her to make sure she gets home okay?"

"Not at all. Celeste said she and Don would keep an eye on the kids for us. I'll be right behind you, Em."

I didn't have time to think, much less respond to her—I was running on full medic autopilot. After hanging the IV bags on the hooks overhead, I took my seat across from Colin and went to work helping Carter stabilize him. Joe slammed the back doors and we were en route to the hospital that Colin normally worked—Bienville.

It wasn't until much later, as I sat near the helipad watching the medical helicopter whisk Colin off to a larger, better equipped facility that the full weight of the situation hit me. He barely clung to life, his beautiful wife was gone, and it all happened at *my* wedding. The curse was still intact. I let out a disheartened sigh as I fell to my knees. The whirl of the helicopter blades tossed my hair about, each golden-blonde strand whipping solidly against my face. I began to wail; the roar of the helicopter's engine concealed the sound of my anguish. I was sick and tired of the relentless pain, death, and trauma. For half a second I considered ditching everything and running as far away from Louisiana as I could.

Connie hugged me tightly, not letting go until the air ambulance was a tiny speck on the horizon. "Are you all cried out, sweetie?"

I nodded, pulling away to wipe my face with the corner of my shirt. "I guess we should get back to Greenleaf."

"Are you sure you're ready? There's no rush."

"I appreciate the offer, but no. I need to check in with Holden and I can guarantee that Celeste wants to have a full spread prepared for anyone and everyone who responds. I suppose we should offer to help her."

Connie's lip curled upwards. "That sounds like your mom for sure. I can picture her outside with a silver tray filled with coffee and beignets, chasing down the crime scene guys. 'Excuse me, Coroner Blenman, could I interest you in some refreshments? If beignets aren't to your liking, I have a full buffet inside,'" she said, giving her best impression of my mother.

I had to join in. "I hope that Eggs Benedict with homemade hollandaise, fresh seasonal fruit, as well as grillades and grits will be sufficient. I do wish I would've had more time to prepare, but I'm afraid it's the best I can offer with such short notice. Don, please tell the Coroner that we would have offered much more variety if we'd had more notice," I mocked.

As soon as Connie saw me crack, she started giggling. "I'm so happy to have a friend who appreciates gallows humor."

"Me, too. I'm really sorry that you and Bert keep getting dragged into my messes."

"It's not like you're doing it on purpose, Em!"

"I know, but I still feel responsible."

"Well, cut it out! No more apologies."

It wasn't long before we turned into my driveway, which was now filled with a variety of emergency vehicles. I took a cleansing breath before going inside for an update.

"You're home! How's Colin? Are you hungry? I cooked breakfast for everyone," Mom said, rushing toward me with Kimberly in her arms. Connie and I exchanged a quick knowing glance.

Andre barreled around the corner and smashed heavily into his mother's shins. Connie shuffled back, flailing her arms to keep her balance. "Did you miss me, son?" She laughed as she scooped him up and he leaned forward, eyes unblinking with his precious little lips poking out in duck face. He patiently waited for a smooch. Connie and I couldn't help but laugh.

"No, Mom. I'm not hungry right now, but I'll get something soon." I took Kimberly long enough to give her a soft kiss on her forehead. "Is Holden still out back?"

"As far as I know," she answered.

"Let me check in with him and then I'll come get the baby. I'm sure that you and Dad could use a break."

"No need. It's nearly her nap time and she's been no trouble whatsoever. Go and do what you need to do and don't worry one iota about this little sweetheart." She took Kimberly into her arms and gently patted her back.

"If you see Bert out there will you tell him that I'm taking Andre to the park? It'll do him and me good to burn off some of this energy. I have my cell phone if you guys need me."

"I'll be sure to tell him. You have fun 'swiding down', little guy!" I squatted down and puckered up for a kiss. Andre's duck face reemerged and I giggled when I accepted the show of affection from my adorable godchild.

"Be sure to call me if you find out anything," Connie insisted.

"I promise," I said as I made a shooing motion toward the front door. As soon as she was gone, I went in search of Holden. He was talking with a group of uniformed officials out back. I caught his eye and he quickly finished up his conversation.

"How's Colin?" he asked.

"Critical, but stable. They airlifted him to DeSoto."

"That's good." He cupped the back of his neck with his palm. "Emily, I need to talk to you about something. Maybe you should sit." He pulled out one of the patio chairs, and with a sinking feeling in my stomach, I slowly took the offered seat. Rapid and random thoughts plagued my mind until one stood out more than the others. It was the memory of getting the phone call the day Pete was shot. Our positions were far too reminiscent of that day so I jumped from my seat.

"Can we sit on the swing instead?" I asked.

Holden looked slightly confused, but agreed nonetheless. "We're pretty sure we know what happened. Of course, we won't be certain until we can interview Colin, but I'd say the odds are pretty good that this theory is accurate."

"Tell me."

"I will, but first, you need to know that there was a third casualty."

"You found another body?" I asked with surprise.

"Not me. A fisherman did. Brad was floating in the

bayou not far from here."

"Brad's dead?" I asked with disbelief before briefly zoning out. *Could it be true? After years of being stalked, threatened, and near-death more times than I cared to count; was my nightmare finally over?*

Holden's voice snapped me out of it. "I'll explain about Brad in a minute. I'll start from the beginning, based upon the evidence we've found. When the detectives searched the pockets of Colin's jacket, they found a note jotted on one of our wedding napkins. Miranda asked Colin to meet her in the boat shed for sex."

I gave him a confused look.

"Brad was already in there when Miranda arrived. Colin came in later and found Brad sexually assaulting her. The men fought and Miranda tried to help Colin. She was fatally wounded in the process; the coroner seems to think a broken neck. Brad took advantage of the confusion and drew a weapon. Colin lunged for the gun, but Brad fired at the same time. Even though Colin was hit, he still had enough momentum and weight on his side to throw Brad off balance. Brad hit his head and was knocked unconscious as he fell into the water. His body floated out of the shed and into the bayou. Colin, too weak to go for help, curled up next to Miranda and stayed that way until Bert found him this morning. The coroner has already come and gone so the people you see out there are detectives finishing up with the crime scene."

"It's all too tragic to fathom. My heart breaks for them, Holden."

He hugged me tightly against his chest. "I know, baby. I know."

I pulled away to look at him. "I can't say that I'm sorry about Brad, though."

"Yeah, you aren't the only one. Are you okay?"

I gave a half-smile as I nodded. "I'm fine."

He hugged me again. "I'm almost done out here. Why don't you go inside and visit with your parents?"

"Okay. But before I go… Holden, I don't ever want a day to pass without me telling you how much I love you."

His expression morphed from his stern, straight-laced work face to one of softened, heartfelt endearment. "Don't you worry about that. I know how much you love me. You realize the feeling is mutual, right?"

"When you look at me like that I do."

He rose, leaning in to give me a gentle kiss on the forehead. "See you in a few minutes."

I watched as he walked across the yard to the group of detectives standing near the crime scene. So many thoughts flooded my mind. *Brad's gone. How is it possible to feel so horrible, yet so relieved at the same time? These constant conflicting emotions are draining me. Wait, even though Brad's gone, it's not like all is resolved. Donovan's still out there. Would he come after me? He didn't seem to have a personal vendetta. He got his money and his drugs. Maybe he's on a beach in Mexico, never to be heard from again. Not everyone carries a grudge to the extent that Brad carried his. Donovan may very well leave us alone. Besides, his resentment was directed at Roberta, not me. But, what if he comes after Holden?* Refusing to succumb to the "what-ifs", I went inside to see my parents.

2

A week and a half after the incident, Connie agreed to keep the baby for me so I could visit Colin in the hospital. With a full diaper bag slung over one shoulder, my purse dangling from my elbow, the baby carrier in my hands, and my keys precariously dangling between my teeth, I opened the door to find my mother-in-law, Luciana Dautry, standing on the front porch. As usual, everything from her perfectly styled hair to her custom tailored clothing oozed sophisticated perfection. The expression on her face told that the jeans and t-shirt combo I wore was unsatisfactory to her. Ignoring her condescending gaze, I looked past her to the massive security guard/driver decked in dark sunglasses and a designer suit. He was just as intimidating as ever.

I quickly pulled the keys from my mouth. "Luciana. What a surprise."

The relationship with my mother-in-law could best be described as guarded. When we first met, she called me a whore, and even went as far as forging paperwork and having me arrested so I'd stay away from her son. Once Holden returned to town, she supposedly had a change of heart. Ever the optimist, I tried to give her the benefit of the doubt. Holden—not so much. He repeatedly warned me that she was up to no good.

"I'm sorry to stop by unannounced. Obviously, I've

caught you at a bad time. I'm on my way to visit Stephen's gravesite and I hoped to visit with my granddaughter for a little while before going to the cemetery."

Shuffling the load I was carrying, I moved aside to let her pass. "Sure. I'll run my errand later. Please, come inside," I said with far more enthusiasm than I felt. The security guard remained in place. "You can come in, too."

"No, ma'am. Mrs. Dautry, I'll return to the car until you're ready to depart."

"Are you talking to me Mrs. Dautry or her Mrs. Dautry? Maybe you should come up with a codename for her," I joked.

He wasn't amused in the least. "My statement was intended for Luciana Dautry," he said dryly.

"I see," I said, suddenly uncomfortable. I nervously cleared my throat.

"If you'd prefer I come some other time, I can do so," Luciana offered.

"No, no need for that." I put the car seat on the floor and started to detangle myself from the variety of straps that ran across my body. Luciana looked at me curiously.

"Later, Tank," I said, reaching over to swat the door closed.

The security guard used his gargantuan foot to stop it midway. "Are you referring to me?"

"Wow, you have zero sense of humor. Yes, I was referring to you and I'm sorry if you were offended. What should I call you?"

"Dick."

I laughed. "Let me guess! The last name is Head? You *do* have a sense of humor! Good one. No, really. What do I call you?"

His nostrils flared. I turned to glance at Luciana and

was instantly mortified when I noticed the look on her face.

"Dick is a great name—very strong and professional sounding. Are you sure I can't get you something. Tea, lemonade?" I quickly rambled with embarrassment.

Without a word he turned on his heel and walked to the waiting SUV.

"I'm sorry if I offended him, I just meant to…"

Luciana stopped me by holding up her hand. "He's probably the crankiest security guard ever, but he does an excellent job. I can't complain."

I squatted down and unbuckled Kimberly from her seat. "I know it's incredibly forward of me but I have to ask. Why do you have a security guard with you all of the time?"

"I'm sure you know that my father's oil investments made him quite wealthy. He was always concerned that someone might try to kidnap me for ransom, so as far back as I can remember my mother and I had security with us when we went out. Oh, the trouble I got into the night I met Stephen at that football game! My father was furious when he found out that I went unprotected. Stephen promised him that he'd never have to worry about that again, so even after we married, I was still expected to call for security when I went out alone. I find it much easier just to keep him on staff full-time."

"Wow, I can't imagine living under lock and key like that. Oh wait! I have had a taste of it. I didn't like it," I said, passing Kimberly to her.

She looked surprised.

"Is something wrong?" I asked.

"I can't say that I've ever met anyone quite like you."

"Should I be offended or flattered?" I pulled the filled baby bottles from the diaper bag.

"Not offended."

"But not flattered, either." I finished her sentence for her. "Follow me. I'm going to put these into the refrigerator; you can have a seat in the den. Can I offer you something to drink?"

"Anything would be fine. Please don't go to any trouble."

She was lovingly smiling down at Kimberly when I came back with a tray of cookies and two glasses of freshly made strawberry lemonade.

"Where is your mother today? I would like to make amends with her, as well."

"She and Dad are in Baton Rouge for the day."

"Will you please pass on that I was sorry to have missed her?"

"Certainly," I said, taking a seat across from her. "So what is it about me that you're so unsure about?" I bit into one of the cookies.

Luciana practically choked on her lemonade. "Your straightforwardness, and the fact that you're willing to give me another chance after I treated you so horribly. I wish your husband could be as understanding."

"I can't speak for Holden, but I generally try to offer forgiveness. Sometimes I'm not so successful, but I try to remember that no one in this world is perfect and that people can change."

"How nice." She smiled broadly.

"Yes, but as nice as forgiveness is, I *never* forget," I said, looking her straight in the eye.

She sat rigid in her seat, her smile fading to a mere superficial grin. "I understand."

I shifted to a more neutral tone. "If you don't mind, would you tell me more about Holden's father? He doesn't speak of him often."

"Unfortunately, Holden probably doesn't have many memories of him. He was so young at the time of the accident, and then Stephen went to live in a private facility. Prior to the accident, Stephen was gone much of the time on business."

"It must have been difficult for Holden."

"It was. I wish he had better memories. He rarely visited him when he was in the facility. I'm afraid his father didn't have much of an impact on his life."

"I think he may have had more of an impact than you realize. Did you know that Holden credits the accident for his career choice? He wanted justice for his father and for his brother."

"Does he now? He never divulged that to me. I just assumed he was being rebellious," Luciana said.

"He told me that the drunk driver who caused the accident was never found and he wanted to do everything in his power to make sure that didn't happen to another family. He knows that he can't save them all, but he wants to try."

A trace of something flashed across Luciana's face. What was it? Fear? Guilt? Uncertainty?

"Well, that's quite admirable, wouldn't you say?"

"Absolutely," I agreed.

Luciana smiled down at the baby. "It still amazes me that she looks so much like her father. Many of Holden's features came from his father, but his build, it's just like my father's. He was a tall, muscular man who commanded full attention just walking into a room."

"I assume that your father has passed on?"

"Oh, yes. Fifteen years ago."

"I'm sorry. You were obviously close to him."

"Thank you. I was close to him. My mother wasn't around much. I honestly can't say why. I wasn't allowed to talk about her."

My brows furrowed.

"Don't fret about it. It was a different era. I made peace with it all a long time ago. I was Daddy's princess and I grew up receiving anything I ever asked for. Before he died, he made sure that Holden and I would want for nothing. In fact, little Kimberly will be well provided for, too."

"That's nice to know, but perhaps you should discuss that with Holden."

"You mean to tell me that you're not in the least bit interested in learning about your husband's or your child's net worth?" she asked, skepticism in her tone.

"As long as she's healthy, has food to eat, and a roof over her head; I'm happy."

Luciana slowly looked around the room, arching one eyebrow high in the air. "Really? So if you lost all of this and were forced to raise your daughter in a tiny shack, you'd be okay with it?"

"I'd like to think so. It wouldn't be ideal, but…"

Luciana smirked. "Oh Emily, I get the feeling you'd be singing a different tune if you found yourself forced to live in near poverty."

"Okay, so I'm fortunate to have wealthy parents. Notice the use of the word 'fortunate'? I'm grateful for what we have," I snapped.

"I never implied that you weren't. I'm just saying that there's no need to play martyr with me. You're family now, so naturally, I'm sure you have questions about assets—especially since you and Holden didn't so much as discuss a pre-nup."

I angrily stood. "Is that what you're here for? You're worried that I'm going to try to drain you and Holden dry? I have no idea how much money Holden does or doesn't have, and I mean it with the utmost sincerity when I say *I don't care*. Every time I try to bond with you, you insult me! I'm done. Get out," I said, reaching for the baby.

She twisted away from me. "Stop that! Would you kindly take your seat?"

"Why is it so hard for you to believe that I'm a good person with no ulterior motives?" I asked, slowly moving away from her.

"Because every person I've ever come in contact with has wanted something from my family. It's sad, but true."

"You know what? I do want something from you. I want you to be a decent mother-in-law to me and a loving grandmother to Kimberly. But, that's where it ends."

"That's *all* you want?"

"That's all. I swear."

She sighed heavily. "I suppose I should believe you."

"Thank you. That means a lot to me. It's time for Kimberly's bottle. Would you like to feed her?"

"I'd love to."

"Great. I'll be back in just a minute."

On the way to the kitchen I mumbled to myself about Luciana's insulting speech, but once I got in there I stopped and took a deep breath. Once my full composure was regained, I warmed a bottle and carried it into the den. Luciana, though quiet, was all smiles as she fed the baby. Kimberly finished eating and Luciana rose from the sofa.

"I've enjoyed seeing both of you. Thank you for allowing me to visit even though I dropped in unexpectedly." She handed the baby to me and rummaged through her bag. "Here. This is the paperwork for Kimberly's trust fund. I've set it up so she will have access to a portion when she turns eighteen, then at various milestones in her life, she'll receive allotments. If you wish to simply hand the paperwork over to Holden, so be it. If you'd like to peruse it, that's acceptable, as well."

"You didn't have to do this, Luciana. Does Holden know you've set up a trust for Kimberly?"

"No, but it's set up quite similar to the one his grandfather established for him."

"I see. Thank you for looking out for her future well-being."

"She's family, and we Balladeno's take care of family. Goodbye, Emily. I hope we can get together again in the near future—perhaps for dinner?"

"Dinner sounds lovely. I'd be happy to cook."

"You cook? How interesting."

"I suppose that means you don't."

"I tried once. I wasn't very good at it. Ask Holden," she said with a contagious smile.

"I'll do that."

"Goodbye, Emily and goodbye sweet, sweet Kimberly. Nonna loves you. It's okay if she addresses me as Nonna, isn't it?"

"Sure," I said, shrugging my shoulders.

Dick was standing at the door when I opened it. The imp in me wanted to antagonize him a little bit more, but the sedate mother holding her sleeping newborn decided against it. Dick was spared that day, but I'm pretty sure he snarled at me when he turned to walk away.

I put Kimberly in her crib and called Connie to tell her that I'd bring the baby over later in the afternoon. She wanted a play by play of Luciana's visit, but Andre took a dive off of her sofa, so she had to go. The envelope Luciana gave me was on the coffee table. I thought about calling Holden to discuss it with him, but curiosity got the best of me. I broke the seal and glanced over the paperwork. *Legal mumbo jumbo. More legal mumbo jumbo. Turn the page. When Kimberly turns eighteen she'll receive a lump sum of one million dollars and an additional million every five years after that.* My mouth went dry. *Upon completion of a college degree one million. Marriage-one million. One million at the birth of each child. Luciana said Kimberly's trust was set up similar to Holden's. Dear God, how much was my husband worth?*

I put the documents back in the envelope and waited a few minutes before dialing the phone.

"Hello, gorgeous. Calling to tell me how much you miss me?" Holden asked.

"I miss you terribly, but that's not why I'm calling. Your mother stopped by today."

His tone changed. "Really? Was she on her best behavior?"

"So-so. Nothing to get upset about though," I quickly threw in when I heard him grumble.

"What did she want?"

"To visit with Kimberly and to drop off the paperwork to her trust fund."

"Really? Was she fair with Kimberly's portion?"

"I think she was more than generous."

"Tell me about it."

"Basically, once she turns eighteen, she'll get a million, then every five years after that the same. Plus, she'll get a million for every special event that occurs in between."

"Eh, I guess that's good. I wouldn't be surprised if she ups it later on down the road."

"Are you kidding me?"

"Sweetheart, you can't even fathom how much my

mother's worth."

"And you're only now telling me this?"

"I thought you knew."

"No! Why would I?"

"I don't know? Are you curious to know how much I get for my birthdays?" he teased.

"No, that's between you and your mom and whoever controls all that stuff."

Holden laughed. "I love you. I'll be home around five-thirty."

"I love you, too. I might be at the hospital visiting Colin. Connie's going to keep Kimberly for us."

"Okay, I'll pick her up on my way home. Please be careful on the road."

"I will."

"Hey, Em…"

"What?"

"Two million every birthday."

"Holden! I told you not to tell me!"

"Oh well, too bad." I could still hear him laughing when he disconnected the call.

~.~.~.~.~

A shiver went through my body as the automatic doors of DeSoto General Hospital swooshed open. The ban against me had been lifted long ago, but it still felt awkward crossing the threshold. I made a beeline for the elevator and sighed with relief when the car stopped on the sixth floor without any interruption. I stopped for a second outside of Colin's door before gently rapping. When I got no response, I pressed the latch and slowly opened the door. His eyes opened.

"Emily, come on in," he said, his voice still weak.

"Hi! I didn't mean to wake you."

"Don't worry about that. All I ever seem to do is sleep."

I smiled. "How are you feeling?"

"I won't lie, it hurts."

"I'm sure it does. You've been through a lot."

Colin nodded. "Sit down and tell me what I've been missing. Any breaks in the case?"

"No, I'm sorry."

He closed his eyes and turned away from me.

"I wish I had better news. I would've visited sooner, but I got a surprise visit from my mother-in-law."

His eyes flew open. "Lucifer Dautry?"

"It's okay. She wasn't too harsh this time. She brought a very nice gift for Kimberly."

"Well, sounds like you two are making progress. You must be winning her over with your charm."

"More like tormenting her with my charm. She gets uncomfortable when I'm nice to her."

Colin let out a chuckle, though he was soon coughing and guarding his abdomen. "Damn this sucks!"

"Any clue as to how long you'll be here?"

"Actually, I'm glad you brought that up. They'll be releasing me in a couple of days and there's something you should know."

I looked at him curiously. "What is it?"

"Once I'm released, I'm going back to the beach. I'm putting the house on the market and I'll be staying at my uncle's resort until I'm well enough to decide what to do next. As much as I like Green Bayou, it's too painful to even consider staying here without Miranda." He worked to choke back his tears. It took all I had not to join him. "I really loved her, Emily."

"That's obvious."

"Really? Do you think she knew how much?"

"I'm sure she did, and I know that she loved you just as much."

He closed his eyes and let out a slow, deep breath. "How long until the pain gets tolerable?"

I looked out of the window. "It depends," I said softly. "Everyone has their own way of grieving. As much as I love Holden, not a day goes by that I don't feel sad, guilty, or upset about losing Pete. If you remember, I was housebound for six months after his death. There's no telling how much longer that would've lasted if Holden hadn't gotten involved."

"No one can possibly understand what this is like unless they've lived it."

I slowly nodded. "I hate that you're going to leave town, but I understand why you're doing it. Will you promise to keep in touch?"

"Of course." He reached for my hand. "You've been a good friend to me."

"You're just saying that because I kept you in business. Who's going to stitch me up now?" I teased, trying my best not to cry.

"I guess I should leave an instruction manual for the new doctor, or at the very least, a warning to watch out for the Boudreaux clan."

"That was one hell of a Thanksgiving, wasn't it?"

"One that I'll never forget."

"How long until you move?"

"As soon as I'm released. My uncle's hired a moving company and the house is supposed to be cleared out by tomorrow." He suddenly got quiet.

"What's wrong?"

"I don't remember much about what happened in that boat shed. Just vague bits and pieces."

"Maybe you should talk to a therapist, Colin. It's something that will take time and help to work through."

He nodded slowly.

"I'll miss you," I said, giving his hand a slight squeeze.

"I know. It's getting late. Stop worrying about me and get on home to your baby and your husband."

"Hey, I'm supposed to be the bossy one!"

He smiled. "I learned from the best."

"And don't you ever forget it." I leaned over and gently kissed his forehead. "Bye, Colin."

"Bye, Em. Now that Brad's gone, I hope that your life will finally settle down."

"Me, too. So far, so good." I said, giving him two thumbs up and a grin. As usual, my comment was premature. Would I ever learn to keep my big mouth shut?

3

Dad was sitting at the kitchen table, deep in conversation with Holden, and Mom was finishing up a gravy to go with the scrumptious smelling pork roast that was smothered down with lots of onions and bell peppers.

"Hi, my sweet girl! Would you mind setting the table?"

"Sure, Mom. Supper smells really good!" Before getting the plates from the cabinet, I bent to give Holden a quick kiss.

"How's Colin?" he asked.

"As well as can be expected," I answered. "He's moving back to Gulf Shores and will be staying at his uncle's resort. The house next door is going to be on the market within the next week or so."

"I'm sorry to see him go, but I understand his reason," Holden commented.

I nodded as I helped Mom serve dinner. Once I was seated, all eyes were on me.

I put down my fork. "What? Did I miss something?" I asked warily.

"I need to talk to you," Holden said.

"I don't like it when you start conversations like that, Holden Dautry. What's up?" I looked to my parents for clues, but they offered none. Dad was shoveling in rice and gravy like nobody's business and mom was concentrating a little too hard on the roll she was buttering. I tried to brace myself for whatever was about to come out of Holden's mouth.

"You remember that I promised to keep you better informed of departmental situations, right? What I'm about to tell you is *not* public knowledge."

"Okay," I said cautiously.

"I have information from a very credible source that Donovan Guidry didn't make it out of the parish. I know where he is and we'll be taking him down soon. But, I don't want you or the baby anywhere around when we do it."

"What? As if! It's not like I'll be in the squad car with you when you make the arrest. Why would you want me to leave?"

"Because if he gets away, this will be the first place he comes."

"So why don't Kimberly and I stay at your house?"

"I don't want you out there alone. Crusher Landry worked for Donovan, so he may very well know where my house is located."

I sighed. "What do you two know about this?" I asked my parents.

Dad looked up from his plate long enough to briefly glance in Holden's direction, then went right back to shoveling food. Mom, who was still buttering the same roll, finally put down her knife and took a bite.

"Oh, come on! Just tell me!"

"I want you and the baby to go with your parents on a road trip. It won't be too far away, I'll know you're safe, and you'll be going to a place where you'll have lots of fun."

"Where are we supposed to go?"

"To Morgan City for the Shrimp and Petroleum

Festival," Dad answered excitedly. "I used to have tons of fun when I went as a kid and your mother's excited about seeing the arts and crafts exhibits. It'll be a blast, Doodlebug."

I gave him an unsure look.

"Bert's going to be with me, so Connie and Andre can go with you guys," Holden said.

That got a smile out of me. "Okay, I'm slowly warming to the idea."

"And your father and I are more than happy to watch the kids so you and Connie can enjoy listening to the bands and whatnot," Mom said.

"Okay, I'm in!" I said excitedly.

"There's one more thing I need to tell you about the trip," Holden said.

"Great! Here comes the bad news! Don't drag it out, just tell me."

"Roberta will be going, too."

"That's not so bad. We've been getting along pretty well lately. She's Donovan's primary target; it makes sense that she should come along," I said, finally relaxing enough eat.

"Alphonse is going with you guys. He requested time off so he could personally protect her."

I dropped my fork. "You're the Sheriff! Deny his vacation request!" I fussed.

"I can't do that. He's worked for the department over ten years and has only taken vacation twice, and one of those times he was forced to take it. He'll be in his own quarters. He told me that he bought a tent so he'll be able to 'hear, smell, and sense a prowler much better than staying in the RV.'"

I rolled my eyes.

"Come on baby, his senses are now 'poaned'." Holden

tried his best not to laugh.

"He did not," I said, shaking my head at Alphonse's newest vocabulary flub.

"And he's more 'millagent' than ever. He's 'demoted' to this." Holden was spot on with his Alphonse impersonation.

I laughed so hard tears started to fall. "Oh, Holden! Please don't make me spend my Labor Day weekend with him!"

"It's a small sacrifice to make so that your husband can have peace of mind knowing that you and his child are nowhere near the danger zone. Will you do this for me, please?" he pleaded.

"Ugh, cut the drama. Okay, I'll go! But be warned, I'm going to drink lots of Hurricanes and I'm going to dance to the bands like nobody's business."

"If that's what makes you happy then dance away. Just don't do it provocatively and no dancing with anyone handsomer than I am."

I gave him a sensual smile. "I seriously doubt such a man exists."

"Is that so?" he asked, sliding his seat closer to mine. He cupped my cheek, using his thumb to gently stroke my lower lip.

I kissed his palm, my eyes never leaving his. "It's a fact."

Dad loudly cleared his throat. "Okay you two, save it for later."

"Leave them alone, Don!" Mom snapped. "It warms my heart to see them so in love."

"Yeah, we're newlyweds, Dad. We're entitled," I huffed as I scooted my chair back to its original position.   "So when are we supposed to leave?"

"We pull out tomorrow around lunchtime. It shouldn't

take us more than a couple of hours to get there, so I figure we'll be enjoying ourselves by mid-afternoon. I reserved a spot at the local campground for us and you, Connie, and the kids will stay in one of the cabins. There's a beach, boating, and lots of other fun things to do. Even though the festival technically starts tomorrow afternoon, we'll likely relax at the campground and wait until Friday to go. How does all that sound?"

"It sounds good to me. I hope it turns out to be as fun as you say it will be."

"It'll be as much fun as you make it, Doodlebug. Laissez les bon temps rouler!"

Later that evening, I gently placed a sleeping Kimberly into her crib in the nursery. She stirred slightly and quickly drifted off once again. I smiled down adoringly at my precious baby for several minutes before finally going into my bedroom. The shower was still running. I pumped several globs of moisturizer into the palm of my hands and rubbed in onto my legs.

The bathroom door swung open and when the steam slowly cleared, a nearly nude Holden was slowly revealed to me. One towel was fastened around his exquisitely chiseled mid-section; another he used to vigorously whisk beads of water from his hair. His tanned biceps bulged when he raised his arms to smooth his dark hair down. Seeing him in such a state caused my pulse to rapidly accelerate. I slowly stalked him with my eyes as he made his way to the dresser and pulled out a pair of sleep pants. He was tying a knot in the drawstring when he caught me staring at him.

"If you come on over here I'll let you do more than

look."

I smiled. "What if I don't want to go over there?"

"I noticed the way you were looking at me; you want to," he said with a suggestive smirk. His eyes darkened and his fingers slowly twirled the ends of his drawstring. "I promise to make it worth your while."

There wasn't a chance of me turning down that offer so I eased from my seat and slowly moved towards him. As soon as I was within reach he swiftly tugged the ribbon that fastened my robe. His fingers lightly drifted across my shoulders and it fell into a satiny pile at my feet. He turned me away from him, draping one arm across my chest, the other around my waist. Once my body was molded against his, he trailed slow, sweet kisses across my upper back and down my neck. I felt a combination of sensations: the warmth of his breath, the softness of his lips, and the bristly coarseness of his facial stubble—it made me quiver. He released me from his hold and I turned to face him. I offered my lips up to him, but he pulled away.

"I want you to get in the bed, face down," he requested.

"What? Why?"

"You don't have to know everything, Emily. Just do it."

My nostrils flared and I held my held my head high, but he wasn't intimidated in the least. With a huge grin on his face, he nodded toward the bed.

"Fine." Convinced I'd give him a taste of his own medicine, I concentrated on each step, carefully putting extra swing in my hips. Hoping to tantalize him further, I slowly crawled across the mattress and settled face down under the covers. My skin prickled with the anticipation of Holden's touch.

I looked back to see Holden walking out of the bathroom. "Hey! You missed my sexy walk," I complained.

"Hey, yourself! I didn't miss a thing. Stay on your stomach like you are. No peeking."

I rolled my eyes and huffed out a disappointed sigh before interlacing my fingers and letting my head rest on my hands. Unexpectedly, the covers were pulled from my body and tossed onto the floor. I was about to protest when I felt Holden's big, strong hands slowly gliding up and down my back. I moaned loudly when I felt the exhilaratingly warm oil spread across my skin.

"Feel good?" he whispered into my ear.

"Mmmm hmmm"

"That's what I want to hear."

I inhaled the musky vanilla aroma from the massage oil as he thoroughly worked on every tense, tight muscle of my neck, back, and legs. I was the one getting massaged, but when he leaned across my body to rub my calves, it was very obvious that he was enjoying it, too.

"Why Mr. Dautry, I do believe the beast has come to life."

"Mrs. Dautry, the very sight of you is enough to unleash the beast," he whispered.

I rolled to face him. "Let me give you a rub down?"

"No way. Tonight's all about you," he said, pouring more oil into his hands. "I'm glad you turned over. Now I get to massage some of my favorite parts."

I let the pleasure wash over me as he firmly kneaded my arms and shoulders. My body drifted into a deeper and deeper state of relaxation. The next thing I remember, it was morning and Holden was staring down at me.

"You fell asleep," he fussed.

"What?" I sat up to wipe the sleep from the corners

of my eyes. "Fell asleep during wha... Oh!" I said sheepishly.

"I can't believe you fell asleep! What a blow to my ego!"

"Wait, you stayed up all night staring at me?"

"No, I woke up ten minutes ago when your snoring reached unbearable levels."

"I do not snore, Holden Dautry?"

"Then there's a buzz saw hidden under our bed."

My mouth hung open with indignation. "I can't believe you said that!"

He started to laugh. "Did you sleep well? I'm guessing you did."

"I did." I curled up next to him. "You should be flattered. The feel of your strong hands on my rigid, tense body..."

"Save it," he said jokingly.

I sighed loudly. "Kimberly and I have to leave you today."

"I'm not happy about it either, but at least I'll know you're safe with your family and that's a huge relief to me. It's only for a long weekend and I'm sure you're going to have a great time. Relax and try to enjoy yourself."

"Yeah, you'll know where *I* am and that I'm fine, but I'll have no clue as to how *you* are," I remarked.

"I promise to check in with you as often as possible and remember, Bert's gonna be with me. It's not like I'm running out there all alone."

"That's true. I guess that does make me feel a little bit better."

Holden kissed the top of my head. "Stop worrying. Everything's going to be fine. I'm going to lock that scumbag up for a very long time and hopefully I'll get the big man who's running the show at the same time. Whoever this guy is, he's been at it for a long time and he has a lot of puppets doing his bidding—judges, politicians, law enforcement, councilmen. You name it, he's got an inside man. If I can get Donovan to flip, a long chain of corruption will be broken."

"I understand your zealousness, but Holden, you're going after someone very powerful and that really scares me."

"If I turn my back on this, I'll be no better than every person on his payroll. This has gone on long enough. Someone has to take him down."

"Promise me you'll be careful. You have a young daughter and a new wife to think about."

"Baby, I love you guys way too much to leave you. I'll take every precaution possible."

"I heard that from Pete and you know how that turned out. I couldn't handle going through that again. I want you alive and in one piece when I get back. I'm going to hold you to your word, Holden."

"I've got something you can hold."

"Don't you dare try to change the subject!" I snapped.

"Okay, you win. I've heard your concerns and I've promised to be extra careful. That's all I can do."

"I suppose you're right. I'm really going to miss sleeping in *my* bed, you know?" I said with a sad sigh.

"Emily, you're going with your parents. End of story."

"Jeez, whatever you say, *Sheriff*," I joked.

"That's right and don't you forget it. I call the shots around here, little lady," he teased.

"Ass!"

"What did you call me?"

"I said gas. I hope my dad remembered to fill up with gas today. One less stop we'll need to make."

"I'll pretend to believe you.""I love you, baby," I said super sweetly.

"I love you too, Angel Lips."

4

The place was an absolute madhouse when I finally made my way downstairs. I peeked from the doorway of the back stairwell and found Mom and Connie making brunch while cackling about the upcoming trip. Dad, Bert, and Holden were at the table speaking just as loudly. Kimberly sat atop Holden's lap, turning her little head to look at whomever was speaking. Not to mention, an amped up Andre who steadily pinballed between the adults and the furniture! Bert, not missing a beat, continued his conversation with Dad while reaching out to catch an empty coffee mug Andre knocked over. I tiptoed back up the stairs.

As quietly as physically possible, I slowly crept down the front stairway, but was disappointed to find my path blocked by an overwhelming amount of luggage. *Get prepared, Emily. This is going to be one hell of a trip!* There was nowhere to run and no place to hide—my best option would be to simply embrace the madness. I plastered the largest grin I could muster on my face and took off for the kitchen with purpose. A chorus of cheery greetings welcomed me.

Connie clasped her hands in mine and eagerly jumped

up and down. "How exciting is this? We're going to have so much fun!"

"I know!" I exclaimed, trying to match her tempo.

"Nee-Nee!" Andre yelled right before he plowed his body into my lower half. I threw my arms out to catch my balance.

"What have I told you about that, Andre Peter?" Connie scolded.

"He's fine," I said, bending down to scoop the rambunctious toddler into my arms.

His little arms went around my neck and he squeezed tightly. "I miss you, Nee-Nee." He pulled back with his famous puckered lips ready to go. I had to laugh.

"Nannie missed you, too. Are you excited about our trip? I hear there's going to be lots of rides for you to have fun on."

He nodded emphatically. To his delight, I plastered his little face with kisses before putting him back down.

"Hey, Doodlebug!" Dad yelled over the rest of the chatter. "What's the name of that boy you got caught swimming naked with when we stayed in Grand Isle that time?"

There was dead silence as all eyes turned on me.

I flushed ten different shades of red. "Dad, we weren't naked and why are you telling that story? That happened when I was in high school!"

"We were talking about surprises in the water and it came up," Dad said defensively.

"If you two weren't naked, why did the mystery man get pinched by a crab in that super-sensitive spot, darling? You've been holding out on me, Emily," Holden said with a grin.

"Mom, please tell Dad to stop with the embarrassing

stories," I pleaded.

"Wait, why don't I remember that story?" Mom asked. "Are you sure you're not confusing it with the time the Coast Guard rescued her? She was nearly naked that time. How is that cute, blonde headed man you dated after he rescued you during the buoy incident? What was his name? Clay! Do you still keep in touch with him? Is he still in the Coast Guard?"

"Oh, my God! Can we please leave?" My cheeks burned like fire.

"No way! Now I've got two stories that I want to hear! Don't you want to hear 'em too, Bert?" Holden expectantly arched an eyebrow my way.

"I must say that I'm quite eager to hear all about Emily's debauchery-filled younger years," Bert answered.
I sighed heavily while shaking my head. "I plead the Fifth. Move on to a different topic, please."

"Don, surely you'll be happy to elaborate for us?" Holden asked.

"Fine!" I interrupted. "If you're going to hear the stories, you're going to hear them from me! Sometimes the facts tend to get twisted when others retell the stories." I shot my dad a look. He just smiled. "Coast Guard story, okay. We were staying in Biloxi and I rented one of those little kayak things. Instead of going out a little ways and running parallel to the shore, I paddled straight out from the beach. I was having so much fun that I completely lost track of time. I figured I needed to return the kayak so I looped around to start back. Problem was I couldn't see the shore and in my panic, my paddle went overboard. Instinctively, I tried to grab it, but when I did, the boat flipped and started to sink as it filled with water. Unfortunately, my bikini top got caught on something in the boat, so my only choices were to continue to get pulled underwater or lose the top. After I ditched it, I swam to a buoy that was bobbing not too far away. Then, as if it wasn't terrifying enough to be stranded all alone miles from shore, I suddenly remembered the possibility of sharks. I wasn't about to become shark bait, so I climbed up the buoy and latched on for dear life. It seemed like hours before I finally heard the sound of a motor. I wasn't about to miss an opportunity to get rescued, so I yelled and screamed until I grew hoarse. A Coast Guard vessel pulled up next to the buoy and thankfully, I was rescued. The end."

"And this Clay guy?"

"I hear someone outside." I practically ran to the front door, leaving a trail of moans and groans in my wake. *Why do my friends and family get so much pleasure from my embarrassment?*

A huge pickup truck with a tiny travel trailer was pulling into the driveway. My eyes narrowed as I tried to place the vehicle. Roberta popped out of the passenger side and ran up to me. "Hey, Emily! I'm so excited about our trip, aren't you?"

"I am, but what's this?" I asked.

"This here is a top of the line, pull-behind travel trailer, Emily." Alphonse affectionately tapped the side of the small camper.

I didn't realize it at first, but after hearing his description, I knew exactly where Alphonse had acquired his new possession.

"Grant sold it to you at the ESMR surplus auction, didn't he?" It was the tiny trailer that Chuck and I had used as a station after the tornado.

"He certainly did. I got it for a steal, too. Now me and Berta got a place of our own! I know I said I was gonna protect ya'll better in the tent, but I got to thinking about it.

If I'm gonna be in a tent, then I'm gonna be clean on the other side of the campground. This way, I can be right next to y'all."

I wasn't about to tell him that Connie and I were going to be staying in one of the waterfront cabins while Mom and Dad stayed in the RV. "That's wonderful, Alphonse. Do you want to come in for a bite before we head out?"

"Nah, I'm going to stay out here and run through my checklist." He pulled a pencil from behind his ear and tapped it on the clipboard.

"Okay, then. Roberta?"

"I think I'll stay out here with my Honey Bunny just in case he needs help with anything." She sidled up to him, gently nuzzling her cheek against his shoulder. I was thinking about how lovely it was that the two finally discovered each other when Alphonse suddenly jerked away from her. *The amount of physical contact Alphonse can sustain with Roberta must've increased. She's able to touch him for at least two minutes now.* Shaking my head, I returned to the kitchen.

"What was that all about?" Connie asked.

"Alphonse and Roberta have arrived."

"Great!" Connie said, putting away the last of the dishes. "Okay, is everyone packed, fed, burped, changed, and milked?"

"Connie!" I snapped incredulously.

"Is what you were doing upstairs while your mom and I fixed brunch supposed to be a secret?"

"First of all, I'm not a cow, Connie!"

"I know, but if I said pumped, well, it could be taken so many different ways. You know men use pumps to…"

"Don't finish that sentence! Kimberly's drinking formula now, so no more 'milking'. I was taking a shower and making sure everything was ready to go. If it's okay with you, may we please load up now?"

"I'll buckle the princess into her seat," Mom volunteered.

Holden softly kissed the top of Kimberly's head and handed her over to Mom. Dad and Bert loaded the piles of luggage into the storage compartment of the RV. Eager to help, Andre held out his little arms until Bert gave him one of the smaller totes.

"Come with me," Holden whispered in my ear.

"Why? What's wrong? Is this about the Coast Guard thing?" I asked, following him into the kitchen.

He laughed. "No. This is about us being apart for nearly a week."

"Need I remind you that this is all your doing?"

"It's a necessary evil."

"Are you saying you're going to miss me?" I asked teasingly.

"Terribly. I can't stop thinking about last night. You fell asleep before we got to the best part." He opened the door to the large, walk-in pantry and nodded that I should go inside.

"Oh, no. I know what's going to happen if we go in there."

"You act as though it's a bad thing." He suggestively pushed his body against mine while his fingertip gently traced the outline of my lower lip. He shut the door behind us.

"It's far from bad, but I've got a load of people waiting for me and a father itching to get on the road, so…"

Holden's lips settled on mine and there was nothing gentle about the kiss—it was pure passion. His hands laced through my hair as his tongue greedily tangled with mine. I edged against his leg and knew right away that I wasn't the only one suddenly feeling turned on. His hands left my hair and slid down my back to cup my rear. I gasped when he lifted me onto his rock hard thigh.

"Come on, Em. We'll be quick," he pleaded, his voice raspy with desire.

"Kiss me like that again and I don't know how I can resist."

A devious smirk swept across his face, and once again he tormented my senses. In addition to the knee-buckling kiss, his strong hand went under my shirt and pushed aside the cups of my bra. His fingers instantly created an inferno down below that made me squirm with anticipation. I pulled away from his kiss to breathlessly whisper, "Stop."

He raised my shirt and his tongue leisurely roamed where his fingers had recently been. "You don't really want me to stop, do you?"

My body betrayed me, my back arching deeply in response to the pleasure I was feeling from Holden's warm mouth. "No, don't stop," I breathed.

"How long do you think we have?" he asked, his fingers fumbling with the button on the waistband of my jeans.

"Emily! Where are you?" My mother's call may have been faint, but the high-pitch carried it to our hiding spot.

Absolutely frustrated, I rested my forehead against Holden's shoulder. "None obviously." I sighed heavily, stepping away from Holden to make sure that I was presentable.

"What am I supposed to do with this?" Holden asked, pointing to the bulge in his pants.

"Emily Clothilde! I know you're in here! Answer your mother right now, missy!" The shrill voice sounded much closer than before.

"Never mind, hearing that just took care of it," Holden said, adjusting himself.

I laughed and gave him a quick kiss on the lips. "I suppose I should answer her."
Her call went from shrill to eardrum busting.

"Please do!" he insisted.

I cracked the pantry door to slowly ease into the kitchen. "I'm in here, Mom!"

"I've been looking all over for you! Why wouldn't you answer me? I was starting to worry that something horrible had…" Her rant stopped when Holden came out of the pantry smiling and tucking his shirt into his pants. Her cheeks flushed bright crimson. "I…uh….I."

"Sorry about that, Celeste. Your daughter's insatiable. She can't keep her hands off of me."

Mom's jaw dropped to the ground and I slugged him in the chest—hard. "Holden Dautry!"

"Awww, come on. You know I'm just messing with you. We were saying a quick goodbye. That's all," Holden said.

At first, Mom's eyes darted with uncertainty, but the redness began to fade from her cheeks and she let out a strained chuckle. "You kids sure keep me going." She waggled her index finger at us then gave Holden a kiss on the cheek. "I don't want to rush you, but your father's getting quite antsy, Emily."

"Okay, Mom." I thrust my hand out to playfully shake Holden's hand. "Mr. Dautry, I wish you lots of luck on your quest for the bad guy. Please be careful. I'll see you in a few days. Adieu, dear sir."

He grinned broadly, tugging my hand so that I'd fall into his arms. He dipped me low to the ground and gave me another sweet, passionate kiss. He made sure I was steady on my feet before he backed away. "I hope you have a marvelous time, Mrs. Dautry, but not too marvelous of a time. Remember that your loving husband will be stuck here pining for you."

"Oh, you two!" Mom said, extending her arm and playfully dropping her wrist. She left to wait outside, but we weren't far behind.

"Ready to hop to, Doodlebug?" Dad called from the driver's seat.

"Ready, Dad," I answered, climbing the steps to the RV. I reached my hand out to cup Holden's cheek. "I love you."

He smiled and kissed the palm of my hand. "Love you, too. See you in a few days, Angel Lips." He closed the door of the RV and thus began the *longest* ride of my life.

~.~.~.~.~

Mom and Connie talked incessantly the entire two and a half hours! I started the trip sitting between them on the sofa, but I had to turn my head so frequently to keep up with the conversation that I got dizzy. To the recliner on the opposite side of the RV I went. Dad sent me a sympathetic gaze in the rearview mirror. I answered with an indifferent shrug. Kimberly and Andre were both sacked out in their car seats. Suddenly, I missed those days of yesteryear when I'd simply wake to find out we'd arrived at our destination. Longing for a change of scenery, I moved to sit in the cushy passenger seat next to Dad.

"So, this is Morgan City?" I asked when I noticed the large, wooden sign stating such.

"That it is, Doodlebug! Almost to the campground."

For a while, we were driving along a grassy levee to one side and cypress tree-filled swamp on the other. The trees were fewer and further between until finally the swamp opened into a vast lake glittering like diamonds in the sunlight. At the far side of the lake, I saw the cabins. They were elevated houses on pilings, with screened-in gathering areas underneath and wrap-around decks across the upper level. It reminded me a lot of the beachfront cabin Connie, Bert, Pete, and I stayed in when visiting Gulf Shores. Excitement started to build when I thought of how relaxing it was going to be to sit on the upper deck with a steaming mug of coffee while watching the boats glide through the water. *Maybe this wasn't such a bad idea.* With a smile plastered on my face, I settled contently into my seat.

After we stopped at the front office so Dad could check us in, he dropped us off at the cabin before he and Mom went to park. From what I could see from the porch, it looked like Roberta and Alphonse were going to be camped out about halfway between Mom and Dad's slot near the marina and our cabin. Close enough for us to see them, but not right next door where I could almost guarantee there would be non-stop, constant visits. *Yep, this is going to be nice.*

Not even an hour later, we were all settled in and unpacked. The only downside to Alphonse and Roberta's spot was that it was near the playground—right where Connie and I were headed with the kids. As we approached, I noticed Alphonse tinkering around outside. He wore only jeans and a pair of sunglasses, which offered anyone walking by an unobstructed view of his milky white skin and the thick vest of jet-black hair that traveled down his torso and into the waistband of his jeans. Sweat copiously trailed down his lanky body while he worked to chop firewood with a hatchet. My stomach rolled in revulsion.

"Am I the only one who thinks he looks like a hairy, albino eel?" Connie quietly asked.

"Goodness, no. I was trying to think of an accurate

description, but you beat me to it. I was going to say an emaciated Maverick from *Top Gun*. You know, during the volleyball scene, but only if Maverick had been of Mediterranean descent."

He wiped the fluid from his brow with the back of his hand, swiftly shook it from his fingers, then glanced our way. "Oooo-wee! Dis' a nice place ain't it, Emily?" Alphonse yelled loud enough for people in the next state to hear.

Embarrassed by the looks we were getting from the surrounding campers, I quickly raised my hand in an awkward wave. Connie and I double-timed it with our strollers to his tiny travel trailer, before he could cause a bigger scene.

"Yes, it's a very nice place, Alphonse. Where's Roberta?"

"I'm right here," she said, stepping out with an icy glass of lemonade. "Here you go, Honey Bunny. Don't want you getting dehydrated on me, my big, hard-working stud." She sidled up to him, giggling as he took a long chug.

"Honey Bunny likes," Alphonse purred, pulling her in for a very moist embrace. I shot Connie a look that said, "Ewww." She returned with a cough to cover her gagging.

"We're going to take the kids to the park. See you two later." I was gone in a flash, Connie right on my tail.

"Wait! I'll come with you!" Roberta yelled from behind us. "Is that okay with you, H.B.?"

"Of course it is, Sugar Blossom."

"I'll miss you so much," she said with a pouty lower lip. Alphonse responded with a playful growl.

"You know what? We changed our minds," I yelled over to them.

"We did?" Connie whispered.

"We're going back to the cabin to change into our

swimsuits. We decided to take the kids to the beach."

"Oh, my gosh! I just bought a new swimsuit for the trip! I'm going to change and I'll meet you there!" Roberta eagerly shouted while jumping up and down.

"Look what you did now," Connie huffed. "She'll probably show up in a set of pasties and dental floss."

"Well, would you rather see Roberta sunbathe or Alphonse chop wood?"

"Neither."

"Too bad. It's beautiful out here and I want to bask in the sunlight! Just ignore her."

"Easier said than done," Connie said, clicking her tongue and sighing.

Even though we had to dress ourselves *and* our children, we still made it to the beach before Roberta.

"You see, you worried for nothing. She probably decided to hang with H.B.," I teased Connie.

"What's up with the H.B. thing? I don't get it."

"H.B. Honey Bunny. Get it now?"

Connie stopped fumbling with her fold-up lounger to give me a look. "And it doesn't bother you in the least that you picked up on that so quickly?"

"No, why should it?" I asked, making sure the sun canopy on Kimberly's stroller was doing its job.

"Oh, forget it!" she exclaimed, sinking into her seat. "Andre! Sunscreen time, little boy. Arms out!" Andre knew the drill and turned at the appropriate times to get maximum coverage from the spray. "Now, go build Momma a beautiful sandcastle," she said, passing him a little plastic bucket and shovel. Andre was more than eager to play in the sand.

I'd just settled in to my lounger to enjoy the sweet breeze blowing off of the lake when I heard, "Hey! There you are!" I guess Roberta hadn't changed her mind. It took all I had to keep my mouth closed as she approached.

Oh, Connie had it so wrong when she predicted pasties and dental floss! A cheery Roberta was making her way toward us, dressed in what appeared to be an authentic replica of a circa-1917 swimsuit. The mouth dropping part came later, compliments of her companion, Alphonse. I thought the jeans and no shirt situation was bad, but it was nothing compared to the bright green banana hammock he proudly donned. His body was slick with oil that matted down the thick hair of his chest and abdomen, while bushy patches poked from the apex of his thighs. Black dress socks, sandals, and a smear of zinc oxide on his long, beak-like nose completed his ensemble.

"What the fuc…" Connie started.

"You mean fudgerdoodle?" I quickly blurted.

"Fudgerdoodle my ass. I'm ready to leave."

"Oh, just keep your eyes closed and enjoy the breeze," I fussed.

"Enjoy what? The breeze? How am I supposed to enjoy the breeze if I'm busy trying to keep my lunch down…" Connie rambled under her breath as she quickly reclined back in her chair and threw her arm over her eyes.

"Is this seat taken?" Roberta asked, giggling.

"Nope, you're fine," I said, moving some of my things so she could set up next to me.

"Heck, I'm the luckiest man on this here beach. I got three fine women under my protection. Who's ready for a swim?" Alphonse asked from the head of Connie's lounger. She slowly opened her eyes and jerked back violently when she realized she had an unobstructed view of Alphonse's undercarriage.

"You go on ahead, Snooglepuss. Us girls are going to

chat," Roberta said with a large grin.

"Alrighty then. Yell if you need me." He barreled forth and dove into the water. That's when we made the unfortunate discovery that his swimsuit was a g-string. Connie mumbled something under her breath that I'm pretty sure I was lucky not to hear.

"He's one heck of a man, isn't he?" Roberta said, slowly licking her lips as she openly admired Alphonse's water play.

Connie sat up. "Look, you need to spill. We all know he's incapable of lasting beyond two minutes, so it's obviously not about sex. What gives?"

"What do you mean? Alphonse is amazing," Roberta answered.

"In what way is he amazing?"

"In every way, silly!" Roberta singsang.

"Elaborate please," Connie insisted.

"Well, he's protective, he treats me like a queen, he puts no pressure on me for sex, he's funny, and kind... The list goes on and on."

"You seriously never had *any* other man with those qualities show interest in you before?" Connie blurted.

"Connie!" I snapped.

"It's okay, Emily. No, never in my life has a man treated me as good as Alphonse."

"But we're talking like hundreds of guys, right?"

I sat up to scold Connie once again, but Roberta made a shooing motion with her hand. "It's okay, Emily. Really, I don't mind. I've never had girlfriends to talk to. This is kind of fun and refreshing. Isn't this what girlfriends do?"

"Yes!" Connie answered at the same time that I said, "No!"

"I mean, they do, but usually after they get to know each

other pretty well. It's not typical to get an inquisition after only a few brief meetings," I explained, arching my eyebrows at Connie.

"Nonsense! I say you get it all out in the open so we can spend the rest of the day talking about more important issues. Please, do go on, Roberta," she requested.

"Wait, wait, wait! What issues?" I asked.

"It's irrelevant right now. Spill, Berta."

Roberta sheepishly smiled, then retold the story of her tragic childhood and the less than friendly welcome she got into adulthood. Connie's eyes were wide by the time she finished.

"I guess I can see why you're attracted to him," she said softly.

"Yes, he saved me in more ways than one," she said with a sigh. Her gaze drifted to the lake and a goofy smile spread over her face as she watched Alphonse frolic in the caramel colored water. "He's my hero."

"How long are you gonna make him wait until you give it up to him? I've read some articles about premature ejaculation, so I can give you pointers about things you can do to start increasing his staying power," Connie said matter-of-factly.

"If you're going to continue to hang around us, you need to know that Connie's sensor button is broken," I said apologetically.

"No, I just say what's on my mind. If more people did that, there would be fewer cases of peptic ulcers and high blood pressure," she said.

"And more cases of broken noses and facial fractures from being socked in the pie hole!"

"Has anyone ever told you that you worry too much, *Celeste*?" Connie teased.

"Oh, that was harsh! Keep it up and you can bunk with Celeste!" I warned.

"I didn't mean to cause friction between you two," Roberta interrupted.

"You did no such thing! We're just having some fun," I explained. "But, would you please answer her about whether you want the advice or not before she pops? And fair warning—she doesn't sugarcoat anything," I said.

"Uhm, sure. I'd love to hear your advice. Truth be known, I miss having intimate contact with a man. I'm curious to know how different it will be with someone I have feelings for."

Connie excitedly clapped her hands. "Yay! Andre, stay here with Nannie and be good for her, okay? Mom has to go get a banana from the cabin for Miss Roberta."

"Her's hungry?" he asked.

"Starved," Roberta answered. She and Connie shared a knowing look before doubling over with peals of laughter. *Oh great, Connie's successfully corrupted another one!!*

5

The Shrimp and Petroleum Festival was turning out to be quite a good time. We spent the first day touring the arts and crafts booths set up under the large bridge that connected Berwick to Morgan City. Mom was like a candy-filled toddler, rapidly bouncing from booth to booth. After several long hours of hearing how much she needed the majority of the offered wares, Connie and I grew tired of following her around. We parted ways, leaving Mom and Dad to shop while we brought Andre to the kiddie rides.

The next day, Roberta and Alphonse were supposed to come with us to listen to music in Lawrence Park. Connie banged loudly on their camper trailer, impatiently tapping her foot. Alphonse answered the door wearing only white ankle socks and a wide-open, very short, red robe.

"We're sorry to have interrupted. We'll come back later," Connie shot out.

"Wait! Where y'all runnin' off to in such a hurry?" Alphonse yelled after us. "You ain't interrupted nothin'. I was ironin' my jeans to make 'em all streamlined and such."

"You take your time! Just meet us at the park later!" I yelled, slipping into the driver's seat of the rental car and slamming the door as quickly as possible. Connie grunted loudly then pantomimed scrubbing her face.

"Drive! Now!" she yelled.

"What's wrong with you?"

"I need to erase what I just witnessed from my brain. I swear, if I see one more inch of that man's flesh," she screeched.

"Oh, no! You're going to bear with it just like me! It's seared in my brain and I'm not going to suffer alone!"

"Alcohol! We need lots of alcohol!"

"Mom and Dad have the kids, Roberta and Alphonse are busy getting ready, and our husbands are on the prowl for bad guys. Shall we party, my friend?" I sang.

"Yes, we shall! Now quit talking and drive faster!"

Fifteen minutes later, we were parked and making our way to the massive stage set up in the gorgeous oak tree-laden park. The first band played a mixture of modern and retro hits. Connie and I sipped on Hurricanes, laughing and watching the festival-goers dance in an area near the stage. Connie was beside herself when she overheard that the next band to play specialized in Cajun music.

"Oh my gosh! Zydeco! Line dance time!" Connie yelled, jumping up and down with excitement. She hurriedly drained the little bit of red liquid that was left in her cup, tossed it into the nearest can, and dragged me onto the dance floor.

"Are you drunk or is this some secret passion of yours that you never told me about?" I yelled over the song.

"Both!" She jumped right into line, perfectly following the other dancers in our row while I awkwardly stood around trying to figure out what in the heck I was supposed to be doing. A good looking man wearing perfectly fitted jeans, a golf shirt, and baseball cap approached me.

"You look lost. Would you like me to show you how it's done?" he asked. I noticed tufts of mahogany colored hair peeking out from the edges of his cap.

"I'm not much of a dancer. I'm just going to wait for my friend over there," I said, pointing to a spot in the crowd.

"Why sit on the sidelines and watch everyone else have fun? Let loose! That's what this festival is all about." Slight wrinkles framed his dark green eyes when he smiled broadly.

"I can't promise that I won't step on your toes. If I agree to let you help me, you do so at your own risk," I warned.

"Challenge accepted. I keep a pair of steel-toe boots in my truck—just in case. I'm J.T. Babineaux," he said with a lopsided grin.

"Emily Dautry."

"Are you from around here, Emily?"

"No. My *husband* and I live in Green Bayou. What about you?"

He held his hands in a surrender position and chuckled. "Okay, you're married. I promise to be a perfect gentleman. Is he here with you? Should I ask his permission for a dance?" He anxiously looked through the crowd.

"No, he's not here. He had to stay behind for work."

"Well, I'm glad I don't have an irate husband to deal with. To answer your previous question, yes, I was born and raised here." One of his hands rested on my waist while the other hand clasped mine. "Are you ready to learn the Cajun Waltz?"

"I guess," I said nervously looking around.

He laughed. "Would you relax? Watch me." He shuffled his feet as he counted, "Long, short, short. Long, short, short."

I emulated his steps and before I knew it, we were

whirling gracefully through the crowd.

"You have a beautiful smile," he said. "It's much better to look at than that nervous grimace you were wearing earlier."

"It's because this isn't nearly as difficult as I thought it would be!" I yelled over the music. "Thank you for being such a great teacher."

"My pleasure," he said, twirling me twice before drawing me back toward him.

"Looking good, Mr. Mayor!!" An elderly gentleman in a pair of plaid Bermuda shorts exclaimed as he danced his Muu Muu clad wife closer to us.

"I heard you'd made it back from your trip. Bless you, J.T., for helping all those poor souls," the woman said.

"You're the Mayor of Morgan City?" I asked. He smiled at me.

"Thank you, Grace, Ed. Will I see you tomorrow at the Blessing of the Fleet?"

"You sure will, J.T. Why don't you stop by for dinner on Monday? You look like you could use some fattening up."

"As much as I appreciate the offer, I'm afraid that Marilyn Barnes beat you to the invite."

"Tuesday then?"

J.T. threw his head back as he laughed. "Very well, I'll see you Tuesday evening."

"And feel free to invite a date if you wish," Grace said, smiling her approval at me.

"Thank you. I'll keep that in mind," he said before we danced away.

"Sorry about that. This town has been trying to get me hitched since I took office."

"I'm still stunned that you're the Mayor," I blurted.

"Did you think that we don't have personal lives? I'm not sequestered in City Hall, you know?" he teased.

"I know, it's just that I never... Never..."

"Expected a politician to be so down to earth and charming?"

"You have to be charming to get elected, so that part I get. I'm sorry, I guess when people say 'Mayor' I envision an old man in a suit and tie," I said as the music stopped.

"Glad I could help break the stereotype." The band began to play a much quicker tune. "Ready to learn the Cajun jitterbug?" J.T. asked.

"Sure! But first, will you tell me about the Blessing of the Fleet?"

"Basically, it's a boat parade in the river. It's really nice to watch. The festival king is on one boat and the queen is on another. They meet bow to bow in the middle of the river and toast to a successful harvest."

"They do that on shrimp boats?"

"It depends. This year they're using crew boats. Actually, would you and your friend like to join me? I've been invited aboard the King's vessel. I can guarantee you all the boiled shrimp you can eat, a nice ride on the river, and at least mediocre company," he said.

"It sounds great, but I have to know why... I mean we just met, and you seem really nice, but I don't understand..."
"You don't understand why out of all of these people I picked you to receive dance lessons and free shrimp?" he asked.

"Exactly," I said with a shy smile.

"Intuition."

"What?"

"Okay, here's a very quick bio. I was a high school athlete who got a full paid scholarship to a very good school.

I earned a degree in physical therapy, played with the pros for a bit, became a hometown hero, ran for mayor, obviously won, and here I am."

"That in no way explains why you singled me out of the crowd," I said, my eyebrow arched.

"I knew you weren't from around here and I wanted you to feel welcome."

I shook my head. "Try again."

"You're going to make me say it?" he said, that lopsided grin back on his face.

I nodded.

"Okay," he said. He blew out a deep breath and his cheeks flushed red. "I noticed y'all as soon as you entered the park. Then once you confirmed that you were married and unavailable, I figured I could get some of the matchmakers off of my back and actually have some fun if I was seen around the festival with you. But please don't get weird on me. I promise nothing but straight up, in no way uncomfortable, one hundred percent strict acquaintanceship…and dance lessons," he threw in as an afterthought.

I couldn't help but smile. "Well, the jitterbug song is over. What's next?"

"Cajun two step. Ready?" I heard the relief in his voice. "I guess so."

J.T. was not just a great instructor—he was amazing! Before the evening was over, I considered myself quite the skilled dancer—or maybe it was just the plentiful number of Hurricanes that flowed through my blood that made me feel that way? Regardless, I had a great time. Connie and I barely talked that night. She had more dance partners than I could count, so when she came to me at eight-thirty that evening complaining that she was pooped, I knew she wasn't exaggerating. Her forehead rested on my upper arm and her body slumped against mine when I introduced her to J.T. Without looking up, she offered him a half-hearted wave.

"Fireworks will be starting in half an hour. Would you like to follow me to City Hall to watch them? We can cool off in the air conditioning for a while then sit on the balcony and watch the show. They shoot them from a barge in the river so we'll have a great view."

"I don't know you, but you said the magic words! I'd give my left nut, if I had nuts, for some air conditioning," Connie said, lifting her head to fan herself.

I didn't fuss; I just gave her a look. I was going to apologize to J.T., but he was laughing so hard that I wasn't able to get a word in.

"Y'all come with me," he said, still chuckling. "City Hall is just around the corner."

We followed him deeper into downtown where we openly admired the historic buildings that had been refurbished with murals reflecting the glory of yesteryear.

"You people seriously believe in multi-tasking. City Hall, Courthouse, and Fire Department all in one?" Connie said, staggering slightly as she pointed to the sign attached to the cupola of the stately orange brick building that had beautifully arched windows and brilliant white trim.

J.T. laughed. "Sort of. Yes, there is a fire station in the building and this also serves as city hall, but it's no longer a courthouse. Come on inside and we'll get something cold to drink."

"Ah! Air conditioning! You *are* my friend!" Connie exclaimed as soon as we walked through the door.

J.T. fished around the pockets of his well-fitting jeans and pulled out some money. "There's a vending machine around the corner. What can I get you ladies to drink?"

"Anything cold," Connie said.

"Water for me, if you have it," I requested.

"Sure thing," he said.

"Wait! Before you go, I need directions to the powder room," Connie said, wriggling.

"Down the hall, on your right," J.T. said, obviously amused.

"Thanks! Em, you coming with?" She anxiously bounced up and down while squeezing her knees together.

"It's something we girls tend to do in pairs," she explained.

"I have four sisters. I know all about it," he said with a smirk.

"Good!" Connie said, pulling me down the hall with her. I offered J.T. a sort of half smile in apology. She barreled through the bathroom door, smacking it so hard against the wall that the *boom* echoed all the way down the hall. She had her shorts and panties down before she entered the stall. Seconds later, I overheard a long sigh of relief.

"Better?" I teased while primping in the mirror.

She stumbled out tucking her tank top into her shorts before buttoning them. "You have to tell me the secret. Is it a jewel-encrusted cootchie, super-potent pheromones, or what? Spill."

"What in the hell are you talking about?"

"You! How in the hell do you keep getting these gorgeous men to fawn over you?"

I shook my head and went back to primping. "You delivered my baby, you know there's not a thing that's jewel encrusted down there."

"I know I'm married, but crappy crustacean on a cracker, that J.T. is some fine!"

"It's not like I'm trying to date him. I'm married,

too!" I snapped.

"Yeah, to the magna cum laude graduate of 'Sexy University'. How could I forget?"

"Bert is a *very* good looking man," I said sincerely.

She stopped washing her hands and looked up as if she were contemplating it. "He is pretty hot," she agreed.

"Come on. Let's go watch some fireworks, but you better be nice!"

"I'm always nice!" Connie snapped as she danced her way down the hall way to the beat of the music wafting in from the park.

We found J.T. on the balcony overlooking the river and the fireworks show started a few minutes later. We could hear the crowd that lined the riverfront "ooing and awwing" at each new flowering explosion of brilliant color. No one said a word, we just soaked it all in.

Once the show was over, J.T. insisted on following us to the car to make sure we made it safely. "I hope you ladies had a nice time tonight."

"We had a great time!" Connie yelled. "I can't wait until next year's festival! You can bet I'll be back!"

"I think she stood a little too close to the stage," I explained.

"I'm glad to hear you had a good time," J.T. said loudly as he laughed. His face beamed with pride.

"We're supposed to meet you on the wharf tomorrow morning for the Blessing of the Fleet, right?" I asked.

"That's right. I'll see you ladies tomorrow. Be safe on your drive back to the campground."

"J.T., you've been so nice to us, I'd like to return the favor. How would you like to come back with us after the Blessing? My dad can grill some steaks while we talk and relax around the campfire."

"I never turn down steak. Sounds great. I'm looking forward to our non-date," he chided.

Connie popped her head out of the car and through gritted teeth, animatedly suggested, "Em, you can't forget to warn him about the extra baggage we have."

"What? What baggage are you... Oh, yeah. I suppose I should caution him about Alphonse and Roberta. They are slightly... What's the word I'm looking for?"

"Slightly my ass! They're annoying as hell!" Connie interjected.

J.T. laughed. "I'll make note of it, although you shouldn't worry. I'm used to dealing with all sorts of people. I'll see you two tomorrow." He waved as we pulled away.

"He is so nice!" Connie said. "What's up with that?"

"I have no clue. Did he make a pass at you?" I asked.

"No, not a one. What about you?"

"Nope. He taught me a few dances and that's all. Maybe's he's just really nice."

"Maybe, but out of all of the people that were crammed in that park, why did he pick us?"

"He told me that the townspeople keep trying to set him up and he's tired of it. That's why he wanted to hang out with a married woman. They'd think he was courting someone and he'd be able to enjoy himself. I guess we should be a little more attentive when we see him tomorrow. Are you thinking that might not be the real deal?"

"I think you need to pop back into the present, my friend. Courting? What the hell? This isn't 1895, you know. As far as the being attentive thing, I think that's a really good idea, especially considering the fact that you're a shit magnet."

"That has never been proven!" I snapped.

"The hell it hasn't! Shall I recap?"

"No! There's no need. You're right. I'm a shit magnet."

Connie slumped down in her seat and started to mumble, "Damn right. I know what I'm talking about. You need to start agreeing with me from the start then there wouldn't have to be all this extra dialogue."

"You want to say that to my face when we get out of this car," I joked. Connie flashed me a smile as we pulled into the driveway.

"I'll say it to your face, your hand, your foot, any body part you pick, witch!"

"Tell it to my ass," I said, shaking it briefly before I jogged up the steps.

The kids were fast asleep by the time we got back. Mom and Dad went back to their camper, and I jumped into the warm and inviting shower. I tried calling Holden before drifting off to sleep, but there was no answer. I hoped and prayed that wherever he was and whatever he was doing, he was safe.

6

The sun was just beginning to set when J.T., Connie, and I arrived at the cabin after a long day on the water. We were still going on about what a good time we had aboard the crew boat when J.T. and I joined Mom on the screened in porch underneath the elevated cabin. Kimberly was happily watching Andre play peek-a-boo with her from inside her play yard. The sounds of the children's laughter gently floated through the night air. Without a doubt, I'd never grow tired of that sound.

After Mom finished interrogating us about the Blessing of the Fleet, I brought J.T. outside and introduced him to my dad. The introduction wasn't necessary.

"Well, if it isn't J.T. Babineaux!" Dad said, putting down the spatula he held in his hand. "I used to watch your games faithfully! I sure was sorry when you blew out that knee. But, I hear you did some really good things overseas. Stand up man! Yes, stand up for sure!" Dad said, thrusting one hand into J.T.'s for a shake and giving him a solid pat on the shoulder with the other. "Nice to meet you, son."

"It's nice to meet you, too. So you're a sports fan?"

"Oh, I'm more than a fan. I used to play college ball

back in the day. You wanna hear a humdinger of a story about why I had to give it up?" Dad asked.

"Excuse me. I should go up and check on the kids," I said practically in a full run. I had absolutely no desire to hear the old "college prank injury" story for the five hundredth time. I took a seat next to Mom on the swing. She looked over at me, smiled sweetly, and lightly pushed my hair out of my face. Connie joined us.

"What did I miss?" she asked, plopping on a nearby chaise and wrapping a sweater tightly around her body.

"Nothing, unless you want to hear Dad's 'Rougarou' story. He's downstairs telling it to J.T. right now," I answered.

"Oh, no! Poor J.T.! Is it me or does it get longer every time he tells it?"

"Darling, it's not you," Mom said with a sigh. "The first time he told it, it took about thirty seconds. What are we up to now, Emily?"

"Uh, about twenty minutes, I think."

"Poor J.T.," we said in unison.

After dinner, the darkness rolled in thick as tar. The children were fast asleep and nestled snugly in the play yard on the screened in porch while the adults enjoyed the crisp night air. We were huddled around a roaring campfire and still laughing at Connie's rendition of Alphonse's scuffle with the old lady at my wedding when J.T. excused himself to go to the restroom. The door had no sooner closed behind him than a park official came rolling up in a golf cart.

"I'm sorry. Are we being too loud?" I asked.

A woman who looked about my Mom's age smiled broadly as she exited her cart.

"Oh Emily, this is Carol. She's visited quite a few times. Carol, this is my daughter, Emily," Mom said.

Carol had a mix of blonde and gray hair that was straight as a board and cut in a shoulder length bob. Her blue-green eyes looked friendly and familiar even though I'd never met her before. I instantly wanted to like her. She wore a khaki polo shirt with the park's logo and a pair of black shorts that stopped right at the knee.

"Hi, Celeste. Emily, it's nice to meet you. I'm sorry it took me a while to get back with you, but is it okay if I go on up to take care of that leaky pipe?" she asked, lifting a large, black tool bag from the back of the cart.

"We have a leaky pipe?" I asked Mom.

"Carol pointed it out when I was putting Kimberly down for her nap earlier. It's not horrendous, but all that water constantly dripping will add up over time."

"Oh, okay. Is there anything we can do to help? I hate that you have to do this so late."

"Oh, no. You folks just keep on enjoying yourselves. I won't be long," Carol assured.

"Are the little one's in the way?" I asked as she opened the door to the screened porch.

"Not at all," she whispered. "I promise to be as quiet as I can." She walked to the far corner and squatted down to work on the pipe.

"Thanks. I'll let you work. Just let us know if you need anything."

"Sure will," she whispered. I couldn't put my finger on it, but an uneasy feeling washed over me.

I gently closed the latch on the door and met J.T. as he was coming down the stairs. I pushed the feeling aside as we walked the few yards to the campfire and reclaimed our seats. We were just in time to hear the end of one of

Connie's crazy patient stories.

"That's one thing I miss about working on an ambulance. I don't have stories to contribute anymore!" I said.

"Like the baby oil in the kiddie pool story! That one still cracks me up! Oh, oh, oh! Or the time you went shrimping!" Connie cackled.

J.T., though clueless, still looked amused. "Since this is Shrimp and Petroleum Festival weekend, why don't we hear this shrimp story that has Connie rolling?"

"I'm going to tell it!" Connie yelled in between shaky breaths. She wiped some tears from the corners of her eyes.

"You weren't there!" I snapped.

"But Chuck told me the whole, unedited version. This is what happened..." Connie started.

I noticed Carol walking to the golf cart and that uneasy feeling came back. "Wait, Connie. Hold up a sec. Is everything fixed, Carol?"

"Yeah, everything's great. Y'all have a nice night. Good to meet you!" she said, putting her tool bag into the back of the cart then climbing in.

"Who's that?" J.T. asked once she took off.

"Carol, one of your park workers," I answered.

"Emily, this isn't a very large city and I spend a lot of time here at the park. I know all of the workers here and she isn't one of them," J.T. said.

"Mom, didn't you say she's been around several times? Maybe she's a new hire?" I suggested hopefully as I felt panic starting to rise.

"No, with the economy, we've had a hiring freeze in place for a while," J.T. answered.

The blood drained from my face. "The babies!" I bolted from my chair faster than my feet could manage. I almost hit the ground, but somehow managed to regain my balance and continue toward the porch. I threw open the door. Andre lay nestled in a corner, but Kimberly was nowhere to be found.

Every bit of me wanted to sink to the ground and wail to the world exactly how much pain I was feeling, but the fighter in me said, "Hell no! Get that bitch!" I was gone in a flash, running after the golf cart as fast as I could pump my legs.

J.T. zoomed by me in his pickup. Brake lights lit up the night. "Get in Emily! I've got the police dispatcher on the phone and she's sending every available unit. Unless she's in a boat, there's only one way in and out of here. I'm on my way to block it. I doubt she rode out in a golf cart so chances are she's still in the park."

I jumped into the cab and he positioned the truck in such a way that any vehicles that wanted access to or from the park would have to wait for him to move or ram him to get by. Nervously biting my fingernails, I repeatedly scanned the park in search of anything out of place. A bit of movement, a bobbing light, a strange noise... *I need to call Holden! He's going to be devastated!* I pulled out my phone, praying I had enough breath left in me to explain what was going on. My heart was pounding so hard I thought it would beat out of my chest.

There was no answer—straight to voicemail. "Holden, it's Emily. I need you to call me right away." I tried Bert's phone. Nothing. Tears started to flow as my mind pictured every heinous act this mystery woman could do to my daughter. I felt as though I couldn't catch my breath and the lights in the distance started to blur. *Keep it together, Emily! You're not going to do your daughter any good if you lose it! Deep breath in, slow breath out. Oh God! Where is she?*

I spotted a line of blue flashing lights coming around the bend and a fleeting sense of relief came over me. More people to search for Kimberly, but would they find her before something horrible happened? J.T. moved his truck to a nearby parking space then ran to meet up with the Sergeant who was getting my version of the story.

"You've given us really good descriptions. I'm going to step over here for a minute to assign duties to the officers. I'll be right back with you, okay?" he said.

I gave him a mechanical nod of the head. My body was there, but my brain refused to function. People were talking, yet I couldn't concentrate on the words long enough to comprehend what they were telling me.

"We've called in the detectives. They should be here shortly. This officer is going to stay here and guard the gate. I'd like for you to take me to your cabin. You said she was working on a pipe. We may get some fingerprints and hopefully we'll be able to identify her."

I gave another compulsory nod. The officer opened the passenger door of his car for me and I glanced over at the only source of light inside—a computer screen. The call notes were still glowing. *Missing child. Missing child. Missing child.* I read the words over and over. *I need my baby! I've already lost so much in my life. How would I ever recover from the pain of losing a child? It won't happen. If she's gone I'll... Stop! You haven't lost her for good! She's missing. People are searching for her! Stay strong! I have to stay strong for her.*

"...from?" I heard the last word of the Sergeant's sentence.

"I'm sorry. What?" I asked as he slowly navigated the narrow path.

"I'm guessing that you're here for the festival. Where are you from?"

"Green Bayou."

"Do you have a recent picture of the baby?" he asked.

"Yes, quite a few on my phone and some in my wallet."

"Good, I'll need those."

Another obligatory nod.

"My husband. I tried calling him but I can't reach him. He's Sher…" Radio communication cut my sentence short.

"I've got the subject in custody and the baby is fine. What's your twenty so I can meet you?" a female voice sounded over the radio

"Cabin Three," the sergeant said into the mic on his collar.

"Ten-four. I should be there in a few seconds."

I climbed out of the car only to find that my legs wouldn't support my weight. My parents were quickly on either side of me, helping me to my feet. Connie grasped my tear-stained face.

"What do you know? Is it bad? Tell us!"

"They found her and she's fine," I said in between sobs of gratitude. Connie hugged my neck so tightly I thought for sure she'd snap it. The sound of gravel crunching turned our attention toward the road. I loosened myself from my parents' grip and ran to the approaching car. A female officer opened the passenger door of her vehicle and another female officer stepped out gently cradling a still sleeping Kimberly.

"I can never thank you enough!" I said, wiping the tears away so I could carefully examine every visible inch of my daughter.

"Just part of the job, ma'am. I'm glad it all worked

out for you and that we were able to find her so quickly."

"Seconds felt like days to me. I pray I never have to feel that ever again," I said, planting butterfly kisses all over my sleeping baby.

"Mrs. Dautry, I know you've had a really rough night, but would you mind coming down to the station with me to finish up your statement?"

"Mom?" I asked weakly.

"We'll all be here and none of us will let her out of our sight. You have my word, sweetheart. Go do what the officer asks so that nasty woman can be put behind bars where she belongs."

I nodded.

"I'll drive you to the station," J.T. volunteered.

"You've done so much already. I'll be fine with one of the officers," I assured. My voice still wasn't very strong. Hell, even I doubted that last statement.

"I insist. Plus, I know the Chief. I hired him myself, so maybe I can get some things expedited."

"Okay. I'll go with you, J.T. It means a lot to me that you'd go to so much trouble."

"Think nothing of it," he assured.

I reluctantly kissed and hugged Kimberly goodbye before getting into J.T.'s pickup to meet the Chief at Morgan City Police Department.

~.~.~.~.~

We were silent the entire trip to the simple, white brick police station that was situated next door to a doughnut shop. If I hadn't been in such a somber predicament, I might have found that amusing. I was escorted through a side door and ushered into a conference room where I sat alone while J.T. left to find the Chief. I checked my phone. Still nothing from Holden. *Damn! Where in the hell is he? I need him now more than ever and he's a no show.*

I heard voices coming down the hallway—heated voices, so I quickly pocketed my phone. I couldn't make out actual words, but the tone led me to believe that whatever that conversation was about, it warranted a queasy stomach. A tall man with broad shoulders and strawberry-blonde hair kept his back to me as he leaned in the doorway. He talked in hushed tones with J.T.

The conversation ended and he turned to enter the room. Yes, my queasy stomach had indeed been warranted. I ran to him in an instant, clinging to him for dear life while sobbing onto his chest.

"Oh, my God! Jackson! I've never been more scared in my entire life! Someone kidnapped Kimberly and I can't get in touch with Holden, but luckily we found her before anything bad could happen..." I pulled away, quickly wiping the tears from my eyes. "Wait a minute. What are you doing here? Where in the hell have you been? You had me thinking you were dead in the swamps somewhere and the entire time you! You! You left town without finding out if the baby was yours! Why am I hugging you?"

An utterly stunned J.T. stood in the doorway and Jackson slowly approached him. "May I have a few minutes alone with Emily, please?"

"Sure," he said, slowly backing away so Jackson could close the door to the conference room.

"Emily, please sit down."

"You stole from Atchafalaya Parish's evidence locker and gave it to druggies! How in the hell did you land a job as Police Chief?"

"I'm going to explain everything to you. Please stop

looking at me like that. I didn't turn rogue or anything; just hear me out."

Though I tried to hide my jitters, they made an unwelcome appearance when I tried to pull a chair out from under the table. The banging of my knees against the underside of the table sounded like staccato drum beats. Jackson put his hand on top of mine and I looked at him with desperate eyes. "How could you do that to me?"

"Em," he said, coming forward. "I had to. It was for the best."

He reached for my hand and held it tightly. I guessed that he was searching for the right words to begin his story.

"Why don't you start by telling me why you helped supply the Guidry gang?" I suggested.

He released my hand and ran his fingers through his hair. "Okay. When I accepted the job in Green Bayou, I wasn't officially released from the FBI. I was asked to assist in the investigation of a major crime ring that is running out of the parish."

"The same ring Holden's trying to break up? He told me that there were bigger fish out there than Donovan Guidry."

"Yes, that one. Donovan was getting his stuff from someone. I only gave Donovan's group enough to appease them, gain their trust, and hope for some intel. It was all legit, Emily, and it kept Brad away from you. It was win-win."

"Why did you leave town so suddenly?"

"You decided to be with Holden and I knew that the baby wasn't mine. I submitted my DNA sample to the lab months before she was born. Once I got the letter stating that I wasn't a match, I figured it was best to back out of the picture and let you and Holden get on with your lives."

"Why didn't you let me know?"

"Because you would've tried to stop me. You envisioned this happily ever after where you and Holden look on as I happily walk hand in hand with your daughter through some brightly colored field of flowers. Or perhaps it was our laughing it up at dinner parties and family gatherings. I knew that wasn't going to happen. I said I'd be happy being 'Uncle Jackson', but that could only happen if Holden was out of the picture. It's not right that your happiness would be shoved in my face on a daily basis. Not too long ago, the life that you two share was supposed to be my life. Can't you see my point?"

My heart was heavy. "I do see your point and you're right. It was very selfish of me to wish for that fairytale." I sat back and mulled over what he said for a few seconds. "You know me so well. I did picture family dinners and gatherings, never once taking into account anyone's feelings but my own." I started to tear up. "Wow, how deluded am I? I'm so sorry, Jackson. Honestly, I can't say anything negative about you or the way you handled the situation now that the rose-colored glasses are off. I think it's time for me to pull my head out of the clouds."

Jackson slowly shook his head. "I always loved the way you tried to see the best in everyone and everything. Hey, look at me."

My eyes slowly drifted upwards.

"I'm okay. You're okay. We're both okay. Isn't that what's important?"

I gave him a half smile. "I suppose. Are you really okay? You didn't even let me know that you were alive," I said with spunk.

He leaned forward, squinted his eyes, and stared me

down. "You're not going to let that go, are you?"

I shook my head. He grinned.

"Here's what happened. I got back from my trip, found out you'd had the baby, and went to the lab to pick up the copy of my results. When I saw that I wasn't a match, I did some soul searching. I realized that I had no one left in my life. No wife, no girlfriend, no family. I didn't want to be a loner anymore. I decided to try to fix the relationship with my mother. I found out that there was an opening for police chief here in Morgan City and applied for it when she agreed to go to counseling."

"Your mom still lives in Morgan City? I thought she'd moved away."

"No, she's been here for quite a while. She was still delusional when it came to Kent, but with the counselor's help, she's slowly starting to see the light. I went with her to some of her sessions and we made quite a bit of headway. Until…"

"Until what?"

He sat back in his chair and nervously ran his fingers through his hair again.

"Jackson?"

He took my hand in his. His thumb slowly stroked my wrist. "She had a major setback. A meltdown. Emily, you can't even begin to know how much I hate to tell you this, but it was my mom who kidnapped your baby."

It took a second for what he was telling me to sink in. "Excuse me."

"I didn't get the full story from her yet. She's going through booking and processing right now, but the woman they arrested tonight is my mother, Hollyn Sonnier."

"I don't know what to say. I'm in complete shock, yet I have a thousand questions. Was she stalking me and I wasn't even aware of it? How scary is that? Why? Why would she do that?"

"I don't have the answers you want, but I promise you that I'm going to do all in my power to get them for you. I don't believe she was stalking you; I was in pretty constant contact with her. I don't have a clue why or how any of this came about."

As upset as I was with Hollyn, I sympathized with Jackson. He was once again betrayed and alone. A knock at the door startled both of us. A rather short, stocky guy with spiked hair poked his head inside.

"Excuse me, Chief. I have a red-headed woman out here that refuses to leave unless I bring her to her friend, Emily. Should I arrest her?"

"Is that where you're holding Emily? Is she in that room? I demand to see her right now! My husband is the Chief Deputy of Atchafalaya Parish Sheriff's Department. You'd think that some professional courtesy could be extended this way. Hello! Do you hear me?" I could hear Connie snapping her fingers.

"Ah, Connie. Bert took my slot? Good call," Jackson said, crossing his legs in front of him as he interlaced his fingers and placed his palms behind his head. "Want me to mess with her?"

Hell, I could use the tension breaker. "Kimberly's safe and I may never get this opportunity again—yes!"

Jackson mouthed "Go along with it," to the officer in the doorway. He nodded that he understood. Jackson cleared his throat and did his best to disguise his voice. "I don't give a rat's ass who her husband is! No one comes into my department demanding anything! I run this place! Tell her she's got thirty seconds to vacate the premises or you'll mace her!" he yelled.

"Did he just tell you to mace me? Oh no, I want this on video! Where's my phone? I know the mayor of this town! Shit, I don't have his phone number! I saw his truck outside. J.T.! Where are you, J.T.? I need your help!"

"Shut her up! If the mace doesn't work, tase her!" Jackson yelled in his fake voice.

"Tase me! Tase me! I know my rights and that is excessive force! I'm going to own this department! Mark my words! Emily, I'm going to get back there one way or another! Are these Neanderthals holding you hostage? You can sue, too!"

Jackson was working so hard to contain his laughter that he was the color of a ripe tomato. "Please show her in before she blows a gasket," he whispered.

"Is it wrong of me to admit that I'm a little scared?" the officer joked.

"I know that woman well. You *should* be scared," Jackson said in a soft, yet ominous voice.

"Great." He turned away from the door and could be heard as he walked down the hall. "Ma'am, I need you to calm down."

"Calm down! You want me to calm down! Why is your hand near your gun belt? He's going to tase me! Help! Help! Police brutality!"

"Ma'am, no one's going to tase you. I always rest my hand on my belt. Come with me."

"What? Follow you to some dark room with only a hole in the floor so you can beat the hell out of me with a rubber hose or something! I don't think so, mister! You'll have to forcibly take me because I refuse to move!" she screamed.

Jackson, with tears in his eyes, nearly fell out of his chair. He used his fake voice again, "Don't bring her to the hole, we only just got it cleaned up from the last guy! Do what you gotta do in cell four!"

"Don't you come near me! I mean it! You better stay away!" Connie insisted.

"On second thought, she sounds pretty cute! Bring her in here so I can check her out before you lock her up!" Jackson yelled.

"Oh hell no! I'm not about to become anyone's jailhouse bitch! Mace me, arrest me, whatever! But, you are not about to confuse me with a crack whore! I'm an upstanding, professional member of the medical community and I... Hey, get your hands off of me! Don't touch me! Let me go! You can't make me! I have rights!" Connie's voice got higher pitched and louder as the poor officer dragged her closer to the room. Her hands locked on each side of the doorframe and she refused to enter.

"Is all that really necessary?" I asked Connie's back. She whipped her head around when she heard my voice.

"Emily!" she said with a sigh of relief. She ran into the room and hugged me tightly. After a few seconds she pulled away, finally noticing Jackson. It was almost as if her internal dialogue was being written across her forehead. Her face showed all the emotions she was feeling as she put the pieces of the puzzle together. "You no good son of a bitch! You set me up! What in the hell are you doing here?" She slugged him hard in the chest as she asked in a tone that was a mixture of anger and amusement.

"Hi, Connie. It's good to see you, sweetheart," he said, giving her a warm hug.

"It's good to see you, too. Do you know how worried this poor woman was about you?" she snapped.

"We've already had that conversation," I admitted.

"Are you okay, Em?" she asked, walking over to

stroke my hair in a way that seemed quite maternal.

"I'm fine. Are you ready for another shocker?" I asked.

"Why not? Let me have it."

"Jackson's mom, Hollyn Sonnier, is the person who kidnapped Kimberly."

"Oh, my gosh! What! Why? What's the motive?"

"We've asked all the same questions, but we don't have any answers yet."

"Hopefully, we'll know soon. This is going to be an informal, off-the-record interview. Do you want to sit behind the two-way mirror?"

"Can I do that?" I asked.

"I'll let you, but I only want you to listen. You can't participate or interrupt. Connie, you can sit with Emily if you'd like."

"Absolutely. Thank you, Jackson," she said, giving him a look.

Something about their exchange caught my attention, but I couldn't quite put my finger on it. Jackson spoke up before I could figure it out.

"Okay, let's get you two set up in your places before I send for her." He led us down the corridor and then hooked a right before punching a code into the door lock. "This is where you'll be. Don't leave this area until someone comes to get you, okay?"

Connie and I both nodded our understanding.

"I'm going to go ahead and send your friend, the Mayor, home as soon as he finishes his statement. Unless you would prefer him to be here?" His arched eyebrows told me he was curious as to what exactly my relationship with the mayor was.

"No, send him home. We only met yesterday at the

festival. He's a really nice guy who has befriended the entire family."

Jackson nodded. "Okay then. Let's get this thing rolling."

7

Though we were fidgety, Connie and I were silent as we stared into the empty interrogation room. I stopped wringing my hands and pulled the phone from my pocket—still nothing from Holden. A sigh escaped and Connie looked my way.

"Don't tell me you still haven't been able to reach him," she whispered.

"I'm sure it must be something important if he's not answering," I whispered back.

"I'm not going to say a thing," she said, making the "lips zipped" sign with her fingers as she crossed her legs.

"Thank you," I offered.

"Do you want me to call the dispatcher over there and try to track him down that way? I don't mind because Bert's not answering either."

"I thought you weren't going to say anything," I teased. She cut me some eyes. "No, it's fine. If Kimberly was still missing, I'd say, 'yes'. She's fine, I'm fine, you're fine, we're all fine, so no. Just leave it be."

"Okay, if that's how you want it," she said, carefully inspecting her nails.

"It is."

She sat up and leaned closer to me. "You know what happened the last time you couldn't get in touch with him.

You don't want a repeat of the whole Roberta situation again, do you?"

I gave her a look to show my annoyance.

"Subject dropped," she said.

The door on the other side of the mirror opened and Hollyn Sonnier was escorted in by a uniformed officer. Jackson entered right behind them. Once she was seated, Jackson nodded to the officer. He closed the door, leaving Jackson and his mother alone in the soft fluorescent glow of the ecru colored room.

"What happened, Mom? I thought we were making such great progress. Why did you take that baby?"
Hollyn hung her head low while slowly picking at her thumbnail.

"Mom, please talk to me. I can't help you unless you tell me what happened."

A palpable silence hung heavily in the room as Hollyn began to slowly rock back and forth.

"Where did you get that shirt you're wearing?" he said, referring to the polo shirt with the name "Carol" on it.
Hollyn finally looked at Jackson. She had a sheepish expression on her face. "Someone bought it for me."

"What are you talking about? Who bought it for you?"

She nervously looked around the room. "Can I speak freely in here? They aren't listening to me, are they? They said God sent them to me. Maybe they'll know I told you about them and then they'll come for me."

Jackson moved closer and took his mother's hand in his. "Mom, this is me and you. No one else. I want to help you, but I can't unless you tell me exactly what happened. Why would someone want to get you?"

"I'm so scared, son," she garbled right before she burst into tears. "They might come get me since I didn't do what they wanted."

"Who, Mom? Who might come to get you?"

"The big, ugly men. They stopped by my apartment a while back. At first they told me they was church people, so I felt obligated to let them in. After a while, they asked me if I knew what the Bible said about revenge. I never was a godly woman, so I told 'em I didn't know. They asked if I wanted to be a holy person. I kept thinkin' how proud you'd be of me if I started doin' things with the church, so I asked them to explain it to me. They asked me if I ever wanted revenge for anything and I told them about how my baby boy was killed in cold blood by some cops."

"Mom, you know that isn't how it went down," Jackson said softly. "We've discussed this many times at therapy."

"Well, it was what I was feelin' in my heart at the time," she snapped. "One of them even looked like your brother, God rest his soul."

"We'll talk about what they looked like after I get the full story. Go on."

"They told me that the best way to get revenge would be to take something from the person who killed my boy. I told them he was already dead—killed by some psycho lady, so he got his. They said that wasn't good enough. They said my baby boy wouldn't rest in peace unless the woman who hurt him paid for what she did."

Jackson snapped to attention. "They said that? How did they know about this woman? Did they mention anything else about her?"

"I told them the whole story! How else you think they knew!" she said, getting more irate by the second. "They told me that I should take her baby 'cause she took mine and they was right! It's only fair!"

"Mom, what were you going to do with the baby?"

Jackson asked softly. Obviously, he was using a soothing tone to help abate her fiery mood. It worked. She eased back in her seat and answered the question.

"I wanted to give her to some deserving family, and those men told me they knew just the right people. Supposed to be a real upstanding couple that couldn't have no baby of their own."

Jackson backed away from the table, leaned forward in his seat, and planted his palms on his thick thighs. "You had to know that stealing that baby was wrong," he said softly.

"I did," she said, crying. "Soon as I got back in that golf cart I knew what I did was wrong. She was just a sweet, innocent little baby laying there all peaceful. For a baby to be sleeping so sound, without a care in the world, she must have a really good momma. See, you and Kent were restless little ones and rightfully so. I was a horrible momma to you boys," she sobbed.

Jackson reached to a side table and removed some tissues from a box. He handed them to her then gently patted the top of Hollyn's hand. "Let's not dwell on the past. You're making an effort now and that's what's important. Finish telling me about the guys. How were they supposed to get the baby to this deserving family?"

Hollyn began nervously rocking back and forth in her seat; her arms were crossed over her chest. "They were going to meet me at the marina. I was supposed to bring the baby to a blue boat in the fifth slip."

"Was there a specific time that you were supposed to meet?"

"Nine-thirty."

Jackson glanced down at his watch as I peeked at the wall clock to my left. Eleven-twenty. They would be long gone by now. I let out a sigh of frustration.

"But I couldn't do it. I hid out by a group of campers until the blue lights of the police cars zoomed by. I surrendered right away. Gave them no trouble and handed the baby right on over, safe and sound. I tried to do what was right. I wanted to make you proud of me even though I messed up. We only have each other now, my boy. Jackson, how bad did I mess up? I don't want to be without you."

"You messed up pretty bad, Momma. Have you been remembering to take your medicine like the doctor told you?"

"Them men told me that medicine wasn't the way to be healed. They said I needed to lean on God and he'd make me all better."

"How long has it been since you've had your pills?"

"About a week, I think. Maybe longer."

"You can't stop taking your medicine without the doctor's permission. You could make yourself really sick. Why didn't you tell me about these men sooner, Mom?"

"They told me the only way everything would work was if I kept everything to myself. It would jinx my healing if I talked about it."

"So they told you which baby to get. How did you know where to find her?"

"They told me exactly where to find the baby and made me practice what I was gonna say when I got to the place over and over."

Connie and I turned and looked at each other, confused looks on both our faces. She mouthed, "What in the hell?" and I shrugged.

"That's how I knew for sure they must've been sent from God. They knew too much. Stuff only someone with real spiritual connections would know."

Jackson propped his elbow on the table and gave his

mother his undivided attention. "Like what? Give me an example."

"Like the details of your brother's murder, I mean shooting. They knew the name of the girl who he was chasin' after, the name of the boyfriend who killed him, where she lives, when she would be in town, and where she'd be staying once she got here." She leaned forward and wriggled her index finger in a "come here" fashion. Jackson did so and she whispered something to him that Connie and I couldn't hear. He listened intently then sat back in his chair and ran his fingers through his already mussed hair. He looked at her with sad eyes and slowly shook his head. Hollyn began to sob.

"Momma, listen to me," he said, hurt showing on his face. "I can't let you go. You need help and you need to be held accountable for what you did."

She lightly palmed his cheek, desperation bright in her eyes. "Please, baby. Momma can't go to jail. I'll do anything you want me to. I'll do extra therapy sessions. I'll let you watch me take my medicine every day. I won't talk to anymore strangers. Name it, my darling, and I'll do it. I only just got you back. You all I got, baby. I can't lose you. I'll die without you."

"Please stop crying. I'm going to get you the help you need, but first, we need to talk to a lawyer and a judge. No matter where you are; I'm not going to leave you. I'll still be here for you, Momma."

Witnessing Hollyn's frantic pleading and watching Jackson's pained reaction to his mother's plight broke my heart. Connie had tears in her eyes. It was easy to see that Hollyn's pleas were genuine and that her problem was mental instability, not malice.

Jackson stood to leave the room. Her hands eagerly

grasped his arm. "Don't leave me, baby! I'm scared! I need you! You're all I have left! I'm sorry for what I done! I need you, baby! Don't leave!" Her sobs turned into full-on wails. I couldn't take it anymore so I left the room.

Jackson found me in the hall with Connie, who was gently rubbing my back to console me. He reached for me and I stepped into his waiting arms. They were warm, comforting, and familiar. He gently rocked me back and forth as we stood in the hall. His chin rested lightly on the top of my head.

"I never meant to upset you, Emily. I figured you'd want to hear what happened. That may have been a bad decision on my part. I'm sorry."

I pulled out of his embrace. "You shouldn't be apologizing. Can we talk in private somewhere?" I asked, clearing my throat and pushing the hair that had fallen in my face behind my ears.

"Sure. Let's go into my office," he said, leading the way. Instead of taking a seat behind his desk, he sat in the chair opposite me. "This isn't over. I'm going to find out who manipulated her. I'm also going to find out how they knew all the details behind the incident with Kent and how they knew you were in Morgan City. Probably most important to know is the motive behind trying to take the baby. Maybe money? Maybe they were going to hold her for ransom or try to sell her. I fully intend to find out."

"I trust you, Jackson." I took a long, deep breath. "I don't want your mom to go to jail."

"What? Emily, she took your baby."

"But like you said—she was manipulated into doing it. I've had to deal with my fair share of psychiatric patients, and I don't see malevolence in her. I see hurt. She needs help coping with the loss of her son, even though he *was* a serial killer. Jackson, I know that her mental issues go way back, and I don't see how putting your mom in prison is going to help. It may make things worse. I'd rather see her in a psychiatric hospital."

"Emily, you don't have to say that because she's my mom."

"I'm not." I assured. "I'm doing it because it's what I truly feel. How do we go about making it happen?"

"There are no guarantees, but maybe if you speak to the judge…"

I replied before he could finish his sentence. "Consider it done."

"I don't know what to say," Jackson admitted.

"You don't have to say anything. It's obvious that no matter what her issues might be, your mom loves you, Jackson. I hope that one day you two will have the kind of relationship that you're longing for. The kind of relationship that you deserve."

"Do you have any idea who might be behind this?"

"I have my suspicions," I answered.

"Are you thinking that it might be the spiteful prick of an ex-DA who just so happens to be on the lam?"

"Great minds think alike. He said *he* didn't have anything against me; that I was kidnapped for Brad's amusement. Brad's not a concern anymore, but Donovan did say that he would make Holden pay for shutting him down," I answered.

"How did he know you were in Morgan City?"

"Well, it's not like we went quietly into the night. I can't imagine that it would be that terribly hard to follow a huge RV loaded with people who insisted on stopping every few minutes at each damn landmark between Green Bayou and Morgan City. Not to mention, right behind us a miniscule travel trailer being pulled by a monster truck with a custom horn that kept playing, *Blue Bayou* at every stop. Obviously, the toothpick or his busty, blonde girlfriend has a thing for Linda Ronstadt."

Jackson looked confused.

"Alphonse and Roberta," I explained.

"Together? Friends, right?"

I shook my head. Jackson gave me a look as if to say, "Yeah, right!"

"Oh, my gosh!" I gasped.

"What? What's wrong?" Jackson asked with concern.

"No one has seen them since yesterday. We thought it was because Connie showed Roberta a trick to keep Alphonse from prematurely… Well, we figured it was because they were… You know!"

"Having sex?" Jackson said with a repulsed look on his face.

"Yes," I confirmed. "But they weren't. They didn't. They were supposed to meet us and they never showed up! Donovan was after Roberta. We need to get to that trailer, Jackson!"

He already had keys in his hands and was nearly to the door when he said, "Let's go. You and Connie can ride with me." He stopped at the dispatcher's cubicle and spoke to the officer who was sitting at a nearby desk filling out a report. "Follow me to Lake End Park, Jerome. I might need your help."

"Yes, sir," he said, jumping to his feet and following us out of the door. We quickly loaded into Jackson's duty vehicle and were at the tiny camper in a matter of minutes.

"Emily and Connie, you two stay here," he said right before gently closing the door to his unit. He and Jerome had a brief conversation then carefully made their way to the

dark camper. Once Jackson nodded to signal that he was set, Jerome tapped on the door with the butt of his flashlight.
No answer. He waited a few seconds then tapped again. Silence. He gave Jackson a hand signal and readied to draw his weapon. "Police department! Open up!" he yelled loudly and clearly. Still nothing.

Jackson moved in closer and Jerome tried the door latch. It swung open and Jackson shined the beam of his flashlight inside. He and Jerome entered the tiny trailer, guns drawn. Within seconds, Jerome was out of the camper and using the microphone on his lapel to communicate with the dispatcher. He rapidly approached the car.

"Oh, this can't be good," I mentioned to Connie.

"Chief Sonnier said that he needs you to grab the medical bag from the trunk of the car," he said, pushing the button to release the locking mechanism. "I've called for an ambulance. They should be here soon."

Connie and I jumped into action, she took the bag and I hastily made my way to the camper. The space was too confined, so Jackson and Jerome peered in through the doorway. Poor Alphonse's limp body was slumped backwards in a folding chair. His arms and legs were bound and a section of duct tape covered his mouth. He was still wearing the too short robe, which was laid open to reveal a note that had been pinned directly to his bare chest. "She is... ?" was all it said. His eyes were closed and his head cocked at a bizarre angle, a small trickle of blood from the wound on his chest was the only obvious injury. I touched his neck to check for a pulse and found it weak and thready. His skin burned like fire.

When Connie removed the tape from his mouth, Alphonse slowly began to stir. His eyes struggled to open and his lips tried to move. "Water..." he finally got out.

I ran to the mini-refrigerator. He coughed most of the first sip out, but eventually managed to get a good swallow down. We slowly cut away the bindings and were dismayed at how deeply the rope had cut into his wrists and ankles. He was going to be in tremendous pain once he became fully conscious and blood returned to his previously bound appendages. I silently wished for the ambulance to hurry up. Pain medication is what he needed and I didn't have any. My wish came true. The ambulance arrived and two uniformed medics took over. They headed for the hospital with sirens blaring, Jerome followed.

"I'm going to walk back to the cabin to check on the kids," Connie insisted.

"Nonsense. Just give me a few minutes and I'll drive you as soon as another officer gets here," Jackson said.

"No need. It's not far," she said with a smile. "I'll give Em a call once I get there."

She and Jackson exchanged the same look they did in the interrogation room, then she took off down the trail. I still couldn't figure out what it was about so I made a note to ask Connie about it later.

"Make sure you call so we know you made it okay," Jackson called to Connie's back.

She turned and smiled. "Cross my heart," Connie said, making the sign before continuing to briskly walk away.

Jackson and I were suddenly alone. "She hasn't changed a bit," he commented.

"Something is up with her."

Jackson smiled. "You think?"

"Yeah. I'm not sure what it is, but something is definitely different."

"I'd ask you to go on, but the detectives are here," he said, nodding to the car that stopped inches from his SUV.

"Hopefully we'll find some clues that will lead us to Roberta."

"Let's hope," I said under my breath.

Jackson entered the camper. "It looks as though we have another kidnapping to deal with." He pointed to little notes scrawled in blood that had been scattered in various places around the camper. *Dead?* said the one secured to the cabinet door with a fork. *Missing?* said the one on the dinette set. *Hurt?* was written on one left in the bedroom. *MINE!* was written on the final note that was directly above the door and held in place with a stiletto knife. A long lock of what appeared to be Roberta's hair was casually draped across the blade.

I felt as though someone had thrown me into a freezer. My hands trembled and the blood rushed from my extremities. Jackson wrapped his arm around my waist and helped me out of the door.

"The fresh air is going to make you feel better," he said, softly guiding me to sit at a picnic table. With my eyes tightly closed, I nodded.

He gripped my upper arms. "Look at me," he requested.

When I opened my eyes, his face was inches from mine. His voice was calm and smooth as silk. "You're okay and Kimberly's okay. You did nothing to provoke this, so don't even think of beating yourself up. We don't know that Roberta's dead or that she's even injured. That blood could be from Alphonse's wound and was likely used for intimidation purposes. It appears we might know one of the men that visited my mom," he said, releasing me so he could stand upright.

"Donovan?"

"Yes. Looks like his grudge runs much deeper than we

thought. I suppose I should contact Holden so we can network on this one."

"I can't get him to answer his phone. He and Bert were supposed to be searching for some drug dealer. I haven't heard from him since we left Greenleaf to come to Morgan City."

Jackson looked agitated. "So much for all the 'I learned my lesson and I'm going to devote my time to being there for my family,' talk he was dishing out when he got back to town. Dammit! Why does he always do that?"

His outburst left me stunned. I stumbled over my words. "I…I don't know…"

"I'm sorry. I shouldn't have said anything." He turned away, his gaze now on the unmarked police cars that were pulling into the park. "The rest of the detectives are here and they'll be busy processing the crime scene. Let me drive you back to your cabin."

"You don't have to do that. I can walk."

"I'd rather you didn't." He looked as though there was something more he wanted to say. Finally, it came out. "Emily, will you come with me? Somewhere we can talk."

I probably should've insisted that he bring me home, but curiosity got the best of me. I knew I'd be accepting his invitation. I felt nervous, excited, and sort of like I was doing something illicit. "Let me check on Kimberly first," I said, pulling out my cell phone. Connie assured me that Kimberly was fast asleep and she promised to call if she needed anything. I was able to relax a little before I left with Jackson.

8

Jackson took a right out of the campground and not even a mile farther he turned onto a small, gravel path that opened into a larger shell parking lot. He stopped so we faced the lakefront, shut off the lights, and cracked the windows. A cool breeze blew off the choppy lake causing the little waves lapping at the rocky shore to sound like a lullaby. We sat in silence just listening and watching the moonlight illuminate the rough waters.

"Come with me," Jackson requested, opening his door. Unsure of what was about to happen, I slowly walked around to the front of the car. His hands encircled my waist and he lifted me to sit on the hood. I let out a startled *whoop* as I reached out for his shoulders to steady myself. He smiled broadly.

"Why don't you lean back and relax?" he insisted.

I turned my body so that my back rested against the windshield and my legs reclined across the still warm hood. Jackson fumbled around inside the car, reemerging with a thick, black uniform jacket. He wrapped it around me and hopped up to sit beside me. He interlaced his fingers and rested the back of his head on his palms. I glanced over, waiting to hear the real reason he wanted to talk to me.

"You and Holden didn't waste any time getting married." Jackson's tone was in no way acidic or negative. Actually, it was quite matter-of-fact. It was the words themselves that threw me. I'd expect something like that to come out of Holden's mouth, but not Jackson's.

"It wasn't really something we planned," I said, stumbling on my words.

"So it just *happened*?" he said with a smirk.

"Pretty much. It's a long story."

His jaw set, he slowly nodded his head. "Has he been gone a lot?"

"No, not really. Not until recently."

"Honeymoon period must be ending," Jackson remarked.

I wasn't necessarily upset by his comments, but my heart rate began to creep higher. I knew what was coming. It wasn't that long ago that Jackson and I were friends, lovers, and relatively speaking, only minutes away from being engaged. This was an unpleasant, yet necessary conversation that was long overdue.

"You left me, Jackson. You told me to move on," I said.

"Yes, I did and it was the biggest mistake I ever made. I thought that moving away would help me forget, but all it did was make me realize how stupid I was for leaving without a fight. I feel like a fool for pushing you into his arms. I've tried so hard for so long to be the opposite of my brother and now I've become a pushover. I backed away from our relationship because I thought I was being the better man. Good ole' Jackson—does a great job at work and then goes home at the end of the day to what? Nothing but an empty house. Why? Because all I have in this world besides my job is my crazy-ass mother and an old friend who's living my dream life because I handed it to him on a silver platter. As if his money, his charisma, and his career weren't enough! You want to know the truth, Emily? Here's the truth! Holden's always been a spoiled brat who has gotten whatever he wanted, mainly because he manipulated me into feeling sorry for him—like his life was so much worse than mine. And I fell for it again! He had nearly died and was struggling to walk, so once again I felt guilty because I had something that he wanted. You! It's been the story of our lives. I have no right being angry with anyone but myself. I let this happen. But, dammit Emily, it hurts."

I sat unmoving and stunned. Never had I heard such an outburst from Jackson.

He slid from the hood and moved to stand by the water's edge. The frustrated grunt he let out carried back to me on the wind. He turned to face me. "I'm sorry, Emily. You know this isn't like me. I apologize if I'm making you feel uncomfortable. It's just that this has been pent up inside and I have no one to talk to, so it just got to this point..." He let his sentence hang as he turned to face the water again. Without saying a word, I came off of the hood and moved to join him. When I got to where he stood, I saw a solitary tear track down his cheek. I felt a huge lump settle in my throat as I struggled to find the right words to say.

He wiped away any trace of his sadness with the back of his hand as he blew out a long breath. "I'm sorry. I guess that the stress of everything is starting to get to me. Don't worry. I've still got it together. It's just frustrating sometimes and I don't feel like I can vent to anyone. You and Holden were my only friends. I'm sorry I dumped this on you. It's not like you don't have enough of your own problems. I promise, I'm good."

I turned him to face me; my eyes searched his for proof that he was okay. Despite his words, all I saw were fear and regret.

"Don't you dare apologize and please don't lie to me, either. What are you feeling, Jackson?"

He let out a quick, insincere laugh. "You're not a shrink and I'm not Connie. We're not about to sit out here while I talk about my feelings. Next you'll be trying to paint my toenails."

I gave him a sharp shove to the chest and snapped at him. "Be serious! You're hurting Jackson, and regardless of what's happened between us, I want to help you. I still love…"

He quickly spun around to face me. "Say it," he encouraged. "Oh God, Emily please say it because I need to hear it."

My breath caught and my heart melted when I saw his desperate eyes. "I still care about you," I said softly.
"That's not what you were going to say." He gently brushed the wind-whipped hair from my face.

Slowly shaking my head, I lowered my gaze.

He lifted my chin so that I'd have to look him in the eye. "I'll talk to you if you talk to me," he offered.

"You go first," I insisted.

"Agreed." He led me back to the car and we took our seats on the hood. "This stuff with my mom is really starting to take its toll. I knew that she had psychological issues, but I didn't know how bad they were. Then I started to feel guilty because I'd neglected to get her help for so long. We began therapy together and that was when I realized how deluded she truly was. Evidently, Kent had preyed on her fragile psyche. She totally lost touch with reality. Once Kent died, he was no longer able to pump her with his bullshit, and she was kind of like a lost kid in a crowded shopping center. She didn't know who to call for help—especially since Kent told her that I wasn't around because I'd joined some cult overseas as part of an undercover sting."

"Wow! It's obvious that he had issues, but to manipulate his own mother…" I said, referring to the time he held me hostage, torturing and brutalizing me into what he hoped would be submission.

"He needed someone to brag to about his conquests, but there was no one but her. Even though she never met her, she really believed that he was engaged to Sarah and that they were happily expecting a child. It broke her heart when she learned that Sarah and the baby had died. It made me sick to my stomach to hear all of the lies he'd been telling her through the years. Especially the stuff about you."

"What stuff?"

"I think it's probably best that we not go into it. We've already had a long night."

"I think I'm entitled. The woman was manipulated into stealing my child based upon what she believed."

"Fair enough," Jackson said after giving it a little thought.

"Kent had been watching you for a while. He kept telling Mom what a great wife you were going to be for him one day. She was so excited that she started buying things for the wedding. I wasn't sure why she didn't question him about why you weren't coming around until I discovered that he'd found a prostitute who resembled you. Are you sure you want to hear this? It gets really ugly," he warned.

"I want to know."

"I know this because Kent kept a secret storage shed on a small piece of property he bought while he worked for

APSO. Because he put the property in my mom's name, it was never flagged for a search after he was killed. She told me where it was located, and frankly, I haven't been the same since I saw it. There were stacks and stacks of newspaper clippings, notebooks, pictures, the trophies he kept from his victims. The evidence that would help lend closure to the case, I handed over to the authorities. Everything was there in black and white—from his first contact with his victims to the thoughts and suggestions he came up with to make things run smoother the next time."

Despite the heavy jacket I wore a deep chill ran through me.

"Mom got suspicious when he kept going on about Sarah, yet never bothered to bring her by for an introduction. After he became obsessed with you, he wasn't about to make that mistake again. That's where the prostitute came in. He blackmailed her into dressing like you; even made her style her hair like yours. So, even when he held the real 'you' captive, he had the pretend 'you' help him live out his fantasy."

"What happened to the prostitute? Is she still around?"

"I don't think so. He wouldn't have killed her because he still needed her. I went through the old arrest records for known prostitutes in the area. I know who she is, but never could track her down."

"Hopefully, she found out that he was dead and it scared her straight. Maybe she's finally living an honest life somewhere."

"Maybe," Jackson said. "Anyway, as far as I'm concerned, the constant dealing with Mom, finding out the additional stuff about Kent, then losing you and starting all over again in a new department—I guess I underestimated how much it all affected me."

Instinctively, I reached out to soothe him by gently rubbing my hand up and down the length of his thigh. He looked over at me and I quickly drew my hand back. Jackson saw it as a segue to the topic he was curious about. "I've told you my secrets, now you tell me yours. What are *you* feeling?"

"Except for this latest incident with Kimberly, things are good."

"Good? Not great, wonderful, or spectacular?"

"What I said earlier, I'm not sure why I almost said that I…" I turned to face him. "Maybe it was habit? I don't want to give you the wrong impression."

He looked at me uncertainly. "Should I have fought for you? Would I have had a chance? Would it have been worth it?"

"I can't answer that, Jackson." I turned to avoid his gaze.

"I've done so much soul searching as a result of this mess and you know what I realized?" he asked.
I shook my head.

"Holden's a bully and I'm the dumb ass who comes along to clean up his messes while he gets all the glory. This goes way back, Emily."

"Jackson, I don't know…"

"Remember when he barged into *our* house to profess his undying love for you. It's always some big misunderstanding with him and he always comes out golden." I started to raise my hand to protest, but he shook his head. "Please let me do this. I need to say what's on my mind."

I was so conflicted! Was I really supposed to sit back and listen to my former love bash my husband? *Yes, I should hear him out.* Holden's recent return to the very lifestyle he vowed to leave behind did concern me. Jackson was right. The reason he forfeited his opportunity at a relationship was to make the decision easier for *me*. The least I could do was to give him a few minutes of my time to get it off of his chest.

"Okay, go on," I finally encouraged.

"I'm not the type of guy to knock a man's character, especially a man that I've spent so much time with, but all it's ever gotten me is second place. I'm tired of living in Holden Dautry's shadow. It's time for the truth to come out. Nearly all of the positions Holden has held have been bought for him. I have to say that he did a great job. The way he got there wasn't fair, but he did make positive things happen."

"Are you telling me that the Parish President selected him to be Sheriff because he was paid off?"

"Why was Holden picked to be the head of the department,   Emily?"

"Because he was supposed to clean up the mess of the old administration," I answered.

"And who was responsible for the previous administration?"

I sat quietly.

"I'll tell you who—the same old boy network that brought Holden in. Why would they all of a sudden want to 'clean up the town'? Think about it."

"No," I said, sliding off of the car's hood.

"They got kickbacks when Sheriff Rivet was in office so everyone was happy. When Donovan ran things, they still got their cut. Then Holden's mother came in and paid more than Donovan could ever think of dishing out, so they hung him out to dry. Holden's just a pawn in their game and his ego's too inflated to see it."

"But Holden wasn't speaking to his mother at the time

he took over."

"That doesn't mean for one minute that she wasn't his puppet master. Luciana Dautry is one hell of a crafty woman. You know that! Look how she manipulated Holden into giving up on you after his injury!"

"So you're telling me that Holden's not actually in control of his life. That everything that goes on is his mother's doing? I'm not so sure I believe that. His mother hates me, yet she gave her blessing for us to be married. If she had that kind of power, I can guarantee that she would've stopped the wedding."

"You gave her a grandchild—more flesh and blood to mold into whatever she chooses."

I swiftly shook my head. "No! There's no way. I don't want to hear anymore."

"I'm not telling you this to upset you. I'm telling you this to warn you. At this point in time, I don't care if you want to be with me or not." He shook his head. "That's not true, but I don't want you to think that I'm doing this to get you to leave Holden and come back to me. I'm telling you this so you won't get blindsided." He closed the gap between us. "I do still love you, but it's a different kind of love now." I felt emotionally drained. A lot of the points that Jackson made were valid. "I don't think I want to hear anymore," I weakly pleaded.

"Just let me finish with this—I regret that I didn't stand up to Holden that night in the kitchen. I had to back away from the situation to see that I had every right to love you at that time. We had peace, we had fun, we had normalcy. If I got a promotion it was because I *earned* it, not because it was purchased for me. I fought countless people to stop my own brother and I stood up to my mother when that was necessary, too. I'm overseeing her care and treatment, and

I've been nothing but upfront and honest about what she did. I didn't hide a thing. Do you think Holden would've done the same? Where is he right now, Emily? Your daughter was missing and he was nowhere to be found. Who was with you for every doctor's appointment, every ultrasound, every ache and pain of your pregnancy? Me. I was there for you until he swooped in at the end of the fourth quarter and claimed victory. Think about it."

I couldn't argue with him because he was right. Granted, Holden had a legitimate excuse because of his injuries, but maybe I had been too caught up in the fantasy of it all. Holden painted himself to be my knight in shining armor, but how much assistance had that knight received? The dragons he had slain were already dead. He simply propped a boot proudly on top of each of them and then took full credit. I felt my head beginning to throb.

"Jackson, this is more than I can deal with right now. Roberta's missing, Alphonse is barely alive, my baby was kidnapped, you turn up after I feared the worst, and now I'm doubting the character of my husband. It's late, I'm exhausted, and this has turned into something that I can't wait to put behind me. It's too much," I said, walking to the car.

"You're right," he said, quickly catching up to me. He spun me around to face him. "You're right, but I couldn't let you leave here without knowing. My conscience wouldn't let me. I'm sorry that I didn't have better things to say and I'm sorry that you worried when I didn't get in touch with you. I should have known better. I know you're worn out; I'll bring you back to your cabin."

"Thank you," I said, taking off the thick jacket before I slid into the passenger seat.

"I'll be around if you need me. Here are my new

contact numbers," he said, handing me a card. "Don't hesitate to call. I'll keep you up to date on what happens with my mom and with Roberta. We need to stay in touch." I nodded.

He started the car, rolled the windows up, and pulled down on the gear shift. The car gave a slight lurch, but it didn't move. I looked over, my brows furrowed with confusion. He threw the gear shift back into park. "Ah shit, Emily." He slowly breathed in, and took twice as long blowing it out. "I really miss spending time with you."

Maybe it was the desperation in his voice or some of my old feelings flooding back, but those seven words stung worse than the venom of the meanest viper. Tears sprang to my eyes and I struggled to hold them back. I bit down on my lower lip to keep it from trembling. I'd made my decision. I was married to Holden and I needed to honor my commitment to him regardless of what I was feeling at that moment. I swallowed hard and turned to face Jackson.

"I miss you, too, and I'd love for you to be back in our lives...as our friend." I knew those words were going to cut like a knife, but I felt I had no choice. I didn't want Jackson to have false hope that I'd simply pack up the next day and leave Holden for him. Sure, I had some major soul searching to do, but I wasn't about to jump from one gigantic rollercoaster to another.

"Friends," he said softly. "Sure, we'll be friends." He pressed the accelerator and was silent until he pulled into the driveway of the cabin. "I'll let you know if I find out anything. Get some sleep, Em," he said.

"Thank you. I'll try. Good night, Jackson," I answered. I half-heartedly trudged up the stairs and into the cabin completely prepared to face an inquisition from Connie. I actually felt a little let down when it didn't come. She was fast asleep in the front bedroom with Andre and Kimberly in a portable crib right beside her. I smiled at my sleeping friend and felt blessed that I had someone like her to lean on. I gently shut the door and continued to my room. I flipped on the light and before my eyes could focus, a hand tightly clamped over my mouth preventing my scream. I tried to wriggle, fight, bite, yell, but despite all my efforts, the grip got tighter and tighter until I finally quit struggling.

I felt his hot breath in my ear. "Where in the hell have you been?" he whispered gruffly.

"Holden?" Though it was incredibly muffled, I managed to say into his palm.

He whirled me around to face him. "Shhhh," he ordered before lifting me over his shoulder and carrying me out of the door. I tried banging my fists against his back in protest, but all that earned me was a swift swat to the rear. I stopped fighting him and once we got to the bottom step, he led me toward the abandoned beach.

"What are you doing here and what do you mean by scaring the hell out of me!" I hissed.

"I think I'm the one who should be asking the questions. How could you not let me know that our daughter was kidnapped?" he asked through clenched teeth.

"I tried calling you over and over! You didn't answer!"

"Keep your voice down," he instructed as he took my arm and pulled me further down the beach.

I gently rubbed the tender area once he released me; anger showed in my eyes. "Stop manhandling me and I will. Why didn't you answer your phone? Where were you?"

"My phone never rang. I was in the boat with Bert when a dispatcher radios to tell me that one of my deputies has been admitted to the hospital in Morgan City. Imagine my surprise when he goes on to tell me about Roberta's kidnapping and the baby who was taken by the Police Chief's mother. Thankfully, *my* baby was recovered before any harm could come to her. Imagine my further surprise when I found out that this Chief's mother is Hollyn Sonnier and that *you* dropped the charges!" He began to pace. "Then—and here's the icing on the cake—I find out that you're nowhere to be found because you're out somewhere with Chief Sonnier! Am I supposed to be happy? Am I supposed to be understanding and supportive? What do you have to say for yourself?" he demanded as he stared me down.

I quickly closed the distance between us. "What do I have to say for myself? You have some nerve! You sent me out here because you were *so worried* that something would happen to me if I stayed home. Well guess what! You were wrong! You weren't here, and you don't know what I've been through. Yes, Hollyn Sonnier took Kimberly, but we found her very quickly, thanks to the Mayor's connections. We met him at the festival and he has been very helpful and kind to all of us. Hollyn is a very disturbed individual. You weren't there to hear her interview. She needs psychiatric help, not jail time. That's why I dropped the charges with the stipulation that she gets the help she needs. Yes, Jackson is the chief here, but I didn't know that until I got to the police station. He was just as surprised to see me as I was to see him. He drove Connie and me back to the park so we could check on Alphonse and Roberta then we came across the crime scene. I got very upset and Jackson took me away for a bit to decompress. He dropped me off and you know the rest. The end."

"Oh no, Sugar Plum. This is far from over," he said derisively.

"There's nothing more to tell," I said, crossing my arms and turning to face the water.

"Why didn't you call the station and have them radio me?" He spun me to look at him.

I flung my arm to free it from his grip. "Because I shouldn't have to, Holden! You promised me that you were done being in the trenches. You swore that you were a family man who was ready to let the others handle the casework. You lied."

"You didn't tell me to punish me! I didn't lie! I'm not out there every night. There will be a case from time to time that requires my personal attention. That's just a cold hard fact, Emily."

I used my thumb and index finger to massage the bridge of my nose. "Hollyn was manipulated into taking Kimberly," I announced.

"What?" Holden asked.

"Two people visited her and told her that we would be coming to town. They gave her a time and place to not only take the baby, but to drop the baby off. We need to figure out who knew we'd be here so we can catch the person behind all of this."

Holden let out a long sigh. "I wasn't expecting to hear that. The list should be relatively short. Do you think your mom or dad said something inadvertently?"

"I don't know. We can ask them in the morning. I suggested to Jackson that perhaps we were simply followed, but that doesn't explain the prep work that went into getting Hollyn involved."

"We have a lot to think about and it's almost two-thirty in the morning. Neither one of us is going to be at our best. Let's try to get some sleep. Daybreak will be here before we know it."

"You're going to stay the night?" I asked.

"Of course. First thing on my agenda is a meeting with

Chief Sonnier. We've got some talking to do."

"Holden, don't be aggressive. He didn't do anything wrong. He stayed away from us. We're the ones who came into his territory."

"Seriously, Emily! I bust my ass trying to get here as fast as I can because I'm worried sick about you and that's what I hear? 'Be nice to poor Jackson!' You really amaze me sometimes," he said with disgust.

"Not half as much as you amaze me with your callousness! I hope you have a blanket stashed somewhere, because you aren't welcome in my cabin," I said defiantly.

"Try to stop me," he challenged. He stepped so close to me that our lips practically touched. My chest was originally heaving from anger, but inhaling his masculine scent sent my libido into overdrive. Desire flowed between us like electrical currents arcing off of metal. The question was, which one of us was going to break first?

"I have the key," I breathed. "Good luck trying to get in."

His sapphire eyes were so dark they looked like onyx. "I'll get that key from you, one way or another," he assured. I continued to stare him down, unflinching. My tongue darted out to moisten my lips and I noticed his Adam's apple bob up and down. It was all the permission he needed. His arm snaked out to ensnare my waist as he spun me so my back rested against his chest. His big, strong arms wrapped around my upper body and he pulled me tightly against him. "I don't like it when we fight," he whispered in my ear before taking a quick lick.

His tongue was so warm, his breath so hot on my neck, that I felt the urge to strip naked right there. "Why do we have to be so far from the cabin?" I thought out loud.

"I want you so bad," he breathed while his hands

eagerly roamed across my mid-section.

I turned to face him, anxiously anticipating the moment he'd devour me with one of his intoxicating kisses. His mouth was on mine, his tongue separated my lips. It was a hard-fought struggle to remain upright. Without our lips moving from one another's, he lifted me so I straddled his waist then carried me deep into the shadows of an empty pavilion. He set me down and unfastened his pants.

"There's no way we're going to do this out here," I said, nervously looking around. Holden stopped nuzzling my neck and gave the area a quick onceover.

"It's pitch black and all's quiet. If we keep it down, no one will be the wiser." He casually pinned my wrists overhead head and used his teeth to grasp the hem of my shirt. Once the fabric of my shirt was gathered on top of the swell of my breasts, he dipped his head between them and tugged at the cups of my bra.

"Holden, stop," I breathlessly pleaded. "What if a security guard shows up?"

He stopped the exploration long enough to let out a frustrated sigh. "I'm about to blow a gasket over here and you're worried about getting caught. Would you relax?"

"I can't," I answered. "I keep picturing some nasty pervert with inky black hair, scaly skin, and atrocious acne watching us through a night vision scope as he reaches for his asthma inhaler."

"That's what you're thinking right now? Well, that just took care of my issue. Soon as you said scaly skin, down it went like a deflated balloon," Holden joked.

"Just as well."

"Are you trying to hurt me?" Holden asked incredulously.

"Not at all. If we keep this up, it'll be over pretty

quickly. But, if we go back to the cabin, we can take our time," I said, with a devious smirk.

"Good point, Mrs. Dautry. Very good point," he said as he took my hand.

9

Despite the lack of sleep, I was awake by seven the next morning. Holden and I stumbled into the shower hoping to get revitalized, unfortunately that didn't happen until we sat down with a mug of Connie's "thick as syrup" coffee. After a quick breakfast, Holden left for a run through the park while Connie and I sat inside the screened in porch watching the kids play. About half an hour later, a very sweaty Holden returned.

"Hey, baby! Have a nice run?" I asked cheerily. As soon as he walked through the door, I noticed the look on his face and the smile left my lips. "What's wrong?"

His face was so red it was nearly purple, and it wasn't from the exercise. He was pissed! He didn't speak; he simply pointed his fingers up the stairs and gave a quick nod to indicate that I should hastily make my way up there. Though she was silent, Connie's eyes were wide as saucers. She gave me a "what in the hell?" look that I answered with a shoulder shrug. I went up the stairs, Holden right on my heels. He shut the door behind us, threw the morning newspaper onto the kitchen table, and in a quiet, yet daunting tone he asked, "What the fuck is this?"

"I don't know what you're talking about," I said, my

heart rate accelerating.

"This!" he said, pointing to the newspaper.

"I don't know what could possibly be in there to get you so upset. You need to calm down. And, you should never have embarrassed me like that in front of Connie! It was so rude and ..."

"Oh, believe me! After I'm done here, I've got a few choice words for her, too!"

"You'll do no such thing! Clearly, you need to go back to bed." I mumbled, reaching for the paper to see for myself what had Holden in such a state. There in bright, blaring color and plastered across the front page was a picture of me dancing with J.T. I started to laugh.

"This is what has you so upset? That's J.T., the mayor. We were dancing. So what? You told me before we left that you were fine with that."

"Read on," he demanded.

I skimmed the headline. *Morgan City Mayor Lets Loose.* Not that big of a deal. Next, I read the caption. *Pictured left: Offering a rare glimpse into his personal life, a relaxed J.T. Babineaux, Mayor of Morgan City, shows off his dancing skill with a mystery woman. Could she possibly be Morgan City's next first lady? Read the article below for more details.*

"Is this a tabloid?" I asked, turning the paper to the back page. I was shocked to see another photograph of J.T. and me up on the balcony watching fireworks. The angle that the picture was taken from made it look as though J.T. and I were snuggled together as he pointed towards the sky. The damn photograph couldn't have been snapped at a more inopportune time. Even though we were admiring the fireworks display, it appeared as though we were a couple of love sick kids who met with the approving smile of Connie. *Oh, poor Connie.* I wasn't about to let her catch hell over a simple misunderstanding!

"Holden, you can calm yourself down right this minute. Those pictures don't prove a damn thing!"

"They prove that you seem to have had a pretty good fuckin' time in Morgan City!"

"Watch your language, and wasn't that supposed to be the point?"

"What about this! Explain this!" he demanded as he opened the newspaper to one of the inside pages. My breath caught in my chest.

"That's not me. I didn't do that. We never..." I said when I finally recovered from the shock. The black and white photograph was of me and J.T. sharing a passionate kiss on the festival grounds. "Connie was with us the entire time! Ask her! It was all completely innocent!"

"Yeah, I'm going to run on out and ask *your best friend* if you cheated on me with the Mayor of Morgan City. Let me guess what she's going to tell me."

"She'll tell you the truth! Nothing happened."

"So you're telling me that the local newspaper is so hard up for stories that they alter photographs and print them to sell copies?"

"They must because I haven't kissed anyone but you like that since we got married." I kicked out one of the chairs under the kitchen table with my foot and plopped into it, huffily crossing my arms in the process.

"Well, let's get to the bottom of this, why don't we? We're going to the newspaper office and we're going to find out *exactly* where that picture came from." He tugged on my sleeve, pulling me with him out of the door. Jackson was making his way up the stairs.

Holden grunted. "Well, well. If it isn't Chief Sonnier. Coming to visit with my wife, no doubt. Is the mayor down there, too?"

"Holden!" I snapped.

It was obvious that Jackson was surprised by Holden's aggressiveness, but he handled it well.

"Actually, I'm here to see you, Sheriff Dautry."

"About?"

"About the cases we need to network on. Roberta, Alphonse, the baby…" Jackson said, his arms stretched in a "duh" fashion.

I could tell that Holden was torn. Though the passionate side of him wanted to get to the bottom of our problem, his professional side won out.

"Fine. Let me get my stuff and then you can take me to your office," he said, disappearing into the bedroom.

"Emily, I checked in on Alphonse this morning. He's stable," Jackson said loud enough for Holden to hear. "Are you okay?" he silently mouthed.

"Thanks, Jackson. I wondered how he was doing," I answered while nodding my head.

"Call me if you need me," Jackson quickly signaled. I gave him a brief, yet appreciative smile.

"Am I interrupting something? Should I go back in the room to give you two some alone time?" Holden snapped.

"Quit being an ass!" I demanded.

"Oh, you haven't seen ass yet! I want J.T. Babineaux sitting at this table," he paused to look at his watch, "at four-thirty this afternoon. Make it happen."

My mouth fell to the floor. "Excuse me!" I demanded.

With a scowl on his face, Holden looked between Jackson and me. When he saw our faces, his demeanor lightened some. He let out a sigh.

"Would you see if J.T. will agree to meet with us this afternoon, if it's convenient?" Holden requested in a much softer voice.

"I'll see what I can do," I agreed.

"Thank you," he said, rapidly closing the distance between us. He cradled my face in his palms and pulled me so he could whisper into my ear. "It makes me crazy to think of losing you again. I'm sorry I lost my temper."

I didn't answer; I just nodded as I pulled away. Jackson gave me a reassuring wink while Holden was still turned away from him.

"I'll have to catch a ride with you. I was in the boat when I heard about the kidnapping, so I had my guy navigate the channels and lakes until we got into Lake Palourde. It was a lot faster than going back to the boat launch and driving here. He let me off right there at the marina."

"That's fine," Jackson answered. "We have several spare units at the station. I can lend you one while you're here. I think the '76 Impala just got back from the shop."

"Ha! Ha! Always the jokester," Holden said.

I was relieved that Jackson knew how to get Holden back on track after his hot-headed episode. He knew him so well. That got me to thinking about our conversation the night before. Holden sure could act the spoiled brat. But wasn't that all men? I had to admit that Jackson had never displayed that kind of an outburst. *Stop it! You're married to Holden!* I let go of the dangerous thought I was entertaining and followed the guys downstairs.

Connie pounced once they were gone. "Fragrant frog farts! What kinda bug blew up his tight butt?"

"The jealousy bug." I passed her the newspaper. She thumbed through it, her eyes getting larger and larger with each turn of the page.

"Where in the heck did this picture come from? Where was I? Was he a good kisser? He's got those nice, firm lips," she said, pointing to the make out photo.

"It's a fake!" I snapped, bending to pick up Kimberly from the portable crib.

"Oh, yeah! Sure, it's obvious that it's a fake," Connie said, busying herself with wiping a smudge from Andre's face.

"What are we going to do to get your jealous daddy back on track?" I said to Kimberly in a babyish way. I got a huge toothless grin that melted my heart.

"Do you think he's gonna punch Jackson?" Connie asked.

"No! Why would he?"

"You got so mad you punched Roberta. Remember?"

"That was different. She had it coming and I was extra hormonal. I really hope she's okay. I've been thinking about her all day."

"Still no leads, I take it," Connie said.

I shook my head. "Hopefully with Holden and Jackson working on this one together, they'll come up with something soon."

"What about Alphonse?"

"He's stable."

"At least that's some positive news."

"Yeah, I guess. I think I'll take Kimberly for a walk. I really should check on my parents."

"Make sure you take your cell with you," Connie cautioned.

"Got it right here," I said, tapping my pocket after I finished strapping Kimberly into her stroller.

"Good. Tell Mom and Dad I said 'hi'."

"I will. Wish me luck," I joked.

"Good luck. Honey, if Celeste saw the morning newspaper, you're gonna need it!"

~.~.~.~.~

"Emily, a marriage is something that needs nurturing and care. Should I set up a meeting with Father Robicheaux? I'm sure he'll be more than happy to discuss any quandaries that you and Holden may face on your marital journey, including the temptation of infidelity. Sometimes you may find yourself tempted, especially if the object of your attraction is very handsome and in a position of power. However…"

"Mom, I didn't kiss J.T. We only danced. Holden's seen the pictures. We don't know where they came from and you might as well know—please sit down—that Jackson Sonnier is the Police Chief here and he's working with Holden to solve a case."

"Oh, mon dieu! Pourquoi? Pourquoi?" Mom said, tossing her hand to her forehead.

"A little less drama, please," I requested, passing Kimberly to Dad. I don't know which of them was entertained more— Dad by Kimberly's spit bubbles or Kimberly by Dad's over-the-top surprised face.

"Sometimes I believe that you're trying to kill me," Mom fussed.

"I'm married to a Sheriff and I work in the medical field. If I wanted to kill you, I could do it and I'd get away scot free, too," I teased.

She didn't think it was funny. "That is what I'm talking about! Your sense of humor has turned incredibly morbid. I'm quite concerned."

I put my hands on her shoulders. "Mom, I'm not trying to give you a stroke, kill you, or disappoint you. I can only control the circumstances that are mine. I can't help it if I keep getting dragged into everyone else's messes. I love you very much, but I have to track down the mayor to see if he'll agree to meet with me and my husband later this afternoon, so will you watch Kimberly for me?"

"Yes, yes. Of course," she said, still slightly flustered.

I started to leave, but couldn't let the opportunity to tease her a little bit more pass me by. "Hey, you know French, Mom. Holden mentioned something about the possibility of a ménage a trios. Does that translate to a truce or something?"

She went pale, but Dad nearly busted a gut laughing. "You're not funny, Emily. Don, quit goading her," she said sternly.

"Are you sure she's good here with you?" I directed more towards Dad since Mom was still fuming.

"She's great. Kimberly and PePaw are going to be taking a nap really soon on that there hammock. Isn't that right, Kimmiepoo?" She cooed her answer.

"I've got my cell phone. Call if you need, okay? I'm not sure how long I'll be gone. Her diaper bag's loaded with stuff and it's in the little basket under the stoller…"

"We've got this. Go. Don't give it another thought," Dad said.

"Thanks," I said, with a grin. I gave them each a kiss on the cheek and left for the cabin.

~.~.~.~.~

Truth be known, I was surprised that J.T. took my call. I was even more surprised when he started apologizing to *me*. He agreed to meet with us, but insisted that it be over dinner in the busiest, most upscale restaurant in Morgan City. He asked that Connie and Jackson join us, as well. I told him that I'd extend the invitation and he thanked me. Obviously, he had no intention of being alone with Holden.

After I disconnected from J.T., I headed to the hospital. Alphonse looked more pathetic than usual and he was basically inconsolable. As much as I tried to assure him that Holden and Jackson were doing everything they could to find Roberta, he had no desire to hear me or to talk about it. A nurse came into the room and injected some pain meds into his IV. Almost instantly, he fell asleep so I carefully retreated from the room without another word.

The rest of the morning was spent brainstorming theories of what might have become of Roberta with Connie. It was a little strange to not be in the middle of everything. Since Bert was busy running the department in Atchafalaya Parish and Holden was only recently included in the investigation, we weren't privy to much information about the case. I trusted Jackson's ability to lead, so I knew he was doing all in his power to get the case solved. Still, I felt as though I should be helping in some way. I needed to release some pent up angst and there was a beautiful, cypress tree-laden walking path circling the park.

"I'm going for a run," I announced.

"A run sounds perfect. I could sure use some fresh air. You mind if I come with you?"

"Absolutely not. Let's go pound some pavement!"

I changed into a pair of neon running shorts and a racer-back tank then pulled my hair into a tight ponytail before heading downstairs to stretch. It took all I had not to laugh at Connie when she came bouncing down the stairs to join me. The upper portion of her short, cropped hair looked like a wave of copper overflowing the confines of a bowl thanks to the tight, bright yellow headband she wore. Matching the sweatband were wristbands, ankle socks, and shorts. The top she picked was a deep red, which when mixed with all the bright yellow, brought forth images of a tomato orbiting the sun.

"You ready to do this?" she asked, coming up from a lunge to shake out her extremities.

"You know it," I said, leading the way to the asphalt path. We ran along the lakefront first and then passed the marina. We stopped long enough to allow a five-foot gator ample room to slide back into the narrow canal nearby. Once he was well on his way to the other side of the water, we picked up the pace. Soon, the Visitor's Center, the guard shack, and the playground were behind us and we were afforded some shade thanks to the towering trees. Saw Palmetto and cypress knees lined the new area we were in, as well as some really beautiful Louisiana irises. That portion of the trail ended and we were almost back to the lakefront when a snake darted across the path.

"Ack! Holy hell! That's a snake!" I yelled, stopping in my tracks and desperately grabbing on Connie.

"If we don't make any sudden moves, it will just go right on its way. At least it's just a king snake," Connie said with a shaky voice.

It was dead still until it turned its head to stare us down with beady little eyes. That was when my nerves got the best of me. I started running in place so quickly I looked like Jennifer Beals during the *Maniac* workout scene in *Flashdance*! "I said no sudden moves!" Connie snapped, clutching me as she ran in place, as well.

"You're moving, too!" I shrieked. The snake flicked its tongue a few times and slithered on across the path, through the grass, and under a fence. After I finished with my heebie-jeebie, I bent at the waist and pushed out a long sigh of relief.

"What are you getting all worked up for? It was just a tiny, little snake," Connie prodded.

"Don't you even pretend to be all brave and gallant now that it's gone! You were just as scared," I fussed.

"What, no! I thought we were trying to stay warmed up so we wouldn't cramp. I wasn't worried about that snake."

"Oh, no! You aren't going to…" My hearing was still honed thanks to the recent jolt of adrenaline. I quickly turned my head toward the strange noise in the distance.

"Do you hear that?"

Connie angled her head in several different directions before she finally agreed that something was coming from the direction of a pumping station across the way. "Let's see if it gets louder as we get closer."

We jogged the twenty or so yards to the end of the path then stopped to listen. It took a while, but the faint sound of metal pinging was definitely coming from the pumping station. We looked around, but no one was in sight.

"Wanna go check it out?" Connie asked, shrugging her shoulders.

"Why not? It's not too far away," I answered. We moved off the path and headed towards the pond-like area that housed a large metal shed with several huge pipes jutting into the water underneath it.

"I'll bet it's a gator clinking its tail against one of the pipes," Connie guessed.

"Doubtful. Maybe an egret pecking at the metal? Don't they like shiny stuff?"

"I have no clue."

I threw my palm against her chest to stop her from getting any closer to the water's edge. "Oh, my God." All of the moisture in my mouth vanished while my stomach did a nausea-induced flip.

"What? You don't see another snake, do you?" Connie nervously asked while rapidly scanning the area.

I couldn't speak, I could only point. Connie sucked in a sharp breath when she saw the blonde haired woman tied to one of the smaller pipes. The lower half of her body was submerged, but her torso was tethered in a way that kept her hands free. Her head slumped forward and the long, blond hair that spilled forward kept us from positively identifying her.

"Is that Roberta? Ohmahgosh! Is she dead?" she rattled in what sounded like one sentence.

Just then, a tiny wave carried the seemingly lifeless arm across the surface and against one of the pipes. *Ding!* The bracelet she wore emitted a bell-like sound when it made contact with the metal.

Unable to take my eyes from the sight, I frantically dug around inside my sports bra for my cell phone. "Holden! Holden! I need you to come to the park right away! Call for an ambulance, too!"

"Slow down, baby! Are you okay? Is Kimberly okay?"

"We're fine. But this is so horrible, Holden. Is Jackson still with you?" I asked without stopping for air.

"We were on our way back to the park so we're not far away. Emily, where are you?"

"The pumping station off of the walking trail. Hurry!" I cried. He relayed our whereabouts to Jackson and before I had the chance to give any further details, I saw the police unit speeding our way. Connie and I ran to meet them.

"We heard this clanging noise after the snake and we came to see what it was and we found her tied up down there and we're pretty sure it's Roberta, but it looks so bad!" I rambled as Connie and I quickly led Holden and Jackson to the spot.

Another *ding* sounded as soon as we got to the locked chain-link gate that protected the catwalk leading into the metal shed.

"I'll get some bolt cutters from my car," Jackson said, yanking a key fob from a little space in his gun belt and taking off at a full run.

I tried my hardest to get my emotions in check while desperately clinging to Holden. It would be so easy to wail, scream, or sob, but that wouldn't do anyone any good.

"I just saw her head move?" Holden said.

"You saw it, too?" Connie asked.

Holden didn't say another word; he quickly dropped his gun belt, emptied his pockets, kicked off his shoes, and disappeared into the water.

"What's he doing?" Jackson breathlessly asked, returning with the bolt cutters.

"We think she's alive," Connie and I excitedly said at the same time.

"I'm going to help him." Jackson began removing his clothes and tossing them to the side until he was left in nothing but a pair of boxer briefs. "The ambulance should be here any minute," he said, handing Connie his wallet before diving into the canal. He cut into the water with clean, solid strokes which allowed him to quickly catch up with Holden.

"Is it Roberta?" Jackson yelled.

Holden finally reached her. "Yes! It's her!"

Once Jackson was within a few feet of Roberta, he slowed his approach and treaded water in front of her while Holden positioned himself behind her. Holden opened his pocket knife and fervently sawed through layer after layer of rope. Jackson remained in front of her, and though I couldn't make out what he was saying, I was sure he was

127

offering words of encouragement or comfort. Once her torso was freed, she fell forward right into Jackson's waiting arms. Connie and I nervously chewed our lips as we waited for him to bring her in our direction.

"Is she okay?" I called once Jackson reached the water's edge.

"She's weak, but she's talking," Jackson answered. He waited for Holden to start the climb up the steep embankment before he handed her over. Once Holden reached the flat, grassy area that Connie and I were so anxiously pacing, he gently placed her on the ground. I bundled up Jackson's uniform pants and put them under her head and used his shirt as a temporary blanket. Connie went to his car to search for a first aid kit.

I used my fingertips and gently moved the damp, stringy blonde locks from her face. When I saw her condition, I sucked in a hard breath. The color of her skin was a disconcerting shade of gray and her lips were about four shades darker than her skin. She was ice cold. There were gashes all over her face, neck, and arms, but none of them bled. They just laid open, offering a peek at the pale tissues that used to be protected by the skin. Her eyes were rolled back so that only the whites were showing and the word, *SLUT*, had been carved into her forehead. Part of me wanted to cry, but a bigger part wanted to vomit.

"Dear God," I mumbled. "Who would do such a thing?"

"We'll find that out. You just focus and take care of her," Holden insisted.

Connie rejoined us with a small medic bag. It had nothing that would be of use to us, except a survival blanket. We had just finished wrapping Roberta when the ambulance arrived. I was never so happy to see a set of flashing lights! I now knew the wrenching desperation and immense relief our patient's families felt when we responded to their calls for help.

Jackson, draped in a wool blanket, kicked off his wet boxer briefs, slid on his uniform pants, then dropped the blanket to quickly finish dressing. He was lacing up his boots when he looked at Holden. "You're soaked. Go back to the cabin and get showered and changed. I'm going to follow them to the hospital," he said, nodding to the crew that was securing Roberta to the stretcher. "Just meet me there when you get squared away."

Holden, with his hand on the small of my back, nodded and pointed in the direction of the cabin. "Connie, Emily. Let's go."

My feet stayed firmly planted. It wasn't until the back doors of the ambulance closed and it began to drive off that I finally allowed myself to look away. Roberta was finally finding happiness after a life filled with pain and strife. It wasn't fair for her to have to endure another tragedy. Still in shock, Connie and I held onto each other as we followed a dripping wet Holden to the cabin.

Before he got into the shower, he entered the kitchen and began opening and closing all of the cabinet doors. He pulled out a bottle of vodka, filled two juice glasses nearly half full, then added a splash of OJ to each. "Sit and drink this—both of you. It's going to be a long day." He nodded to the drinks he'd set on the table and left us. We needed no further encouragement. Connie refilled the juice glasses once more before we left with Holden for the hospital.

.

10

When Connie and I arrived at the hospital, Roberta was barely clinging to life. The doctors were having a difficult time stabilizing her blood pressure, so only time would tell if she'd survive the day. We were anxiously pacing the waiting room when Holden came in with an update.

"Alphonse is awake. He's still not talking, but the doctor said he should make a full recovery." He rubbed the stubble on his face. "I've never seen the little guy so despondent and depressed. I'm really worried about his mental health."

"Is anyone with him now?" I asked.

"No, Jackson and I told him we'd check back later."

"Maybe I should visit again?" I volunteered.

"I suppose it wouldn't hurt. He's under protection, so I'll have to go with you."

"Connie, will you let me know if there's any change with Roberta?"

"Of course! Please tell Alphonse that I'm thinking of him."

I nodded, let out a pent up breath, and followed Holden into the elevator. Roberta was on the second floor, Alphonse the sixth. He pushed the button and as soon as the elevator began to rise, he pulled me into his arms.

"How are you?" His lips pressed lightly against the top of my head.

"I can't even begin to put into words what I'm feeling. My heart breaks for Alphonse. He only just found someone who appreciates him. And Roberta, she's had such a horrible life and it was finally starting to turn around for her... How could Donovan have done such a horrid thing to them? Holden, that wasn't just spite, what happened to them was the work of someone incredibly evil. Her forehead..."

"You didn't honestly think that Donovan had a huge change of heart once he got away? He shot a man in front of you, Emily. Why would this surprise you?"

"I'm thankful that—for whatever reason—he never released that monster on me." A deep shiver tore through my body.

"Me, too." Once the elevator stopped, he pulled away and placed his hand on the small of my back. I was led down a short corridor where a uniformed guard sat at the end of the hall. He snapped to attention when he saw Holden.

"Sheriff Dautry. I wasn't expecting to see you again so soon. Ma'am," he tossed in my direction with a curt head nod.

"This is my wife, Emily. She's a friend of Deputy Rivet and seeing her might cheer him up some. She won't be long."

"Yes, sir," the officer said, slowly pushing the door open so I could enter.

"Aren't you coming?" I quietly asked Holden.

He shook his head. "We've already visited. I'll be right here if you need anything. You go."

I nervously wrung my hands a few times before Holden

gave my back an encouraging rub. I gave him a quick smile to let him know that it was okay and slowly made my way into the darkened room. The faint hum of an IV pump was the only sound I heard.

"Alphonse?" I softly called while inching closer to the hospital bed. He didn't answer. With bated breath, I rounded the corner and found him staring at the far wall. "Alphonse, it's Emily."

He stirred only slightly, still refusing to look at me. "How's my girl? Is she gonna make it?"

"They're doing everything they can," I answered.

"Yeah, that's what they told me. I want to know what you think. Is she gonna make it?"

I closed my eyes for a minute, unsure of what my response should be. Taking the chair closest to me, I pulled it right to the edge of the bed and sat. "I think she will. She's a survivor."

"I shoulda protected her better. I coulda done more. If she dies, her blood is on my hands. It's like I killed her." His mouth opened, letting out a sound that rocked me to my core—a high-pitched mix between a breathy wail and a cry that told of more heartbreak than words ever could.

"Oh, Alphonse. Please don't cry. You'd never do anything to hurt Roberta and we all know that. There's no way you could've saved her from those two by yourself," I said, trying to control the urge to cry with him.

"They was so mean to her, Emily. So mean. I suppose you want me to tell you about it." He drew in a ragged, shaky breath.

"Of course I want to know what happened. Can Holden come in, too? He really should hear this," I cautiously suggested.

"Will you promise to stay with me?"

"I promise I'm not going anywhere. We've been speculating that Donovan Guidry was behind this. Was he?" Alphonse suddenly stopped crying and a sinister sneer formed at the corners of his mouth. "Mark my words," he stated through gritted teeth, "I may not be the smartest or the strongest man around, but I'm gonna make sure he gets what he deserves."

"I understand where you're coming from, but hopefully that won't be necessary. People from all over the state are looking for him right now. They'll catch him and they'll make him pay," I said encouragingly.

Alphonse carefully shifted in the bed so he could sit upright.

"I want him to be mine." The way he said it combined with dark, sunken eyes and extremely pale skin instantly brought back memories of Brad.

"I'll just go get Holden now." I lurched from the seat and waved him into the room.

"Alphonse is ready to talk," I said softly.

"Okay, let's see what he has to say." Holden pulled a second chair to the side of the bed and took a seat next to me. Before he was settled, Alphonse began to speak.

"What do you want to know first?" he asked.

"How about we start with who did this?" Holden answered.

Alphonse turned his dark, defeated eyes our way.

"Donovan Guidry and some big guy. He was wearin' a mask like them wrestlers on TV."

"Tell me what happened," Holden encouraged.

Alphonse returned his gaze to the spot on the wall. "We was supposed to meet Emily and Connie at the park to listen to some music. Roberta was all excited. She loves to dance, you know?"

I nodded even though he wasn't looking my way.

"She was first one outta the door, but she musta forgot something 'cause she turned around to tell me something. That's when they jumped her. At first, I thought she tripped and fell. She smacked hard against the cabinets and sprawled out on the floor. I went to help her and that's when they stormed into the camper. Donovan Guidry shoved a gun in my face and told me I best not make a move. They shut the door and told us that if we made any noise they'd shoot. Berta was still stunned and not moving, they was looking at her real close like, so I tried to make a grab for my gun. The big guy must be some karate dude or something. He whirled around and kicked my hand so hard I thought it had come off! It didn't, though," he said, holding it up and wiggling his fingers.

"What happened next?" Holden asked.

"He kicked Berta in the ribs and told me that if I did anything stupid like that again, it would be much worse on her. Donovan was telling me all of the horrible things he was going to do to Berta. I tried so hard to get loose from the ropes, but they was too tight. They made me watch when Donovan..." His voice trailed off and tears started to flow. I gently patted the top of his hand.

"I know this is hard for you to talk about, Alphonse. You're doing a great job," Holden said. "Take a breath and go on when you're ready."

Alphonse cleared his throat. "I watched him pull out a bandana and shove it into her mouth. That's when she started to move around. He climbed on top of her, pinning her down. He pulled the knife and cut into her forehead. Her screams were muffled, but God almighty, I knew how much she was sufferin'. I tried to get close enough to kick or something, but the big guy punched me so hard I flipped over backwards. I'll be honest. Stuff got really fuzzy after that. Donovan told the other guy to quit messing with me. He sat me upright—I remember that. I remember the sting of that thing going in my chest. I remember trying to holler when they roughed up Roberta some more. My mouth was taped and I got the hell knocked out of me. I don't remember anything after that until I woke up in the hospital."

"Do you remember anything about when we found you?" I asked.

"Nope. I keep on tryin', but I can't."

"It's okay. You've been really helpful, Alphonse. Why don't you get some rest now?"

"I'll tell you, Sheriff. I been scared before. Emily, you remember how scared we was when Kent Sonnier was going to kill us?"

"I remember."

"You're one of my favorite people ever—even had a crush on you, and all…" Not a trace of embarrassment was in his voice. I, however, was blushing deep red. "…but all of that was nothing compared to how I felt when they said they was going to hurt Berta. I ain't never felt that way ever in my life and I hope I never have to feel it again. I don't wanna live without her."

"I know the feeling. Sounds like you found your soul mate," Holden said, lightly squeezing my thigh before standing. "Thanks for the information, Alphonse. I'll pass on what you've told me to Chief Sonnier. I'm sure he'll send a detective over for a formal statement."

"Can it be tomorrow, you think? I just want to be alone with my thoughts right now."

"I'll be sure he knows that. There's a guard outside your door. Let him know if you need anything."

"Thank you," he said, staring off again. "Can you catch

the lights on your way out? The doctor says if I rest up, I'll heal faster. The faster I heal, the sooner I'll get to visit with Berta."

"Sure," I agreed as I began flipping switches. "We'll see you tomorrow. Rest well, Alphonse."

"I'm glad I helped Pete that day," he threw in as I was going out of the door. "I know exactly how he felt."

Though I couldn't see him in the darkened room, I heard his controlled sobs. Poor Alphonse! I knew all too well what it was like to lose the person who means the most to you. No one should ever have to feel that pain. I eventually overcame, but I had serious doubts about Alphonse if Roberta didn't bounce back from this one.

~.~.~.~.~.~

There was no way that we were going to leave as scheduled. J.T. put in a few phone calls and our stay was extended for another week. Over the next several days, Connie and I took turns visiting with Roberta in ICU. She stabilized, but still hadn't opened her eyes. Connie told me that the last time she visited they wheeled Alphonse in for a few minutes. He really manned up and got through the entire visit without one inappropriate word, phrase, or gesture. Whatever he said to her worked, because not long after, Roberta regained consciousness. She began doing so well that the doctors considered moving her to a private room if she continued healing at that pace. A private room is where I found her the next day.

Her eyes were closed, but as soon as she heard me set the vase of brightly colored flowers on the table next to the bed, she woke with a start.

"Oh, Em. Hi," she said with a very faint smile and an

extremely raspy voice. "You brought me flowers. They're beautiful."

"I didn't mean to scare you," I apologized.

"Don't worry about that. It's been hard to sleep."

"Lots of visitors?" I asked, pulling a chair next to her bed.

"Gobs. I've been visited by people who want to help me, people who want to solve the crime, people who could've been much nicer—that lab lady who draws my blood is not very friendly—and I don't mean to sound unappreciative, but look at me. All the way around, I'm a big, old mess. What I really want to do is lock myself up in a room and never come out. I've been through a lot in my life, but Emily, I don't know how I'm going to get past this." Her eyes were filled with pain and suffering.

"This is still overwhelming. You're recovering from a very traumatic near-death experience and it's going to take some time to sort everything out. Listen to me. It doesn't seem like it will ever happen, but it will get better. They're going to catch Donovan and the other guy and no one will ever have to worry about them again."

She shook her head. "It won't matter if he's found and locked up. He's still going to come after me."

"Why would you say that?"

"Because that's what he told me. He wanted me to be found. He said that's the only thing that kept him from putting a bullet in my head once he finished..." She let out some sort of disheartening mix between a sob and a snort. "He told me that he wants me to live in fear, never knowing if he's lurking behind some building or hiding in a closet. Then he told me that if somehow he does get caught, he'll have someone else to do his dirty work for him. How am I supposed to live like that, Em? What kind of life am I supposed to lead never knowing who's coming to get me or when they're going to do it? If only I had died..."

"Please don't say things like that. That sick bastard needs to be caught and put under the jail." I inched closer to the bed so I could take her hand. "Listen to me. If anyone knows what it's like to live in fear of the unknown, it's me. Giving up seems so much easier than fighting right now because you're emotionally and physically drained. You can't give in to that feeling. You didn't survive everything else in your life to have it all end now that you've found happiness. You're important to a lot of people. We're going to rally together and we'll be here for you, so feel free to lean on us for a while. Someday you'll be there to return the favor. That's how this friendship thing works."

She started to tear up. "That's really sweet of you, but I don't think you've thought this through. What if your being friends with me puts a bigger target on your back? Not to mention, I have the word 'slut' carved into my forehead. How am I supposed to wander around in public with that? I suppose I could wear bangs for the rest of my life, but what if a breeze blows or I get caught in the rain? And what about the emotional scars? If you think Brad's behavior was vile at T-Jacks, that was *nothing* compared to what those two did to me in that pump house."

My breath caught. "Have you told anyone about it yet?"

She slowly shook her head. "The police officers keep asking me, but I feel so ashamed. They even sent in a female hoping it would make me feel more comfortable. I just can't right now."

I was at a loss for words, so I gently squeezed Roberta's hand. After a minute or so, I gave her what I hoped would be a comforting semi-smile. "Would you like me to sit with you for a while?"

"I don't want to keep you from your family. I was thinking of asking the nurse for another dose of pain medication so I can sleep the rest of this day away. But before you go, have you seen Alphonse? Is he doing okay?"

"I did visit with him. He's counting the seconds until he can see you again."

"That's nice." She turned to stare out of the window.

"What are you thinking?" I finally asked when I noticed her fidgeting with the corners of the blanket.

"Should I cut him loose?"

"He'll be heartbroken. Why would you even consider that?"

She slowly turned to look at me. A solitary tear streaked down her pale cheek. "It was videoed. The stuff that happened at the boathouse; they videotaped it. I don't know if they did it for their own sick pleasure or if they intend to flood the internet with it, but either way, there is a possibility that people will see it. Let's say I get my forehead fixed. How am I supposed to live a normal life knowing that people I pass on the street may have witnessed and enjoyed watching my torture?"

I tried to put myself in her shoes, but my mind just couldn't fathom it. "Roberta, what did they do to you?" I asked very softly.

She began to sniffle. "I honestly don't remember most of it because I passed out after a while, but the stuff I do remember..."

I didn't push for answers. Instead, I let her decide what she wanted to say and when she wanted to say it.

"There weren't a lot of people outside, but there were some. I was still stunned from when I fell and hit my head against the cabinets, so I wasn't paying much attention. The big guy wore a mask while he was inside, but he took it off before carrying me out. Too bad I was so out of it that I couldn't get a look at his face. I heard Donovan explaining to the people out there that I had partied too hard at the festival. Obviously, they bought it. No one said anything more. In fact, I want to say I heard laughter." She squinted her eyes tightly as she tried to replay the moment in her head.

"It's okay. Take your time."

"What they did was they mostly messed with my mind. They brought me to the pump house. Once the man sat me on the floor, he put his mask back on and Donovan tossed him this old, ratty satchel. Inside was a long rope and as he began unfurling it, he said things about how good it was going to feel to wrap it around my neck and how fun it would be to watch the life get sucked from me. Emily, I was scared at T-Jack's, but I never knew real terror until I was in that pump house. My head had pretty much stopped bleeding, but I was covered in blood. He wrapped my wrists and then tossed the rope over this large pipe. The balls of my feet were barely touching the floor once he finished hoisting me and it felt as though my arms would pop out of their sockets. He dug through the bag and came out with this huge knife. I opened my mouth to scream, but he slowly shook his head back and forth in warning." She began to cry. I moved from the chair to a spot on the bed and gently embraced her. She rested her head on my shoulder while I softly stroked her back.

"You're safe now, Roberta. You've got a guard at your door and all kinds of agencies looking for them. You don't have to go on if you don't want to. There's time."

"After the stuff you went through with Kent—did you feel better once you got it out or did it make things worse?"

"Both." I answered honestly. "I got very anxious talking about it, but once it was out, I felt better knowing that someone else knew my pain."

She considered that for a minute. "Donovan pulled out a video camera and took a seat on the floor. He said he was going to watch it over and over. Then he told the other guy, 'You know what to do' and he nodded." A little sob escaped Roberta's lips as she closed her eyes tightly. "He used the knife to cut away some of my clothes, making sure he took his time at places like my throat and my wrists. I was trembling so hard, I kept praying the knife wouldn't slip. After that, he threatened to cut off parts of my body and each time I felt the pressure of the knife increase, I'd yelp. They laughed whenever they got me to make a noise or made me flinch. I can still feel that cold blade against my skin," she said with a shiver.

I let out a faint gasp and instantly regretted it.

"I shouldn't be telling you this," she said awkwardly.

"Yes, you should. You can tell me anything. If anyone can relate to this, it's me. Go on, Berta. Get it out."

She zoned out, but I intently listened as she finished telling the rest of her story. The more she told, the more nauseous I felt, but I didn't let her know.

"...Donovan loved seeing me weak and helpless like that. After what seemed like a lifetime, he stood up and told the other guy to move out of the way because it was his turn. That's when my body finally gave out. I lost consciousness, only regaining it briefly when they put me in the cold water and tied me under the pump house. Donovan grabbed a fistful of my hair and smashed my head against the pipe. I don't remember anything else until I woke up in the hospital."

Taking a tissue from the box on the nightstand, I lightly wiped the tears from her face.

"It's going to take some time, but I promise you, it will get better," I said softly. "You'll probably have nightmares and flashbacks for a while, so I can't even begin to tell you how important it is that you see someone about this as soon as possible. A therapist will be able to help you process this in a way that's not self-destructive. You're going to want to blame yourself, but you can't. It's not your fault. It took me a very long time to learn that and I don't want you to go through the same thing I did."

"You still want to help me. Why?" she asked weakly.

"Roberta, we cleared the air between us a long time ago. You're my friend and you'll always be my friend. I care about you and I don't want to see you hurting. If I can help take some of the pain away, then I'm going to do it. There's nothing you can tell me that will make me think less of you or turn my back on you. I don't have a lot of close friends, but the ones I do have are my friends for life."

"I've never had people to lean on—ever. Then Alphonse came around, but I can't tell him about this. Not yet, anyway. It might take me a while to figure this friend thing out. I hope you can be patient with me"

"Don't you worry about it. We've got all the time in the world. I'm here for you. The most important thing for you to know is that you didn't deserve this."

"That's exactly what I was feeling. You do understand." She began to cry once again, and this time I joined her.

Roberta eventually fell asleep. I knew that Jackson needed to hear the information I'd gathered, so I quietly slipped out of her room and called him once I got into the parking lot. He asked me to meet him at the beautiful, oak tree laden park where the festival's musical stage had been set up. I got there within minutes, and since the park was deserted, I slowly swayed back and forth on one of the swings while waiting for his arrival.

A nice breeze blew and the gentle rocking motion of the swing made it even more delightful. I closed my eyes and breathed in deeply as I became totally oblivious to my surroundings. The swing made a slight squeal and groan with every new trip. The cadence picked up as I willed the swing to move faster and higher. Before I knew it, I felt as though I was soaring to the sky and plummeting back to Earth. I hadn't felt that way since I was a little girl! It helped invigorate my weary soul.

When I finally opened my eyes, I spied Jackson sitting on one of the park benches, smiling broadly as he watched me glide back and forth through the air. I stuck out my feet and dragged them across the ground. When I was a kid, I had the exact foot to ground ratio down pat and had a clean, smooth stop every time. My adult dismount was anything but graceful and to top it off, the sudden dizziness that came with it was quite unexpected. Red with embarrassment, I stumbled across the way to join the now chuckling Jackson on the bench.

"Have a few drinks before you came over?" he asked.

"Not a one. What the hell was that about? I never got wobbly from being on a swing before."

"It's part of getting older. Get used to it."

"Are you messing with me?" I asked, turning my head from side to side to restore my equilibrium.

"Nope. Want to get on the merry-go-round so I can prove it? What about the see-saw?"

"No thanks. I'll pass on that one." I shook my head, finally satisfied that I was mostly back to normal.

"So Roberta talked to you today?" he inquired.

"Oh, Jackson. I thought she'd been through a lot in her life, but the hell those mean bastards put her through in that pump house... I don't know if she'll ever be the same again. I think I've talked her into seeing a therapist. She'll need it." His brows furrowed. "What did she say?"

"Most of it was psychological torture, not that it makes it any better. Her scars, except for the obvious one on her forehead, are going to be internal."

"Did she give you specifics?"

"Yes, and unfortunately, the identity of the second man is still a mystery."

"Will you come to the police department so I can tape your statement?"

"Sure. Whatever helps."

He stood up and stretched his arms high overhead, so I stood, too. An awkward look appeared on his face, as if he were struggling with some sort of internal dialogue.

"What's up with you?" I warily asked.

"I know that you had a rough day and that it couldn't have been easy for you to hear the things Roberta told you. If you must know, I was trying to decide whether or not it would appropriate for me to give you a hug."

The tingly feeling in my nose forewarned the imminent shedding of tears. "Appropriate and much needed."

"I figured you were putting on a brave face. Come here," he said, wrapping me in his arms.

"It's kind of creepy that you know me so well," I said with a sniffle.

"Bah, it was just a lucky guess." He pulled away and offered me a smile. "Would you rather we do this tomorrow?"

"No, let's do it while it's all fresh. The more details I can give, the less your detectives will have to grill Roberta.

She's so fragile right now. She doesn't need long interviews or constant repetition of the events."

"My people are pretty sharp, but I'll be sure to talk with the person who will interview her."

"Thank you. So, should I follow you to the station now or should we set a time to meet?"

"We'll meet in an hour. Go get Holden; he needs to hear this, too."

I nodded then stood on my tip toes and gave him a passing kiss on the cheek. "Thank you for everything."

He gave a slight grin. "Don't mention it. I'll see you soon."

11

"What time are we supposed to be having dinner with your friend, the mayor?" Holden asked when he called the next afternoon. He and Jackson were at MCPD working the case.

"I'm not sure if a night out on the town is appropriate anymore—I mean with Roberta and Alphonse being in the hospital. Have you gotten closer to finding Donovan and his guy?"

"Not really. Roberta's still not up to talking. Jackson and I discussed it and we decided that it would probably be better for us to try again in the morning. In the meantime, the detectives are still working on the case based upon the evidence they collected and the interview you gave. As far as the case goes, there's nothing more we can do. And, as for our night out, I don't think you have anything to worry about. Alphonse and Roberta are physically fine and we need to unwind." There was a brief pause. "Hey, you're not trying to keep me from meeting this joker, are you?"

"No! Not at all. I really thought that..."

"I'm messing with you. Never mind the explanations. I want you and Connie to get dressed up and ready to go. I'll be there in a little while to change. Jackson accepted the invitation from the mayor, so he'll be meeting us at the restaurant."

"Will he now? I'm glad that you two are getting along so well," I said.

"We're working together to solve a case so I guess the best term for it is temporary truce."

"Whatever you want to call it, I'm glad it's happening. Okay, Connie and I are going to get ready. I'll see you soon."

"Hey, before you hang up... How are you doing, Em? I know that yesterday was pretty traumatic for you."

My heart melted when I heard the concern in his voice. "I'm okay. I'm better today."

"Good. I'll see you soon. I'm going to stop off at your Mom and Dad's RV to visit with Kimmiepoo for a bit then I'll be at the cabin to dress for dinner."

"Holden, you are *not* calling our daughter Kimmiepoo!"

"Why not? Your dad does it and it's cute." He laughed.

"It won't be so cute when she's thirty-four and she's still known as Kimmiepoo."

"I'm sure she'll outgrow it. Quit worrying so much."

"Oh yeah, tell Doodlebug to quit worrying. Ugh!" Holden chuckled. "I love you and I'll see you soon."

"Love you, too." I disconnected the call and yelled to Connie, "Roberta's stable, Alphonse is making progress, and Holden wants us to go ahead with dinner. Time for us to get dolled up, cher!"

Connie leaned out of the bathroom door. She was wearing a beautiful, emerald green dress with strappy gold heels and her makeup was nearly flawless. "Girl, I was in here getting ready before you finished telling that man, 'hello'. We need some good food and some potent drinks to turn this trip around."

"Yeah, well if you stop to think about it, good food and

potent drinks are what got us into this situation in the first place."

Connie came out of the bathroom and stood in front of me. Her fingers rapidly tapping away as she held her hands on her hips. "Did we have fun that day?"

"Yes."

"Did we do anything wrong?"

"No."

"Exactly! Get your butt in that room and get changed! Now!"

I wasn't about to cross Connie. I took off for the bedroom and didn't come out until I was fully dressed and ready to go.

~.~.~.~.~

The restaurant J.T. picked couldn't have been more inviting. We were ushered through a richly decorated hallway and into a dimly lit private dining room. Soft piano music floated through the air as we made our way to our table. People I'd never seen in my life nodded and smiled as I passed them. Some even acknowledged my presence with a quick, "Hello" or "Nice to see you." I realized they must've recognized me from the photo in the paper and suddenly I wished the floor would swallow me up.

J.T. stood when he saw us and eagerly reached out to shake Jackson's hand. "Chief Sonnier. Good to see you. Connie. Emily," he said with a nod to each of us. "And you must be Sheriff Dautry?"

"Holden," he said, offering his hand to him.

J.T. seemed to relax somewhat after the initial pleasantries were out of the way. "Shall we start with the hot crab appetizer and perhaps a chardonnay?" Everyone was in agreement, so he relayed the request to our waiter who rushed off to fill the order.

We'd barely even settled in our seats when J.T. mentioned the elephant in the room. "I think the best way to handle the situation is to just get this thing resolved as quickly as possible. Sheriff Dautry, I assure you that the pictures that were published were simply the manipulation of some sick individual to cast doubt about the morality of either your wife or myself."

"They sure as hell looked pretty convincing to me," Holden maintained. "Why would someone do that? What would they possibly have to gain?"

"I can't speak for your wife, but it might be a way for some of the older, more influential citizens to let me know exactly where they stand in regards to a certain issue I recently brought to their attention."

"I'm confused. How could your being photographed with the wife of a public official be seen as positive? Are they trying to oust you?" Holden asked.

J.T. smiled broadly when the waiter arrived with the appetizer and wine. As soon as the waiter left, J.T. answered Holden's question.

"It's quite unfortunate, but some of them tend to hold a cheating mayor in higher regard than a homosexual one," he blurted out.

We all stopped what we were doing and stared at J.T. "Why didn't you tell me you were gay?" I asked.

"It's not something I tend to flaunt. I want people to like or dislike me based upon who I am, not my sexual preference. I doubt you start conversations with, "Hi, hetero-Emily here," he asserted. He had a valid point.

"That's true," I sheepishly replied.

"How many people know about your..." Holden left

his sentence hanging.

"Homosexuality? Saying it won't convert you, if that what your scared of," J.T. joked. I knew he was ribbing him, but Holden wriggled uncomfortably in his chair. *Good for J.T.! It's about time someone put Holden Dautry in the hot seat! Given him hell!* I silently goaded him.

"Yes, your homosexuality," Holden choked out.

"Well, most of my family. A few friends. There's a man I've been seeing for a while now, a lawyer from Baton Rouge. Normally, I drive up to visit him, but lately he's been coming down here to see me. One day we were getting breakfast in town and one of the 'tribe elders', as I like to call them, put two and two together. Things have been squirrely ever since."

"Okay, but that still doesn't explain why you zeroed in on Em," Connie shot out.

Poor Jackson, who up until that point looked as though he was about to face a firing squad, suddenly looked on with curiosity.

"Thanks, Connie. I couldn't have worded it better myself," Holden said with a triumphant smile.

"Yeah, Connie. Thanks," I said, heat rising in my cheeks.

"Look at you two. You're probably two of the most gorgeous women I've ever laid eyes on. And you, you little red-headed bundle of piss and vinegar, *you* were the one who first caught my attention."

Connie looked surprised. "Me?"

"Yes, you! I was coming over to speak with both of you, but you took off to go dancing without Emily, so I introduced myself to her. Poor thing looked like a little lost puppy. I love to dance and I noticed that she had a huge honkin' ring on her finger, so it was obvious she was married.

She was beyond adorable with the shy act. Basically, what it boils down to is that I knew there would be no pressure on either of us, and since you weren't from around here, I was sincere with my offer of hospitality. That's it. No ulterior motive—except possibly a friendship down the line if we hit it off, which I think we did?" he asked hopefully.

"I had a blast and I'd love for us to remain friends," I blurted.

"So this is legit. No bullshit—no anything else. You believe it was merely a setup to get you booted from office because some of the old guys around here don't agree with your lifestyle?" Holden asked.

"I do," J.T. maintained.

"And the picture of you two making out on the balcony?" Holden inquired.

"Totally faked. If I kissed Emily that night, I assure you, it was only on the cheek."

"Okay. That's good enough for me," Holden said looking more relaxed than I'd seen him in a long while. "For the record, I have no issue with your sexual preference. The issue I had with you was thinking you were after my wife."

"So how about a big, old do-over? Is everyone okay with that? Chief Sonnier, is there anything we need to discuss? Any questions I can answer for you?" J.T. asked cautiously.

"No sir, Mr. Mayor. What you just discussed has absolutely no bearing on my ability to do my job," Jackson answered.

"Glad to hear it. I don't want this night to be any more awkward than it already is. Please call me J.T. and if you don't mind, I'll call you Jackson?"

"Jackson's fine," he said.

"Good. After this fuddy-duddy dinner, how would

y'all like to go dancing at one of the night clubs in the next parish? Awesome music and a great time are guaranteed!" J.T. asked, expectantly looking from face to face for an answer.

"I think that Emily and I are going to call it an early night," Holden said. I nodded in agreement.

"Well, if you don't mind toting around the spunky monkey, I'm in!" Connie exclaimed.

"Spunky monkey?" J.T. curiously asked.

"Oh no," I breathed when I noticed Connie jumping up from her seat.

She bent her knees to position herself into a sort of demi-plie then wildly waved her arms up and down. "Yep, spunky monkey! Watch out! Oo! oo! ah! ah!"

"Sweetness, you are a hoot! We're going to get along just fine," J.T. laughed. "What about you, Jackson? You in?"

"No, sir. I'm out. I really need to check in on the detectives to see how they're making out with the park case."

"Good man. See, that's why I hired him," J.T. said before changing topics. "So, does everyone know what they want for dinner?" He nodded to signal our waiter.

After an hour or so, I was stuffed, relaxed, and ready to leave. The food was excellent and the company more than wonderful, but I was emotionally and physically drained.

"Don't worry about Andre. I'll check on him before we go back to the cabin. I know how much you love being out and about. I want you to dance til you can't dance anymore, my little social butterfly," I said teasingly.

"Thank ya, honey. Watch out, J.T. I hope you'll be able to keep up with me. I'm an old pro at this," Connie proclaimed.

"Sounds like a challenge. Game on!" J.T. exclaimed.

Holden and I made our goodbye rounds—he led off

with handshakes; I followed behind offering kisses on the cheek. He put his hand on the small of my back and ushered me from the restaurant. I leaned heavily against him. Most of the older people who had been so welcoming when we walked in had left, so I was spared the pageantry on the way out.

Connie was burning the midnight oil with J.T., Alphonse and Roberta were resting comfortably at the hospital, and Jackson was working to catch the responsible parties. The little ones were soundly sleeping in the RV with Mom and Dad, and Holden and I had the cabin to ourselves. After an incredibly relaxing solo shower, I slid into a satiny night gown, shut off the lights, and joined Holden in bed. I rested my head on his shoulder and he rolled to wrap me tightly in an embrace. My fingertips gently traced a path along all the muscular ridges of his tanned chest and abdomen. A contented sigh escaped my lips.

"I'm sorry this trip didn't go as expected," Holden said.

"I hate that Alphonse and Roberta had to go through what they did and I'm sorry those pictures came out. You need to remember that I made vows to you, Holden. No matter what you may hear or see, I don't want to be with anyone but you."

His lips lightly brushed my forehead. "Ah, I should've known better. I completely overreacted. You shouldn't feel as though you need to walk on eggshells around me. If we can't be together, I *want* you to have a good time and to enjoy your friends. You living your life to the fullest is what makes me happy and you can't do that if you're constantly worrying how I'm going to react to a situation. I love you. I trust you—even with Jackson," he said softly. "I still get this jab in the gut when I see you two together, but it's not because I don't trust you. I'm still mad at myself for treating you the way I did." He rolled to lie on his back.

"We don't need to talk about this right now," I said, moving to cuddle with him.

"Are you seriously saying that you're tired of hearing me admit that I was wrong?" he teased.

"Yes, I am."

"Okay, then you pick the topic of discussion," he suggested.

"The Spunky Monkey," I said.

Holden laughed. "Are you wishing we had joined them?"

"No, not really. I wonder what time she plans on coming back?"

"She's fine, Emily," he insisted.

I moved to kiss him softly on the lips. "You really think I'm worrying for nothing?"

"I do. There isn't anyone out there more capable of taking care of herself, no matter the circumstances, than Connie Hebert. How that barely five foot tall, skinny as a rail woman can intimidate six foot four inch men, I have no clue. But, she does it."

His words reassured me enough that I pushed the sinking feeling from the pit of my stomach and finally fell asleep.

~.~.~.~.~.~

Holden and I were nearly packed by the time Connie stumbled out of her bedroom the next morning.

"What in the hell happened to you?" Holden asked without hesitation.

If her smeared, clown-like makeup hadn't made her eyes so heavily lidded, I'd imagine she was doing her best to shoot him an angry glare. Her short, red hair shot straight up in every direction and dark lipstick smudges ran from her lips, up one cheek, and to her temple. She still wore the same dress from the previous night, but it was so wrinkled and stretched out that it looked like an oversized t-shirt. The only thing more shocking than her appearance was her smell! She reeked of booze and stale cigarette smoke. Without a word, she clumsily fought her way to the coffee pot and poured a mug. Well, half a mug since most of it spilled onto the counter. She flicked off the remains of a set of false eyelashes then swallowed two large mouthfuls. She turned her squinty gaze in my direction.

"Why did you let me do that? I'm an old married woman with a kid. Why didn't you just insist I come back here with you?" she croaked.

"You're thirty-two, Connie."

"Ancient. Absolutely decrepit."

"It's the alcohol making you feel that way. How much did you have? And did you start smoking?" I asked, slowly waving my hand in front of my face.

She lifted her arms and gave her body a hearty sniff. "I don't... Oh, what in the hell is this?" she asked, peering down the front of her dress. She dug her hand deep into her cleavage and pulled out a swizzle stick. The confused look on her face made me giggle. Holden, with a broad grin, pulled out a chair to join us. She held her finger in the air as if to say "hold on" and began fishing around her cleavage again. By the time she finished she had the swizzle stick, a rubber bouncy ball, a crumpled up napkin, some blue sequins, a hoop earring, an olive, several coins, and a rock hard wad of chewed bubble gum laid out on the table.

"Want to talk about it?" I asked.

"It was a game that seemed a lot more fun last night when we were all drunk. The guys took turns throwing stuff at me. The person to make it right in the old chest chasm won."

Holden was trying really hard not to laugh.

"What did the winner get?" I asked.

"I don't remember," Connie said, flapping her arms against her hips with exasperation. Her eyes suddenly widened to the size of saucers. "No! No way! Emily! What is this on my ass?" she yelped while hiking up her skirt and pointing her backside in my direction.

"Oh, Connie," I said, throwing my hand to my mouth to keep my laugh from spilling out.

"What is it? Did I get cut, stabbed, burned? Just tell me."

"Tattooed," I said, not able to hold it in any longer."

Holden flew from his seat at the table and came over to where I stood. "Oh, shit!" he said with a hearty laugh.

"What? What is it! What does it say?" Connie asked, desperately craning her neck for a peek, but not getting it.

"It doesn't say anything," I said with a half amused, half sympathetic smile.

"What is it!" she fussed.

"It's not that bad," I said, trying to soften the blow before I told her.

She shot Holden a scowl and pushed away from the table. "You two are no help!" She huffed to the bathroom mirror, pulled up her dress, and shrieked loudly. Unintelligible garble pounded our ears. She stomped back to the kitchen, fire spewing from her eyes. "J.T. is going to die!" she yelled.

Holden stopped laughing long enough to antagonize her further by humming a few bars of a song that threw Connie into a fit of rage. She grabbed Holden by the collar of his shirt and pulled him within inches of her face.

"Yes, I have what appears to be some of the flying monkeys from *The Wizard of Oz* tattooed to look as though they're flying out of my ass! Obviously, I was manipulated into getting that because I *never* would've agreed to such a thing if I were sober. If word of this gets out to anyone, you will answer to me—Sheriff or not! Do you understand?" she said through clenched teeth.

It looked absurd to have the scrawny red head threatening my tall, muscular husband.

"Your breath stinks," Holden said with a smirk.

Connie shot out of the room like a rocket, slamming the bathroom door in the process. I heard the shower kick on, so I quickly went through the cabin making sure everything was packed and ready to go while Holden left to check in with the hospital and the police station one last time before we left town. He also made arrangements for Alphonse's truck and camper to remain on site until he was well enough to return home. He hadn't been gone long when a faint rap sounded at the screen door.

"J.T., you better run," I whispered once I got to the porch.

"Is she upset? I told her to stay away from the queens, but she wouldn't listen to me. They started playing some drinking game where they were tossing things into her dress then she asked them to fix her makeup. One thing led to another, and... I suppose she's upset about the tattoo?" he asked, his mouth scrunched up with uncertainty.

"Oh, she's *really* upset about the tattoo."

"Is that *J.T. the Dead Man* I hear out there?" Connie

yelled, quickly approaching the door wrapped in a bath towel. All traces of the makeup were gone and her deflated hair was filled with tiny droplets of water.

J.T. threw his hands up to halt her forward progress. "I tried to stop you. You insisted."

"I insisted! I insisted on having monkeys fly out of my ass! Come here," she said, lurching toward the screen door.

"Run, J.T.!" I yelled. "I don't know how long I'll be able to hold her back."

"It wasn't my fault!" he yelled as he scurried to his car. "I swear! It was the queens!"

"I'll tell her that once she calms down," I said, struggling to keep my hold on Connie. She was fighting to break free; snorting bull-inspired grunts from way deep down. J.T. tore from the driveway like a bat out of hell. Once he was gone, Connie tightened the towel around her body, raised her nose high in the air, and went into her room to dress. I was sitting on the sofa, flipping through TV channels when the bedroom door opened.

"I was dumb and I have no right to take it out on y'all," she sheepishly announced.

"Connie, I think you're going to be hearing about this one for a very, very long time," I warned.

"I know you're right," she said with tears in her eyes.

"Oh sweetie, come here," I said, hugging her. "A dermatologist will be able to make that disappear. There's no use crying over it."

"That's not what I'm crying about," she said, with a few sniffles.

"What is it?" I asked.

She pulled a strip of photos, obviously from some sort of a photo booth, from her pocket. She headed to the kitchen, pulled some matches from the drawer, and watched as the flames licked the sides of the strip. Once it was nearly gone, she dropped the remaining piece of crispy, black char and washed the remnants down the sink.

"I need you to trust me on this. I'll tell you about it someday, but not now. I need time."

I slowly nodded my head. "Okay, but you know you can tell me anything, right?"

"I know. We'll talk later," she said, waving her hand as she walked away in a daze. I knew I had to respect her wishes, but I wanted nothing more than to know what secrets those pictures had held!

12

Ready to depart on a new adventure, Mom and Dad had barely turned out of Greenleaf's driveway when a long, black car pulled into the drive.

"Holden, your mom's here!"

Even though I had no way to know for sure if she was looking or not, I forced myself to cheerfully wave to the haughty woman who was somewhere in the back of the car. It came to a stop right at the steps of the porch and the usual, bald-headed dude wearing sunglasses and a dark suit stepped from the passenger seat. He opened the back door, extended his hand to help Luciana from the back seat, then nodded for the equally bulky driver to pull away.

"What's up, Dick? Luciana?" I asked. He completely ignored me, but Luciana had a thin smile planted on her lips.

"Emily darling, so nice to see you," she said with saccharin-like sincerity.

Holden popped out of the door holding Kimberly and that was it—we no longer existed. She took the baby to the back porch swing with nary a word to Holden. Her behemoth bodyguard stayed a step ahead of her until she was comfortably seated then I watched with amusement as he gently pushed the swing to make it rock. She couldn't see it, but the look he wore pleaded for escape from this forced humiliation. *She must be paying that sucker pretty damn good money to put up with her snooty crap day in and day out. I wonder if she pays him to sleep with her? Nah, if she were getting some, she probably wouldn't be so crabby all the time. Ewww! Quit thinking gross thoughts about your mother-in-law. As far as you're concerned, Abraham Lincoln was in office the last time she got laid. Okay, that was mean and double gross! Stop it!*

Holden took a seat across from her, but before I sat, I asked, "Would you care for some coffee or tea?" I tried my best to not give away the embarrassment I was feeling about my previous thoughts.

"I think I'll just have some spring water with lemon. Not tap and not that filtered stuff—pure spring water only, please. If you have none, there is some in the car. Shall I send Dick in with you? He knows what I'll drink and what I won't." She snapped her fingers and the hefty man left his post at the swing and followed me to the kitchen.

I pulled out several bottles of water before he finally nodded at one particular brand.

"Do you think she can really taste the difference?" I asked, desperately searching for anything to fill the silence.

"Yes."

Well, he's certainly no talker. I took a lemon from the basket on the counter, washed it, and reached for a knife and cutting board to slice it.

"Why do they call you Dick? Is it short for Richard?" I asked, trying again to quell some of the awkwardness.

"No."

"I can't think of any other name that Dick would be short for?"

"Exactly."

I took a glass from the cabinet and pushed it against the ice lever. Dick stopped me with a simple shake of the head.

"No ice?" I inquired.

"Did Mrs. Dautry ask for ice or did she ask for a glass of spring water with a wedge of lemon?"

"Rude much?" I mumbled under my breath as I picked up the lemon wedge. "Does it matter if it's on the rim of the glass or floating in the water?" I shot back.

"Rim. Mrs. Dautry likes to control the amount of lemon in her water and I heard what you mumbled. One of my many sought after qualities is my excellent hearing."

I suddenly hoped that reading thoughts wasn't another one. I felt my cheeks burn and quickly buried myself in the door of the refrigerator. "Would you like something to drink, as well? I have iced tea, soda, water, beer, wine…"

"Nothing for me, ma'am."

I took out two sodas and placed them on a tray with Luciana's glass of water then started to the French doors.

"It's my finest attribute."

"Excuse me?" I asked.

"My muscle is record breaking size."

"Well, you are quite a large man."

"You have no idea," he said, opening the door for me. Once I caught on that he was referring to his nickname and his innuendo sunk in, I was speechless. I tried my best not to rattle the tray, but Dick was so suave and cool about it all that I seriously began to doubt if I'd heard correctly. Why did I have sex on the brain so much all of a sudden? He casually took his post behind Luciana, once again rocking the swing to and fro.

"This darling has missed her Nonna. See how excited she is to see me?" Luciana turned Kimberly so that she faced me. I couldn't help but smile when I saw her bright, shining face, rosy little cheeks, and sparkling, sapphire eyes. Her dark brown hair was growing out enough for the breeze to blow it around. She was every bit an angel. All that was missing was the halo.

"Did you miss your Nonna?" I cooed. Kimberly rewarded me with a huge, toothless grin.

"Emily, have you any plans for lunch tomorrow?"

"No, ma'am. Later in the afternoon, I plan to visit my friend, Roberta. Unfortunately, she and her boyfriend were attacked during our trip, but she was released this morning. I'll give her time to settle in and I'll bring them supper tomorrow night."

Luciana looked shocked. "Attacked! Was Kimberly ever in danger?"

"No, Kimberly and *Emily* were never in any danger," Holden interrupted. "Thank you for inquiring."
Luciana let out the breath she had been holding and glanced over at me. "Of course I was concerned for your safety, as well."

"Of course," I said matter-of-factly. "Lunch will be fine. Shall I meet you somewhere?"

"I'll send Dick for you," she volunteered.

"It would be so much easier if I met you. You know, with the car seat situation and everything..." I nervously rambled. I had no desire to be alone in the car with Vlad the Impaler, but Luciana shot down every excuse I came up with. "Dick will be here at twelve o'clock to pick you up. I'll have Chef LeJeune prepare a *light* lunch," she remarked as she looked me up and down.

Once she returned her attention to Kimberly, I leaned in close to Holden's ear. "I think your mom just called me fat." Holden blew me off by shaking his head. Dick simply arched one eyebrow high in the air. His super hearing allowed him to confirm what I'd known all along—Luciana was a mega-bitch! I dreaded facing her alone. "Luciana, I promised my friend, Connie, that I'd spend some time with her tomorrow. Would you mind if she came along for lunch? She told me that she simply adores your wardrobe and if she were ever able to spend time with you, she'd be thrilled to get some style tips."

The scowl Luciana was wearing turned into a neutral expression. "I'd be happy to help your destitute friend. I've been meaning to have my assistant toss out last season's apparel. Your friend may help herself to anything she likes." Her comment made me snap. "You misunderstand. Connie is far from destitute. She's a nurse and her husband is Chief Deputy. I assure you, she doesn't need your hand-me-downs. She commented to me once that she appreciated your sense of style. I thought that perhaps you two could have a conversation about the up and coming trends. That is all! No more, no less! I certainly never wished to imply that my friend needed or wanted anything from..."

Luciana interrupted me with her laughter. "Temper, dear. I'm sorry that I offended you with my offer of charity. Most would find that an admirable quality, but you..." I opened my mouth to rebut; she stopped me. "Please feel free to invite whomever you choose. Dick, we'll take our leave now. See you tomorrow." She gave a curt nod in my direction. "Son," she said, lightly kissing him on each cheek. Her tone raised an octave as she gave an animated wave, "Goodbye, my sweet Kimberly. Nonna will see you tomorrow."

I peered out of the door to make sure she and Dick were behind closed car doors before I spoke. I wasn't about to take a chance of Dick overhearing me!

"Your mom hates me."

"She doesn't hate you, Angel Lips. She hates everyone."

"She doesn't hate you or Kimberly."

"That's because the Balladeno blood courses through our veins," he in a mockingly valiant way as he positioned Kimberly so that they were cheek to cheek.

I rolled my eyes. "Whatever. I got the short end of the mother-in-law stick."

"You'll get no argument from me on that one. I love everything about your mother, especially when she gets all beside herself. It's great!"

"You need to quit tormenting my mother for sport," I snapped.

"Me! You're the one who upsets her so much she starts speaking in tongues!"

"It's not tongues; it's French," I said with a laugh.

"I know," he said. "I love you and I love our family." He kissed me on the forehead. "I have an idea."

"What's that?"

"Let's take advantage of this beautiful day. I'll set up the play yard for Kimberly, you grab us a couple of beers, and we'll lounge around near the bayou—just the three of us."

"You mean the five of us?" I nodded my head toward the window.

"Those dirty old men are back! I'll go chase them off," Holden said, referring to the two elderly men tied off to the dock and pretending to fish.

"Oh, leave them alone. They're harmless."

"Liking the attention?" Holden asked.

"No. I feel sorry for them. And unlike your mother, they don't make me feel fat." I ran a hand down the length of my body. "Baby, all of this is for you only."

"On second thought, Kimberly will get mighty cranky if she doesn't get her nap. I'll put her in the crib while you go to our room. Get yourself ready, cause I promise I'm gonna

do a whole lot more than just look at you," he said huskily.
I probably should've slowly sashayed up the staircase, teasing
him with each seductive sway of my hips, but I didn't. My
tank top went flying in one direction and my sandals the
other. I was trying to lower the shades and get out of my
shorts at the same time, which didn't work. I clumsily
stumbled forward, but luckily was close enough to the bed to
have it break my fall. It was as though I couldn't get
undressed fast enough! Under the covers I slid, eagerly
anticipating Holden's arrival.

My breath caught when he entered the room. Regular
trips to the gym combined with my home cooking had added
some much needed weight, as evidenced by the t-shirt that
clung to every muscular ridge like it was painted on. Long
gone was the thin, frail-looking Holden who returned to
town after months at the rehab hospital. His body bore
more scars, but I didn't mind in the least. In my eyes, it
made him even sexier.

"What's on your mind?" he teased as his hand slowly
ran the edge of his waistband.

"I'd tell you, but you'd probably think less of me."

He laughed. "Is that your way of saying that you're
having impure thoughts?"

"Very, very impure," I affirmed.

"Come here."

I started to gather the bed sheet around me.

"No. Leave it."

Once I stood, he quickly closed the distance between us
and laced his fingers in my hair. He gave a gentle tug so I'd
have to look into those striking sapphire-blue eyes of his.
"You're so damn sexy," he growled. "If I acted upon every
impulse I've had to rip the clothing off of that beautiful body
of yours..." He sucked in a breath. "I'm about to kiss the

hell out of that beautiful mouth of yours, and then I'm going to nip, lick, or suck every inch of your flesh. Do you have a problem with that?"

As hard as I tried, I couldn't get any words out. A slight shake of the head was all the permission Holden needed to kiss me so long and so hard that I thought I'd collapse. Just as I felt my knees start to buckle, his strong arms ensnared my waist, pulling me close to his body so he could explore my neck, throat, and shoulders with his tongue. His erection throbbed between my legs and it was his turn to moan when I leaned into it. He never loosened his grip on me, but walked me backwards to the edge of the bed, then slowly moved to be on top of me.

"You still have your clothes on," I breathlessly reminded him.

"If I didn't, this would be over already," he said, planting a series of whisper soft kisses along my lower lip. "You tend to get overeager and then you beg me to do this…" I gasped as he thrust himself against me. "…and then I don't get to do things like this." His tongue traveled a deliberate path down the length of my body, making tormenting detours here and there that left me pleading for more. By the time he finished, I was so exhausted that I didn't even notice when he slipped out of bed to make our supper. *How did I get so lucky as to land a man like Holden Dautry?*

~.~.~.~.~

"She's *your* demonic mother-in-law. Why am I being forced to go with you?" an anxious Connie asked as she peeked out of the window.

"Don't tell me he's here already. I'm still looking for my

other shoe. Do you see it?" I asked with a smiling Kimberly perched on my hip.

Connie turned away from the window, slowly shaking her head. "It's in your hand."

I held it up so she could see that it was empty, but she nodded toward the one that held the baby. Sure enough there dangled the missing sandal. "For Pete's sake! I need to get a grip," I said, passing Kimberly over to Connie so I could put on the shoe.

"Is it her or that mind-numbing sex you had that's making you scatterbrained?"

"You know you're not allowed to use your coital ESP on me."

"There's no shame in it. Your man has the body of Dwayne "The Rock" Johnson, the face of a Calvin Klein model, and from the constant smile and somewhat vacant eyes you always seem to have, obviously he has the bedroom skills to match."

"For goodness sake, don't ever let him hear you talk about him that way. He'll get a swollen head!"

"Swollen head!" Connie started to chuckle. "I'll bet he had a swollen…"

"Shut up, Connie! It's Luciana, okay? She's what's bothering me."

"Quit letting her get to you! She might think she's the queen bee, but she can only be your queen if you agree to be one of her drones."

"Where in the hell do you come up with these things? Wait, aren't the drones male bees?"

"Whatever!" she snapped. "You get my point."

"Yes, I get your point and you're right. If I give her control, she'll take control."

"Exactly! Now let's go. The hulk just pulled up in the

tank."

"FYI, don't ask him why they call him Dick," I said with a shiver.

Connie looked to me with intrigue. "This sounds like a story I need to hear."

"No you don't."

"Oh, yes I do. Tell me or I'm going to ask him!" she teased.

"It's just some possible innuendo that may or may not be accurate. I'm not as crass as you, so I didn't ask him to clarify."

Connie's eyes lit up. "Do you think it's true?"

"I don't know and I don't care. Neither should you." I scooped up the diaper bag and my purse then took Kimberly from Connie. We were walking out of the door when Dick met us on the porch, silently reaching out to take the bags from me. He placed them into the trunk then came around to open the passenger door for Connie and me. I slid in first with the baby, buckling her into the car seat strapped in one of the seats of the limousine. I looked up when I heard Connie yelling, "Oh, no!"

Through the door I saw her hurtling backwards towards the ground. Dick thrust out his arms to catch her against his body, preventing what was sure to have been some nasty bruises.

"Thank you so much. I'm not sure how my shoe got caught, but I'm glad you were there to catch me," Connie rambled as she climbed into the car.

"My pleasure, ma'am," he said, closing the door behind her.

Before he got into the driver's seat, Connie jumped to the seat next to me, her cheeks were beet red. "It was no lie," she whispered.

"What?" I asked, settling back into my seat.

Connie held out her hands a good foot apart then quickly put them down when the driver's door opened.

My eyes widened. "No!" I mouthed.

She nodded emphatically.

"You fell on purpose?" I mouthed again.

She shrugged. "I'm willing to sacrifice myself for research."

I tried to hide my laugh behind a cough. Without so much as a glance back, Dick carefully left my driveway and didn't stop until we approached the thick, concrete wall that bordered Luciana's property. He pulled into a short drive and punched a number into the box that opened a pair of massive iron gates.

"This is your mother-in-law's house?" Connie breathed as we continued down a long, oak-tree lined drive. Dick followed the drive to the right and then after passing a gigantic fountain with water spurting high out of the horns of a trio of bronze jazz musicians, he circled around and stopped in front of the palatial residence.

"Holden's the only child right?" Connie asked once Dick exited the car.

"He is now. His brother died. Remember?"

"Oh, yeah. I didn't mean any disrespect. I just want to make it clear right now that I want to live with you when you two inherit this sucker! How much longer do you think the old bat's got?"

"Connie," I snapped as Dick opened the door for us. I climbed out first with Kimberly then Dick extended his hand to help Connie from the back seat.

"Ma'am," he said in his typical monotone. His face bore no expression whatsoever and his eyes were hidden behind his usual dark sunglasses. After a few unsure seconds, Connie accepted his offering. Once she cleared the door he closed it, made his way to the trunk, and pulled out the baby's diaper bag.

"Darling! You made it!" Luciana, in a svelte black pantsuit and enough gold to fund a third world country, announced from the second story balcony. Her hair was pulled back into a ballerina bun and she donned a pair of dark, over-sized glasses. She looked every bit the glamorous movie star. "I'm so glad that you and your darling friend could join me for lunch. Please come in! Come in!" She retreated from the balcony and I was once again left to ponder whether my mother-in-law had been subjected to a bath in holy water or perhaps an alien abduction?

She came out of the mansion, arms raised to embrace me. After a kiss on each cheek, she pulled away to do the same to Connie before she took Kimberly from my arms. "You look simply adorable today. What a lovely dress. Are you excited to be here? I know I'm excited to have you! No need to dally around out here. Come inside where we can get comfortable! Shall we have lunch by the pool?"

"Lunch by the pool sounds nice," I said with uncertainty, and truth be known, a little fear. I glanced back with the intention of communicating my feelings with a look, but Connie beat me to it. Shock, fear, hesitation, and maybe embarrassment were on her face.

"What?" I mouthed.

She shook her head and started to follow Luciana inside. She was still rambling on about something I was paying no attention to, so I tugged on Connie's sleeve. "Tell me," I whispered.

"No," she whispered back, darting her eyes in a way that signaled she couldn't talk about it right now.

"Dick, will you please tell Chef that we're ready to be served?" Luciana requested as she made her way through room after room.

"Yes, Ms. Dautry," Dick said, suddenly breaking off from the group to do as instructed. Luciana was still a pretty good distance ahead of us, going on about various paintings, tapestries, and other pieces of art that adorned the various rooms we were passing through.

Connie pulled me to her. "He said that I shorted him a few inches."

I gave Connie a confused look, but then the light bulb went off. "He saw you?"

"Duh!" Connie spouted.

I wanted to laugh so hard, but I fought to maintain my composure. "That'll learn ya," I teased.

"You don't think he thinks I'm interested in him? Do you?"

"I don't know, Connie. He's hard to read."

"Oh, great. Just what I need—He-man with a crush. He's gotta be messing with me. He is. He's just messing with me. Isn't he?" she rambled in hushed tones.

"This is the room I've done for Kimberly when she visits with Nonna," she said. I stopped, suddenly aware that I was standing in what could have easily been featured as a "Dream Nurseries" pictorial. Murals were painted on the walls, a large, pink canopy hung to showcase a gorgeous wooden crib, and every toy that might possibly appeal to a little girl lined row after row of shelves. A raised sitting area with a plush loveseat and two rockers stood in the corner while rich, elaborate rugs graced nearly every inch of the shiny floors. Parked in the open walk in closet was a stroller and beyond that, row after row of tiny outfits hung neatly according to color.

"I don't know what to say," I mumbled, still in awe.

"There's no need to say anything. What I want is for

you to trust that Kimberly will be well taken care of whenever she is allowed to spend time with her Nonna. I've lined up some interviews with the most sought after nannies in the country and I'll place the one of your liking on retainer so he or she will be available whenever Kimberly visits. We'll begin screening after lunch."

"Have you discussed any of this with Holden?" I asked, palms up as I shrugged my shoulders.

"What's to discuss. He knows that I won't settle for second best. Never have and never will."

"It all seems very, I don't know, extravagant?" I said.

"I have the means to give Kimberly everything she could ever want in life and I intend to do just that. That's what Nonna's do. They spoil the grandchildren."

Luciana turned her attention to Connie when she piped in. "You know, my grandma died when I was really young. I never got to know her. I always wished that someone would come along and consider making me their adoptive..." I shut her up quickly when I elbowed her in the side. Luciana gave her a bewildered look before ushering us to the back of the house.

The outside was just as impressive as the rest of the mansion—a massive pool with a waterfall, an enormous outdoor kitchen (complete with fireplace), and a guest cottage adorned the well-manicured lawn. The tall cement wall continued all the way around the property, and a large slab with the letter "H" painted in the middle was in a clearing void of the cypress, oak, and pecan trees that were scattered around the property. *Seriously! She has a private helipad?*

I didn't get much time to take it all in because a server was holding the seat out for me. Luciana snapped her fingers and a different person came to the table with a baby carrier on a stand. Luciana strapped Kimberly into the contraption then turned her attention to us. "I should've asked before I placed her in the carrier. Is this acceptable?"

"It's fine," I said with a shrug.

"Good. The menu for today is Ahi Hawaiian Poke Salad. If this is not to your liking, I can have the chef prepare anything you wish."

"No, it sounds wonderful," I answered. Connie nodded.

"Very well." Luciana gave a wave of her hand and we were immediately served our lunch. Dick appeared from around the corner of the house to take his usual place directly behind Luciana. As demanding as she was, I was actually surprised that he didn't cut up her food and feed her.

As soon as Dick settled into his spot, Connie began nervously fidgeting in her chair. Luciana gave her an odd look, yet continued to pick through her salad. Once Connie realized that all of the shuffling to and fro had called unwanted attention to her, she decided to contribute to the conversation.

"My husband, Chief Deputy Bert Hebert," Connie loudly stated as she carefully enunciated each and every word, "would love to borrow your chef for the day."

I was positive that Luciana thought that Connie was short a few brain cells and that suspicion was confirmed when she began talking to her as though she were a young child.

"Isn't it a delicious salad, dear? Does your husband eat them often?" Luciana politely asked.

"Salad! No, ma'am! My husband, the Chief Deputy of Assumption Parish Sheriff's Department," she repeated loudly as she stole a glance toward Dick, "is a serious meat eater. He's a very tall, solid guy who needs lots of protein to maintain his extremely muscular physique."

I couldn't tell if Dick was rolling his eyes or not because of the dark sunglasses, but I was pretty sure he doing just that. Heck, I wanted to roll *my* eyes.

"Well, sounds as though you're very proud of him," Luciana said, looking at Connie even more strangely than before.

"And we're very happy. We have a child. He wants more children. We can't get enough of each other. We're quite like rabbits," Connie rambled.

Luciana's look changed from one of pity to a wide-eyed look of horror. She obviously thought Connie was a certified nutcase, and the sad thing was, I couldn't really prove otherwise if Connie continued to run her mouth.

"Please tell me all about the house. I'm sorry I haven't visited sooner," I said, desperately trying to change the conversation.

Connie pushed her plate aside and put her head down.

"Is your friend okay?" Luciana asked. "Shall I call for the doctor?"

"You keep a doctor on staff?" I asked with shock.

"No, dear. But I can have one here in less than ten minutes."

"Oh, okay."

"Oh, and Dick is a trained medic, but I'm sure your training is comparable."

"Thank you. I'm sure she's fine," I said, dotting at my lips with the napkin and tossing it aside.

I leaned forward to whisper in Connie's ear, "Are you okay?" I saw a slight nod. "Replaying that last conversation in your mind?" I whispered. Another nod. "It's okay. Why don't you walk it off? It's not as bad as you think."

Connie slowly raised her head, a large, fake grin planted

on her face. "May I be excused to tour the gardens?"

"Certainly, dear. Would you like Dick to escort you? His skills may come in handy if you have another spell out there."

"No, ma'am. I'm sure I can manage on my own. I have a phone if I get sick or lost somewhere out there on this vast property that seems to go on and on forever. See a phone." She held it up for everyone to see.

"Bless your heart. That's a very nice phone you have. Enjoy your walk and call if you need," Luciana said, continuing to talk to Connie if she were a young child. Connie practically bolted from the table. I had to admit, I was embarrassed for her. I could only imagine what she was feeling. She definitely needed a chance to reset.

"I'm sorry for that. Connie is usually very collected. Obviously, she's not feeling herself today," I explained. "No need to apologize for your friend. She's rather strange, yet delightful. Dick, will you inform Hannah that she may clear? And it might be a good idea to watch Mrs.."

"Hebert," I answered.

"Yes, you may wish to keep an eye on Mrs. Hebert as she wanders the grounds. But do so via the cameras." He nodded and was gone.

"About the house. It was built sixty-three years ago by my father. It's been remodeled twice in that time period. When Stephen and I married, the east wing was built to accommodate us."

"This is where Holden grew up?" I asked.

"He didn't tell you?"

"No, he never mentioned it."

"Well, he doesn't talk much about his past, does he? Why should he? Having money doesn't guarantee happiness."

"He's mentioned some things."

"Does he talk about his father or grandfather?"

"At times—mostly he speaks of his brother. I know a lot of time has passed, but I'm sorry for your loss. I don't imagine it's easy to overcome the loss of a child."

She removed Kimberly from the carrier. "Walk with me," she insisted.

"I'm sorry if I upset you," I quickly apologized.

"You didn't, dear. I just thought it would be nice for us to take a little stroll."

I followed her down a set of large, flagstone steps and we walked around the massive swimming pool that looked more like a tropical lagoon than a man-made water feature. The sound of water splashing over the artificial rocks was soothing, while the tropical plants that landscaped the area were quite stunning. I had found my new favorite spot to be when visiting with Luciana! We continued our walk around the pool and started toward the large gazebo at the edge of the flower garden. Luciana bent to smell one of the roses before she began to speak.

"That was a very difficult day for me. Probably the most difficult day I ever lived. I'd lost my father the month before, so I was still mourning his passing. My father was a very well-respected businessman—oil."

I nodded.

"Holden was sick, not deathly ill by any means, but not fully recovered from a nasty flu. The nurse suggested he stay home and not attend the baseball game with Stephen, so I made him stay home. Holden was playing with some push cars in the foyer—he used to roll them down the banister to see how far they'd fly—when the bell rang. Two uniformed police officers had come to inform me that Holden's brother, Blaine, had died and that Stephen was in critical condition.

Oh, the money I spent on doctors and rehab hospitals and private nurses! But, I was happy to do it. Stephen's injuries were far too severe and medicine wasn't what it is now, so even though he lived for a while, his quality of life was… Anyway, when I was told of Holden's injuries, a lot of those old feelings reemerged. Have you ever had that happen to you? Where something in the present causes you to feel the same emotions you had in the past because the two situations are quite similar?"

Again, I nodded. *More than you could possibly know!*

"I needed to do anything and everything to save Holden from the same life that ruined his father. He was the only blood relative that I had left—until Kimberly came along." She placed a kiss on the baby's cheek. "It's just the three of us Balladeno's now. Any plans for another, per chance?"

Her question caught me off guard. "No, no. Not anytime soon, no."

Luciana nodded and began the trek back toward the house. "The nanny candidates should be arriving shortly. Shall we move into the front sitting room?"

"Okay," I agreed, following her through the house. I was suddenly worried about Connie. How in the world was she supposed to find us in this maze?

Almost as if she could read my mind, Luciana spoke. "I've sent Hannah in search of your friend. I was going to send Dick, but she seems quite intimidated by his girth. Most people are—he's quite a large man."

Oh, where was Connie when I needed her! Luciana had just provided the perfect setup and I'm the only one here to appreciate it! "I'm sure they are rather intimidated by his size. How long has he worked for you?"

"Ten years. He's an ex-mercenary, so he's not one to

trifle with."

"Forgive my boldness, but why would you need an ex-mercenary bodyguard to follow you around night and day? I understand when you go out because of the threats you say you've had, but even here at your house? The place looks like Fort Knox."

"You can't possess all that I've acquired and not have someone try to take it away from you. The bad guys don't play by rules or follow etiquette, dear. They could care less how much security I have. If they want it, they will try to get it."

"Have there been many attempts?" I asked, suddenly intrigued.

"A couple. But they happened long ago, and rest assured, they were very quickly thwarted."

A waif-thin woman in a navy blue pinstriped pantsuit entered the room. "Excuse me, Ms. Dautry. I hope I'm not interrupting, but the first candidate has arrived. Shall I show her in?"

"Janice, this is my daughter-in-law, Emily, and this little bundle of sweetness is my granddaughter, Kimberly."

Janice stuck her hand out to shake mine then moved to get a better view of the baby. "She is quite a stunning baby, Ms. Dautry. I can see why you speak of her with such pride."

"Thank you, Janice. You may send in the first interview."

"Yes, ma'am. Her name is Beth Harding from New York."

"New York?" I asked with disbelief.

"My granddaughter will always have the very best. I'm going to make sure of that," Luciana said.

"Perhaps there might be someone local? I mean she's just basically going to be babysitting for a bit while we have adult time, right?"

Luciana looked at me as though I'd lost my mind. "We don't scrimp when we have the opportunity to have the best of the best." She held up the sheet of paper that Janice had given her. "Miss Harding is a twenty-three year old who graduated with honors and earned a degree in Education Studies from Columbia University. She minored in French, Italian, and Russian. She's also CPR and first aid trained, as well as a certified lifeguard."

I didn't know what to say. I'd never vetted anyone with such impressive qualifications. It was probably best to just sit silently and watch as Luciana did the questioning. By the time she'd finished with the four candidates, one stood out more than the others and to my amazement, Luciana hired her on the spot. I wasn't sure if I'd ever grow accustomed to this jet-set lifestyle. But one thing was crystal clear by the time I left Luciana's house—she was going to do her best to make sure Kimberly grew up that way and I wasn't too sure how I felt about that.

~.~.~.~.~

After we wrapped up the interviews at Luciana's, Dick drove us back to Greenleaf. Connie shot out of the car before it came to a full stop and didn't bother reappearing until I had Kimberly settled in her play yard. She carefully peeked into the room.

"He's gone, right?"

I laughed at her. "Yes, he's gone." She left the doorway and plopped down on the sofa.

"Did he say anything about me? Did you notice how he kept staring at me? I can't tell if he wants to kill me or have his way with me."

"Oh, Connie! Probably neither. I really think you're overreacting," I said with a chuckle. "Although, you may have learned a valuable lesson about the importance of *letting some things go.*"

"You didn't hear the things he said to me! Whenever he got close enough, he'd whisper lewd things in my ear."

"What! He was never near you."

"Yes, he was! Why would I make that up? You better keep an eye on him. He's a serious perv."

"He's a perv? You're the one who fell on top of him to see if the rumors were true!"

"And now I'm traumatized for life."

"Oh, let it go. How often are you going to see him anyway? Plus, you don't know, maybe he's hard up? I can't imagine he gets much opportunity for boom-boom being at Luciana's beck and call. Unless, our previous assumptions were... Ewww! I'm not going to go there."

Connie let out a full-bodied tremor. "No, please don't. But, I guess you're right. I've learned my lesson and no matter how curious I am, no more checking it out for myself. Some things are better off remaining a mystery. Speaking of surprisingly hung dudes, are you ready to visit Alphonse? You promised we'd stop by."

"Yes, let's go now so we can get it over with. It's been a really long day and I'm beyond ready to call it a night. On the way, we'll stop at Papa Leonardo's and get some pasta to bring to them."

"Alright, let's load everything back up. I sure am glad my mom kept Andre today. Can you imagine us toting all this stuff and a toddler to boot?"

I spied Holden's SUV pull into the drive. "No need. Holden's home." A grin spread across my face.

"Want to postpone the visit?"

"No way. We're going to visit Roberta and Alphonse. If he doesn't have anything else going on this afternoon, he can keep Kimberly," I said, going up on my toes to give Holden a quick kiss as he came through the door.

"Hey, baby. Connie, good to see you. How did things go today with Mother?" he inquired.

"Fine, but I'll have to fill you in later. Are you home for the evening?" I asked.

"I'm all yours, Angel Lips."

"Good! Kimberly's asleep in the den and will probably want to eat as soon as she wakes up. I won't be gone long. Call if you need." I slung my purse over my shoulder and reached for my keys.

"That's it? I walk in and you walk out?"

"Pretty much. I've got social obligations. I love you. Bye!"

"Love you, too. Social obligations..." he said, shaking his head.

RHONDA R. DENNIS

13

Honestly, I was a little nervous about seeing Alphonse and Roberta. Let's face it, they weren't looking so hot the last time I saw them and they both had physical and mental wounds that wouldn't easily heal. Then there was the added layer of discomfort because the last time I was at that house I was trying to save Alphonse's uncle—the sex-crazed Sheriff Rivet. Turning into his drive pulled up repressed memories of Pete; he was with me during that call. Even though I managed to revive the Sheriff, he didn't recover. I remembered the uncertainty that Pete and I felt knowing that a new person was going to be taking over the department.

Now Pete was gone and I was married to that mystery man. Thinking about how much things had changed in such a relatively short amount of time made my head spin. I pushed those thoughts and feelings aside and raised my hand to knock on the door. Alphonse answered with a huge grin and most thankfully, a full set of burgundy-colored pajamas that peeped out the bottom of a velvety, blue robe.

"Berta! Emily and Connie done come to see us!" he called behind him. "Y'all come on in. Come right on in. Thank you for stopping by. Berta's not been herself since the attack. Seeing you two might do her some good. You know she don't really have a whole lot of friends?"

"I hope we can help. We brought dinner." I held up the bag for him to see.

"Well, thank ya kindly, cher! You go on in the living room and say 'hi' while I put 'dis in the kitchen."

He disappeared behind the kitchen door, and Connie and I started in the direction Alphonse had pointed. The living room was dark except for the faint flicker coming from the muted television. A game show rerun from the 1970's flashed on the screen. Roberta, dressed in a heavy, zippered robe and slippers, silently stared.

"Berta?" I softly called. She spun around to face me and I was shocked by her paleness. She practically glowed in the light of the TV. A large bandage covered her forehead and her lackluster eyes had large, dark circles under them.

"Emily. Connie. So nice to see you. Thank you for coming," she practically whispered.

I dropped to kneel next to her. "Roberta, have you been in the house all this time?"

Tears formed in the corners of her eyes when she turned to look at me. "What's the point in going out? I'll never leave this place. I'm a freak."

"You are no such thing! You could use a shower, but you're just as beautiful as ever," Connie offered.

"I'm beautiful? Oh, really? Well you tell me, what's beautiful about this?" she yelled, ripping the bandage from her head to show the scabbed over word *SLUT*. Tears suddenly streamed down her cheeks.

I took her hand in mine and tried to look her in the eye. She kept looking away. "Oh, Berta. Have you consulted with a plastic surgeon yet?"

"How am I supposed to afford a plastic surgeon? I

don't even know how I'm going to pay the hospital bills." She began to sob. "To make money, I need to work. To work, I need to look presentable. No one will ever hire me now. Donovan swore he'd get me back and he did a righteous job of it. I told you I wished he'd killed me and I still do. Maybe then this nightmare would be over. I have nothing left to live for."

"Don't talk like that, Berta!" Connie said with tears in her eyes. "It's going to get better. You'll see."

"I told her I'd pay for anything she needed, but she won't accept it," Alphonse said from the doorway. He walked on through to take a seat on the dark brown sofa.

"Your uncle left that money for you, Big Al. I couldn't possibly take it." Roberta sniffed into a tissue.

"Big Al?" Connie and I mouthed to each other.

"That money don't mean nothin' to me if you ain't happy, Honey Bunny."

"I take care of *myself*," she snapped. "I don't need any man taking care of *my* responsibilities!" A once hopeful Alphonse suddenly looked crushed.

"Do you think it would be okay if I talked to Roberta alone? Connie could give your bandages a quick onceover, Alphonse."

She quickly stood up. "Yeah, come on Big Al. I'll get you fixed up like nobody's business. Where do you keep your medical supplies?" she asked as she followed him out of the room.

I gently patted Roberta's knee in an effort to soothe her. "I can't believe I'm about to say this, but you've got yourself a good, decent man who wants nothing more than to take care of you. Things could be so much worse, Roberta. You told me about those other guys. Alphonse isn't anything like them."

"He only wants to help me because he feels sorry for me. You know that I'm damaged goods. How are we ever supposed to go out in public with me looking and feeling like this? One day the sympathy is going to turn into resentment and then what? He'll leave me and I'll be all alone. Plus, Donovan's going to come get me. Why delay the inevitable?"

"If it were any other man, I'd say that could be a possibility. But Berta, Alphonse loves you more than the air he breathes. Have you forgotten that he's treated you like a queen since the day he laid eyes on you? This is the same guy who got torn the heck up after tumbling off of a scooter at forty-five miles an hour. Why was he in such a hurry? To save us! Then despite his injuries, all he could think about was sitting next to you on the way to the hospital. Don't shut him out. You make him happy. Let him be there for you. He'll feel better because he's helping and when the scarring goes away, you'll feel better, too. That's what couples do; they help each other through the tough times."

"Then I'll feel indebted to him."

"You shouldn't feel indebted if he's offered. Say you were in the position to help him—would you want him to feel bad about accepting help from you?"

"No." She sniffled. "Em, it's more than that."

"What is it?" I anxiously waited for her to drop the news.

"He wants to marry me."

"That's wonderful news, Roberta!"

"I can't do it."

"Why not?"

"The circumstances around our relationship are based on so many negative things."

I cleared my throat. "You do remember how I met my

husband, right?"

"I'm nothing but a no good slut who was stupid enough to think I could change if I started dressing better and dating someone upstanding. The proof's written across my forehead. I should be thanking Donovan Guidry for his reminder." Roberta began to sob once again.

Alphonse shot into the room, practically knocking me over in the process. A confused Connie stood watching from the doorway.

"I don't ever want to hear you talk that way again, ya hear me? The day you agreed to take a chance on me was the happiest day of my life. I felt like I won the lottery the day I met you. You're my angel, my saving grace, my everything. My life would be nothing without you. You wouldn't be the person you are today if it weren't for the things that happened in your past. You're the smartest, kindest, most beautiful woman I ever met and I thank God every day for you. I know it had to be his doing, cause there ain't no way in hell a man like me could ever dream of bein' with a woman like you otherwise. Even if your face looked like hamburger meat, you'd still be my beautiful angel. I want us to get married because I know that I could never in a million years feel for anyone else the way I feel about you. If you want some time to think about it; it's fine. But, I know. I know without a doubt that my life would be nothing without you. Will you please give a little more thought to my offer to help and my proposal of marriage? Please?"

Connie and I looked at each other with tears in our eyes and jaws to the floor. Okay, the hamburger meat part was a little over the top, but did that seriously just come out of Alphonse?

"So, you promise that the only reason you're doing this is because you love me? It's not because you feel obligated or sorry for me?" she quietly asked.

"It's because you're the only person who ever took the time to love *me*."

Connie let out a gasp and I did my best to reign in a sob. We were being total saps, but Alphonse was really channeling his inner Romeo! Roberta looked at me in a way that let me know she was appreciative of our earlier conversation. A smile began to curl at the corner of her mouth and she turned to face Alphonse.

"If the doctor can't fix me, would you agree to a private ceremony?"

"If it makes you feel better, I'll agree to any type of ceremony you want."

"Oh, Big Al! I do love you!"

The scene that followed induced horrendous reflux, so I won't elaborate. Suffice to say, the celebration was so intimate that Connie and I didn't even bother with goodbyes. We very quietly and quickly let ourselves out of the house then practically sprinted to the car.

My phone was ringing so I tossed Connie the keys while I fished out the device. It was Holden.

"Hey there, sweetie. Is everything okay with Kimberly?" I asked.

"Yeah, she's great. Actually, she's taking a nap. Are you ready for this? I just got a call from Jackson. MCPD apprehended Donovan Guidry so I need to get down there. Are you planning on coming home soon?"

"I'm on my way right now."

"Good. I'll see you in a few."

Connie looked at me questioningly.

"Jackson's department has Donovan Guidry in custody."

"Well that should be a huge relief to you, and just

think of how relieved Roberta's going to be when she hears the news!"

"I'm so glad they got him! The nightmare is finally over! Brad's dead and Donovan's behind bars. Life is good." I released a sated sigh.

"I'll tell you what. Let me keep Kimberly tonight. You and Holden can go out or stay in—whatever you want to do. You two need some alone time to celebrate."

"I appreciate the offer, but I don't even know what time he'll be getting back from Morgan City."

"That doesn't matter. Use the time to pamper yourself! Come on! Andre's been begging to have Kimberly visit and Bert's been so busy lately, he hasn't been able to spend much time with our goddaughter. He'll be excited to have her over."

"Okay. I'll bring her over after I get her things packed and Holden leaves for Morgan City. After that, I think I'll stop and get a pedicure."

"You better get more than a pedi."

"Okay, a pedicure and a massage."

"Now you're talking," Connie said with a smile.

~.~.~.~.~.~

Donovan refused to talk so Holden's trip turned out to be a complete waste of time. In the weeks following, Connie and I were busy helping with the details of Alphonse and Roberta's wedding. Her appointments with the plastic surgeon were successful beyond anyone's expectations, so she suddenly had a renewed vigor about her. She was pretty relaxed about the plans, but every once in a while, she'd get really touchy. I sought reassurance from Connie that I wasn't that way with her or mom when they planned *my* wedding.

"Hell, no! You did it right. You see, there were some serious high points to your being knocked up before you got married. You were so sleep deprived by the time the wedding came, you didn't care who did what. Your mom and I did a great job, didn't we?"

"Spectacular," I said dryly because I was trying to decide if her last comment was an insult or not.

"Maybe you should have a talk with Roberta? Tell her to back off and trust me."

"I'm not about to tell her to let you take over. You just like being bossy."

"No, I like being the boss. They are two different things."

"Regardless, you can tell her whatever you want to when she comes for lunch."

"But you really need to sell it for me!"

I laughed. "Fine, I'll do what I can, bossy!"

The phone rang and I was surprised to hear Jackson's voice. "Hi, Emily. I know this is an odd request, but my mom has been making some pretty significant progress at the psychiatric facility. She's been asking to see you because she wants to apologize to you in person. I know it's a lot, but I promised that I'd ask you to come."

"I'm not sure…"

"I understand your hesitation. I won't let you go in alone. I'll be with you the entire time, I promise. I guess that now is as good a time as any to tell you that she hasn't been talking much about the events that led up to the kidnapping. I was sort of hoping that if she were to talk to you, we might get some information to use against Donovan. We still haven't been able to connect him to Kimberly's abduction."

"I was going to have Roberta and Connie for lunch,

but I suppose I can take a trip to Morgan City instead. If it'll help you to charge that sick bastard with trying to steal my baby from me, then consider me there."

"Great. How about you meet me at my house and we can ride over together."

"Okay. I have a few loose ends to tie up here and I'll be on my way. I'll see you in a few hours."

"Thank you for agreeing to do this, Emily."

"I'll see you soon." I disconnected and filled Holden in.

"Do you want me to go with you?" he asked.

"No. Connie's going to keep Kimberly until you get off work. I have no idea what time we'll finish up and let's be honest, Hollyn probably won't say much if you're there, too."

"If that's how you want it, Sugar Plum."

"I think it's for the best. I'll let you know what I find out."

"Good girl." I smiled knowing that if Holden was in the room with me his "good girl" would've been followed by a playful swat on the rear end.

I made sure Connie had everything she needed for Kimberly, insisted that she go ahead and keep the meeting with Roberta, and even told her to offer Greenleaf as the wedding venue. After everything was set, I loaded in the SUV to make the trip to Morgan City.

As I drove the highway around Lake Palourde, things began to look familiar. I followed the directions that Jackson had given me and was surprised to find that his house was one of the beautiful, older two-stories I'd admired from Lawrence Park during the Shrimp and Petroleum Festival. Jackson was reading the newspaper on the front porch swing when I pulled into the drive.

"Wow, I see why you picked this house. I love it." I said, climbing from the SUV. "Living on the water is great , but this view is equally amazing. Kids playing, huge oak trees, a beautiful gazebo, historic buildings all around…"

"I'm glad you like it," he said. "It's not something I'd normally be able to afford, but I made a hefty profit selling the land I had near Holden's. Would you like to come inside and have a look around?"

"Sure! How can I resist?" I asked, as I walked down the well-manicured walkway and climbed the steps to the porch. After a tour of the beautiful home, Jackson and I stood in awkward silence. It was the first time we'd been alone since that evening at the lake.

Butterflies began to flutter when Jackson said, "Emily, can we talk?"

"I guess," I said cautiously.

He held out his hand and guided me into the living room and once I was seated next to him on the sofa, he sat quietly for a moment. The darn butterflies kicked into high gear.

"I want to talk to you about the night at the lake. I was wrong to say those things to you. Of course you made your choice long ago. I guess I didn't realize how much I missed you until you popped up in town. I spoke straight from the heart, something very uncharacteristic for me. I didn't give myself a chance to think rationally and that's why a lot of what I said pushed the limit. You know that I try very hard to remain level-headed and fair. I was neither that night. Holden loves you and you love him—end of story. Holden and I have discussed it and though we'll never be friends like we once were, we've made peace with the past. I know that will make it easier for us to eventually find comfortable ground. The truth is I don't want either of you out of my life. I still remember that promise I made to you when you told me you were pregnant. I told you that I'd be happy being Daddy or Uncle Jackson. I'm ready to be Uncle Jackson to Kimberly—if you'll still allow me, that is."

"But what about the things you said about Luciana buying Holden's positions?"

"Does it really matter if she did it or not? He's done a good job and he does his best to keep things on the up and up. Like I said, everything I was thinking and feeling just came out. Maybe I'm jealous that he has such an abundance of resources available to him? I shouldn't have said anything."

"I'm glad you did."

"I think you suspected that things were swayed in his favor as soon as you found out who his family was."

I stood to look out of the window. "I suppose I did. You're right. Who cares how he got into the position, as long as he continues to do his job well?" I offered Jackson a smile. "I'm really proud of *your* accomplishments. You can say with pride that you have earned everything you've achieved. Morgan City's lucky to have you as Chief."

He moved closer to me. "That means a lot, and it means a lot that you're willing to go with me to the hospital."

"I'm ready to do this. I hope you get the information you need to keep Donovan behind bars."

"We'll see how it goes. Let's hope for the best," he said, extending his arm to escort me outside.

Less than fifteen minutes later, we were on our way up to the seventh floor of the hospital. The elevator opened and Jackson gestured to a set of closed double doors. A camera mounted on a corner wall followed us as we approached the entrance. He pushed the buzzer and patiently waited for an answer. No reply. He pushed it again. Still nothing. I could see concern on his face when he pushed it a third time.

"May I help you?" a metallic voice called through the speaker.

"Chief Sonnier here to visit with Hollyn Sonnier."

"I'm sorry, Chief Sonnier. The floor is currently on lockdown. I'm not going to be able to let you in."

"You do understand that I'm Police Chief, right? I suggest you grant me access or you get a supervisor to talk to me—immediately," he said sternly.

"Just one moment, sir," the tinny voice requested.

A few moments later, a voice that was only slightly less metallic and about two octaves lower came across the speaker. "Chief Sonnier, you are free to enter." There was a loud buzzing noise, then a clicking sound. Jackson tugged at the door and as soon as we were through, it clicked, buzzed again, and locked back into place. To our left was a vacated sitting area, straight ahead was an empty nurses' station, and to our right is what I presumed to be the hall to bring you to the patient rooms. A throng of personnel assembled at the end of the long corridor, so Jackson and I started in that direction. A thin woman wearing dark blue scrubs quickly walked toward us.

"Chief Sonnier, if you'll take a seat in the visiting area, we'll send someone to get you as soon as we get a minor situation under control," she nervously rambled.

"Whatever you have going on down there doesn't appear to be minor. You've got every member of your staff, and then some in my mother's room and I want to know why. Now!" he demanded. When she didn't respond, he moved by her to start down the hall.

She let out a panicky sigh as she wrung her hands. "Chief Sonnier, we're trying to figure out what happened. It seems as though someone mistakenly started a procedure…"

Jackson stopped and turned back to face her. "What procedure and who started it? Quit dodging the questions and tell me what in the hell is going on."

"That's what we're trying to figure out, sir."

Jackson brushed her off and briskly proceeded down the hall.

"Chief Sonnier, you really shouldn't go down there!" she said, running after him. Her attempts to keep him away failed miserably. There was nothing she could do or say to stop Jackson from entering the area. The closer we got, the more we could see pure pandemonium spilling from Hollyn's room. Her heart-wrenching cries could be heard over the manic yelling inside the room.

"We've got a major problem on our hands! If you have a combative patient, you are supposed to call for assistance! Look at the mess you made! Furthermore, this patient has no orders for an IV! Why were you in here trying to start one? And in her foot, no less! You'll lose your license over this one! You're not going to take all of us down with you. You've got some explaining to do to the hospital board! Wait! Where do you think you're…"

At that moment a squat man with wild brown hair, dark mocha skin, and thick glasses bolted from the room. Jackson instantly reacted, launching himself on top of the runner to stop him. During the intense struggle, the wig fell off to reveal a man with golden blonde hair who was able to get one good hit along Jackson's jaw, but that was all. Jackson flipped him over and brought his wrist around to control him. Two security guards rushed down the hall, anxious to help with the apprehension. Jackson borrowed a pair of handcuffs from one of them and pulled the man to an upright position. Still breathing heavily from the scuffle,

Jackson walked him to the waiting area. He used the other pair of handcuffs to secure him to a chair.

"Watch him! And call my department and get some officers headed this way," Jackson demanded as he rubbed at the thick, dark makeup that had transferred onto him. He headed towards his mother's room and I stayed right on his heels.

I was taken aback when I walked in. The room looked like a horror movie set. There were blood splatters on the wall, the ceiling, the bed. A wan Hollyn sat slowly rocking in the middle of a large pool of blood, the IV catheter hanging from her foot still oozing. Every time a staff member would try to get near her, she'd scream, claw at them, and angrily gnash her teeth. She wildly thrashed her legs about, sending blood flying everywhere.

"Everyone out! Now!" Jackson demanded.

"Sir, I don't know who you are but we have this under control. No one is allowed in the area. We're under lock down! Who let this person in?" the nurse snapped to the rest of the staff as she attempted to reach for Hollyn's leg. Hollyn let out a blood-curdling scream.

"I'm Police Chief Jackson Sonnier and that is my mother. I suggest you do as I say immediately or I'll have every last one of you arrested for tampering with a crime scene. Do I make myself clear?" he said in a tone that I'd never heard from him. Hell, I even considered taking a hike with the rest of them.

They quickly filed out of the room except for the nurse who had recently spoken up. "I'm in charge of this floor. I think I should stay."

"No! Get out! Go! You want to hurt me!" Hollyn shouted.

"You heard her. Get in the hall and stay there."

The nurse did as she was told, though she loudly huffed on her way out and angrily crossed her arms over her chest as she leaned against the far wall.

"Momma, it's me. It's Jackson." He slowly made his way into the room with his hands in the surrender position. "It's just me right now, Momma. Open your eyes for me."

Hollyn stopped rocking and slowly open her tightly closed eyes. "Jackson, baby. Did you come to save Momma? Please baby, tell me you're here to save me! He was going to kill me. He said he was. Don't let him kill me, baby. I know I did wrong, but I don't deserve to die. Help me, baby. Help, Momma."

"Shhhh, it's okay. I'm going to help you. I promise. I'm not going to let anyone hurt you. He took a seat on one of the only clean spots on the bed and slowly stroked her untamed hair. "Momma, I've got Emily with me. Can she come in here? You know Emily works on the ambulance. She can make your foot stop bleeding if you let her."

"Emily's not going to hurt me?"

"No, Momma. She's going to make you better."

"You sure, my baby? You the only person I trust. You the only one who never hurt me."

"I promise, Momma. Emily is a good person. Remember how I used to tell you about all the good things Emily did for me?"

"I remember. Emily stole your heart, you told me," she said with a smile. Her eyes lit up when she looked at Jackson. "She made my boys happy. Even your brother loved that girl."

"Let's not talk about Kent right now. Let's get you cleaned up, okay? Can Emily come in and fix your foot?"

"I suppose she could do that. Come on in, sweet

Emily. Let me see you. Oh, you're such a beautiful lady with kind eyes. I know you won't hurt me. I can tell from your aura that you're a caring soul. You'd never hurt no one. You all about the healing."

I smiled as I carefully entered the room. I snapped a pair of gloves from the container on the wall then moved to find tape and gauze in a tray that had been left behind by the nurses. "Hi, Hollyn. This isn't going to take long. I'm going to pull that thing out of your foot and then I'm going to press down for a little while to make sure it stops bleeding. Is that okay?"

"Sure, honey. You do whatever you need. You never gonna hurt me. I can see it. My boy tells me you good people, too. My Jackson, he don't lie. He's a good boy."

"Yes, ma'am. He's a great man. You did a good job raising him," I said while pulling the catheter from the vein in her foot. I quickly covered the spot with a square of gauze, continuing to talk to her as I held pressure. "It's all done. See, that wasn't so bad."

Jackson continued to stroke his mother's hair. She dipped her head to rest it on his chest. "She said I did good. You proud of me, my baby? Momma wants to make her boy proud."

"Yes, I'm very proud of you," he said, planting a soft kiss in her hair. She noticeably relaxed in his arms. The wound had stopped bleeding so I taped a fresh piece of gauze in place. "Has it stopped? Are you done?"

I nodded my head and he scooped his mother into his arms. He was met with a chorus of protests as he made his way down the hall with her. Three uniformed officers met him near the nurses' station, unsure of what was going on. I could only imagine what was going through their minds seeing their chief walking down the hall with a wild looking, blood-soaked woman in his arms.

Jackson spoke loudly and everyone instantly quieted down. "If you are hospital staff, go to your break room—NOW! Jones, you handle the interviews with them as soon as I fill you guys in on what's going on." The staff complied with Jackson's request, all except for the woman who claimed to run the floor.

"Aren't you supposed to be heading somewhere away from here?" Jackson asked.

"You can't leave with her. She's a patient."

"Who's going to stop me? She was nearly murdered in this facility. Do you honestly think for one second that I'm going to let her stay here? I suggest you join the rest of your staff."

"But I… I…"

"Carry on," Jackson said very calmly. She loudly huffed once again, but made her way to the break room nonetheless. He turned his attention to the three responding officers. "The man up front needs to be booked for the attempted murder of Hollyn Sonnier. Roger, find out who he is, why he's in disguise, and why he wants my mother dead. Jones, find out how long he's been working here, if anyone's noticed anything fishy about him, and grill them about how it got to this point. Karen, contain the scene and call in the detectives to look for evidence. If any of you have any questions, call."

They each went their separate ways while Jackson continued down the hall and out of the door. Despite the odd looks we got as we exited the hospital, he kept his head held high and his mother gripped tightly to his chest.

The ride to his house was silent, except for the occasional sniffle from Hollyn in the backseat. She looked almost joyful as she watched the city go by with her hand gently pressed against the window.

"I love being at your place, Jackson! Can I stay for a bit? Please?"

"Yes, Momma. You're going to stay with me for a while," he said quietly.

"My boy! My boy!" she said with great enthusiasm.

"Momma, why don't you sit on the porch for a second? Okay?" Jackson said once we arrived at his house.

"Sure, baby." Hollyn slowly made her way up the porch to gently sway back and forth on the swing.

"Emily, I hate to ask you this…" he started.

"Whatever it is, I'll do it. Don't feel bad about asking me for anything," I said, putting a stop to his apologetic tone.

"I have to get her some clothes and she needs to be cleaned up. I can't leave her by herself."

"Say no more. I'll see that she gets cleaned up while you go to her apartment to get her things."

"Emily, are you sure. You know that she's.."

"I can handle it. She seems to like me and she's not violent unless someone's trying to hurt her. Go. I promise to call if I have any problems. I want to do this for you."

He exhaled a pent up breath. "You're amazing." He lightly gripped my upper arms and grazed a soft kiss across my forehead. He moved past me to speak to his mom. "I'm going to go to your house and get some of your things so you can stay with me for a while. Emily said she'll stay here and help you get cleaned up. Is that okay with you?"

"You're coming back?"

"Yes, ma'am. I'm coming right back. You won't even miss me."

"Emily's going to help me?"

"Yes, Momma."

"I like her. She's such a sweetheart. You should marry

her."

I was glad it was dark since I felt my cheeks begin to flush.

"Momma, why don't you go inside with her, okay? I'll be right back." He opened the door for us. Hollyn entered first, I hung back slightly. She lightly ran her fingers over the chair rails on the walls as she made her way through the house. "Help yourself to whatever you need. Thank you for doing this."

"We'll be fine. Go," I insisted. "Hollyn, are you ready to get cleaned up? Let's go upstairs and draw a bath, okay?"

"Oh, I love bubble baths!" She clapped.

Jackson shook his head.

"What about a regular soak for now? We'll get you some bubbles really soon, okay?"

She shrugged her shoulders and started up the red carpeted stairs, gripping tightly to the dark wood rails as she worked her way up. I followed her knowing full well that Jackson wasn't going anywhere until he was certain I had the situation under control. I entered the bathroom first, quickly confiscating any razors or sharp objects I found.

"I need to do a tinkle," Hollyn said, raising the lid of the toilet.

"Tinkle away," I said with a chuckle. "I'm going to be right back. I'm just going to get a t-shirt for you to wear tonight. Would you like to sleep in one of Jackson's t-shirts?"

"That would be nice. Thank you," she said, taking a seat. I jogged out of the bathroom and into Jackson's bedroom where I placed the potentially dangerous items on top of his dresser before opening drawer after drawer until I found a t-shirt.

I quickly slipped back into the bathroom to find Hollyn

still seated on the commode. I started the water, and once I was sure it was a good temperature, I plugged the hole in the clawfoot tub with the stopper.

"Ready?" I asked, searching through the cabinet for a washcloth and towel. I took a bottle of shampoo with me to the edge of the tub, neatly laying out all of my supplies within easy reach.

"Ready," she agreed, slipping out of the bloody patient gown to ease into the soapy bath water. I pulled a stepstool I found tucked between the sink and the wall to sit on. After lathering the washcloth really well, I handed it to her so she could clean the dried blood from her body. Once she finished, I wrung it out, soaped it up again, and carefully wiped her face. Her eyes curiously stared into mine. I was transfixed with the way they seemed so filled with emotion, yet maintained a guarded distance. They say the eyes are the window to the soul. Well, maybe I didn't want to stare too deeply into that window.

"I'm glad you came by to visit. I wanted to see you. I asked Jackson to bring you cause I just love the way his face lights up when you're around him. Kent used to do the same thing."

"Hollyn, Jackson is a very kind, loving, and generous man that any woman would be lucky to have. But, I'm married to his friend, Holden. Do you remember Holden?"

"That rich boy who lives in that big, ole mansion to the west of Green Bayou?"

"Yes, ma'am. But, he doesn't live there anymore. His mother, Luciana lives there. Holden's all grown up now and he's a Sheriff."

"He's a Sheriff? Isn't that nice. My boy's a Chief and his friend Holden's a Sheriff. They always did like playing cops and robbers. You know, my boy, Kent, used to be a police man, too."

"Yes, I remember," I said with a little more acid in my tone than intended.

She whipped her head around to face me. "My boy hurt you?" she said as more of a question than a statement.

"He hurt me very badly," I answered honestly.

"What he done to you? He told me he loved you. He couldn't wait for me to meet you... But Jackson told me that it wasn't really you he introduced, it was some other girl. Jackson said Kent was sick in the head and that no medicine could ever make Kent better."

"No, no medicine could ever make Kent better. I didn't love Kent. I barely knew him. He kidnapped me and my partner."

"What you talkin' about? How he kidnapped you?"

"Shall I wash your hair for you?" I asked with a smile.

"Okay," she said, leaning her head back. I took a cup I found on the lip of the sink and filled it with water. I carefully poured it over her hair continually until it was good and wet. I didn't answer her question until I began to work the shampoo through her hair and scalp.

"I was at work one day—at the ambulance station. Kent was hiding there and once he made sure that my partner and I were unable to fight him, he took us out to the floating camp he kept in one of the canals off of the bayou." I was very uncertain how far to go with the story, so I did my best to keep the facts to the bare minimum hoping not to upset her.

"Oh, I seem to remember hearing about that, now that you mention it." She stared off to her right as I continued to rinse the shampoo from her hair. "My boy, he killed the man you was with. Didn't he?"

"Yes, ma'am. He did," I said, trying hard not to let the

hurt I was feeling come out in my voice.

"That was wrong of Kent. He wasn't raised like that, no. Your boyfriend, he killed my Kent, didn't he?"

"Yes, ma'am. My boyfriend at that time was a deputy, like Kent. He tried to get Kent to surrender, but he refused. He had to shoot him."

"That boy of mine did have a hard head. He never listened too much when he was a kid, neither. Always giving his momma a hard time. Jackson tried to get that boy on the right track, but he don't listen to nobody. I loved him though. He was my baby boy."

"I understand," I said softly.

"Jackson told me Kent hurt you bad, bad."

"He did."

She scared me when she desperately reached out for my hand, clutching it tightly in hers. "He beat you up bad?"
I nodded, once again desperate to hide the intensity of my emotional pain.

"Jackson don't know this, but I can tell you since you know what it's like." She looked around the empty bathroom as if she were expecting someone to suddenly appear. She began to whisper. "Kent used to hit me, too. He'd come home from work all mad at the world and he used to punch on me something fierce. Told me I was a burden to him and that I should just go away. Every time I'd pack my stuff to leave town, he'd come in crying and tellin' me he'd never do it again. He needed me 'cause I was his momma."

I was shocked. "Hollyn, why doesn't Jackson know about this?"

"I could never tell him! Jackson was always so busy working with them FBI. We didn't even know where he was half the time. Kent told me he was off somewhere working with some cult or something so we couldn't talk to him no more. After Kent got killed, I did something really, really bad. I felt good about it. I knew he wasn't gonna hurt me no more ever again. Then I got to feeling real guilty 'cause I wished bad on my flesh and blood. That's why I told Jackson we needed to get revenge for Kent's killing. Kent might know I was happy he was dead and come back to put some gris gris on me. He might haunt me and make my life miserable from wherever he's at now. If I got revenge, then maybe he'd forgive me for being happy he died."

"But Jackson came home and explained to you that revenge was bad?" I asked.

"Yeah, he said that. But I gave up on it 'cause of more than what Jackson told me. I met up with this woman. She lived a few blocks down from the seawall on the old side of town. For ten dollars a week, she put a protection spell on me. She kept me safe from Kent and all other evil spirits trying to attack me."

"You've been paying her ten dollars a week since Kent's death?"

"Up until them men stopped me one day—them men who told me to get your baby so Kent could rest in peace forever."

"Will you tell me that story?" I asked hopefully.

"This water's getting cold, child. Look my hands are all wrinkly."

I stood with a towel and once I was sure both her feet were solidly on the ground, I helped her dry off and dress in the oversized t-shirt. After clicking on the light to the guest room, I lifted the edge of the thick quilt that was on the bed so Hollyn could slide under. She settled with a comfortable sigh, so I sat next to her.

"Will you finish the story about the men?" I asked.

"Oh, yeah. Them lying men. One day, I was on my way to the spell lady's house and they stopped me. They told me that I was wasting my time going to her 'cause her power was weak. They said they knew the real way to make all this bad stuff be over. They said they knew God's way, which was the only true way. They followed me to my place and started telling me about how God wants us to be equal and since you took my son away from me, I needed to take your baby away from you. I didn't want no part in that 'cause I know what it's like to lose your baby. Baby's make all right with the world. Then them bad things started happening."

"Bad things like what?"

"My doors started opening by themselves. I'd hear strange voices and wasn't nobody home but me. It was Kent. I know it was. Them men kept coming over and coming over. They told me I didn't have to hurt the baby, just take her. Said she was going to go to a family that really wanted a baby but couldn't have none of their own. See, I'd be helping a family and making Kent happy all at the same time. They promised all the bad things would stop."

"How do you think they knew so much about you, Kent, and me?" I asked.

"They said they was sent to me by God. God knows all and we ain't supposed to question."

"When did you know what you did was wrong?"

"When I heard your cries. I heard your big, ole momma heart breaking and it made my momma heart hurt. I knew no other family could ever love that little baby more than you do. I'd have to find some other kind of way to make Kent happy with me."

"Thank you for being careful with her and for making sure she got back to me," I said with a smile.

"I could tell right away that you was a good momma.

When I took her, I knew what I was doing was wrong. That's when I started to think them men might not be from God like they say they was."

"Have you seen these men since?"

"No, not a once."

"Do you remember what they look like?"

"One was real tall and beefy. Solid black hair, slicked straight down. Reminded me of Frankenstein. Always wore dark suits. Oh, and both of them had big, thick beards and mustaches. The other was smaller, but just as thick. His beard was blonde, though. Wore the same dark suit as the other guy. They wore glasses, too. Thick ones."

My heart sank. It didn't take a rocket scientist to figure out they wore disguises.

"Thank you for telling me the story, Hollyn. I know you must be really tired and you probably want to sleep. Before I leave though, I want you to know that I think you should tell Jackson about what Kent did to you. I feel it's important."

"You think it is? I don't think I can tell him. He'll look at me with those sad eyes then he'll get really angry. I don't want to see that. Could you tell him for me?"

"Sure, I'll tell him. You get some rest now. Sleep tight knowing you're safe and no one's angry with you."

"You not angry with me?"

"No, Hollyn. I'm not."

"Oh, bless you child! Bless you," she cried. "I've been so sorry for what I done. Oh, bless you!"

"It's okay," I said, gently stroking her hair. "You know what else?"

"What's that?" she asked hopefully.

"Kent's not mad at you, either."

"He's not? How you know that?"

"Because he told me he's sorry for what he did to us. He knows he was wrong, but he's in a place where he can't come to you to say it. He told me because I was close to death myself when he died. He could talk to me. He said he wanted no more bad stuff to happen to us. He did enough bad things and there was to be no more."

"He said that? When you almost died, he said that?"

"Yes, ma'am," I lied, but it was worth it to see the relief pour over her face.

"No more bad stuff for me or for you. We good mommas, aren't we?"

"Yes, we are. We're good mommas," I said with a smile. I rose from the bed and made sure the quilt was snugly tucked around her. Her heavily-lidded eyes slowly began to close and before I even left the room, her respirations were evenly spaced and steady. My heart went out to that poor soul nestled under the blanket. She bore more pain and heartbreak than anyone I had ever known.

I turned out the overhead light and carefully made my way into the hall. I gasped when I saw Jackson standing in the hall.

"Shhh," he said with his finger over his mouth. He pointed downstairs, so I nodded and followed him into the kitchen. He pulled a beer out of the fridge and placed it in front of me before taking one for himself. "I think we deserve this," he said, pulling a long draw from the bottle. I did the same. He put his bottle down so he could look at me. "I heard what you said about Kent forgiving her. I also heard how relieved she was to hear it. What was that about?"

I let out a sigh. "I'm not sure how to tell you this, Jackson. Dammit, I wish I didn't have to, but it's important that you know.."

He smiled at me. "Still a rambler when you get

nervous?"

"Don't make fun of me."

"I'm not making fun of you. It's cute."

With an embarrassed grin on my face, I shook my head slightly. My tone changed to one that was a mixture of solemnity and dread. "You have no clue how much I hate saying this, but Jackson, Kent used to beat your mother—the way he beat me."

Jackson's face fell. He took another long drink, finishing up the bottle. He walked to another cabinet and pulled out a bottle of whiskey. After pouring himself a healthy shot and knocking it back, he looked at me.

"Go on," he insisted.

I rose from my chair and walked across the kitchen to stand beside him. "She thought Kent was mad at her because she felt relief when he died. She was so tired of being beaten. I know how long it took me to heal. I can only imagine what she went through. Anyway, she was paying a woman to put a protection spell on her once a week. She thought it would ward off Kent's malevolent spirit. Somehow those men, who were obviously just as heavily disguised as the guy from the hospital, found out about it and took advantage of her instability. They used her to get back at me or Holden or the both of us. It's just a little too coincidental that all of this went down at the same time that Roberta and Alphonse were attacked. I think it's a given that all signs lead to Donovan Guidry."

"I figured as much, but he won't talk."

"He's not going to. He's a sadistic son of a bitch." I shivered when I thought about him.

Jackson sat at the table and put his head down. "My poor mom. I always knew she had it bad with Kent, but I had no clue he was beating her. How am I ever going to be able to make up for not being there?"

I walked over and softly rubbed his back. "Jackson, don't play the blame game. That's exactly what your mom did and it literally drove her mad. Look at me." He raised his head to do so, and I noticed that his eyes were weary and bloodshot. I took a seat across from him and took his hand in mine. "It's not about the past anymore. It's about the future. Be there for her. Do you know why she hasn't told you?"

"No, why?"

"Because she didn't want to see the hurt in your eyes when she confessed it. She loves you very much and she'd do anything to keep you from hurting. She may have her off moments, but you can't fake that strong of an emotion. Keep up with the therapy. Keep encouraging her. Keep telling her that you love her and that she did nothing to deserve Kent's treatment. You're her rock, let her know it's okay to lean on you. I think you'll be surprised at how quickly she's going to heal."

"Please come here," Jackson said, extending his hand to me. He pulled me to sit in his lap, encircled his arms around me, and then rested his head high on my chest. "Thank you for being here and thank you for helping with my mom. It means a lot to me. You'll never know how grateful I am."

"I do know," I said, lightly kissing the top of his head. "I know." There was nothing sexual about our actions. He was a friend in need of comforting and I was glad to be there for him. He had so few people that he could trust in his life. I wasn't about to abandon him when he was so vulnerable. After a few minutes of comforting him, I rose from his lap. The clock on the wall read eleven p.m.; I needed to head back to Green Bayou.

"Are you sure you'll be okay to drive back this late?

You can sleep in my room and I'll take the sofa. Or, I can get you a hotel room in town."

"No, I'll be fine. Really. Get some rest and keep me posted on how your mom is doing."

Jackson nodded. "I won't be able to get to sleep until I know you made it home safely. Will you promise to call?"

"I'll call," I said.

"Good. Take care, Emily."

I gave him an appreciative smile.

Jackson walked me to my car and when I glanced in my rearview mirror, I noticed that he waited until I was well down the street before he turned to go inside his house. I knew Holden would be worried, so I gave him a call and explained everything that had happened. When he first answered the phone, he sounded upset, but once I went into detail about the incident with Hollyn, he changed his tone.

"Are you okay?" he asked.

"I'm fine. Tired, but fine."

"Are you sure? Do you want me to come and get you?" he asked.

"No, I'm already on my way home, but you could keep me company while I drive."

"Oh, yeah?" his voice sounded over the speakers. "What should we talk about?"

"None of the Sonnier family, no Donovan Guidry, no hospitals, no turmoil, nothing that even remotely pertains to anything negative," I insisted.

"Can I talk about how lucky I am to have such a caring and outrageously hot wife?"

"That sounds like a pretty decent topic. Do go on," I said, with a smile.

14

Roberta's visits with the plastic surgeon went so well that she was more eager than ever to become Mrs. Rivet. However, when Alphonse and Roberta's wedding day finally arrived, I was concerned that there might not *be* a wedding because of my strong desire to give the bride a pop in the kisser. But, I didn't feel bad about my feelings, because Holden confided that he was a hair away from doing the same to the groom—who happened to be getting dressed at Holden's house. (Even though we're married and live in my family's plantation home, Holden kept his gorgeous, secluded log cabin in the woods for us to use as a haven.) Having the wedding at my house, though my heart was in the right place, probably wasn't the best idea. The worst part was that I couldn't complain to Connie because *she* was the person inciting the madness!

The current crisis, which happened to be the fifteenth of the day since I was keeping count, revolved around the floral delivery. A poor, pimply teenaged guy who obviously knew nothing about flowers was on the receiving end of the Connie/Roberta meltdown.

"These arrangements were supposed to have Fire and

Ice roses! The bouquets were supposed to be Fire and Ice Roses! What color do you think of when I say fire?"

"Red?" the boy asked.

"Yes! And when I say ice, cold, or snow, what color do you think of?"

"Uh, white?"

"Bravo! So if Fire and Ice roses are supposed to be red and white, do you think these yellow ones are in any way close to Fire and Ice?"

"Uh, no."

"Exactly!" Connie yelled. Roberta started to wail and blubbered something about roses. "Get me your boss on the phone, now!" Connie said, extending her cell phone to the shaking teen.

"It's okay," I said to him apologetically. "We know it's not your fault."

"Do not downplay this. The colors are supposed to be red and white, not yellow!" Connie snapped at me.

I shot her a look that said, "Back off, bitch." It didn't faze her. She shook her head, tossed her hand in the air, and started to argue with the person on the phone.

"The colors are supposed to be red and white, not yellow!" Roberta whined.

I rolled my eyes and started to mentally count numbers.

"Why don't you go ahead and start reloading these arrangements. There's no way she's going to accept or pay for these. Thank you...Super Fine?" I said as I read the name tag of the pouting delivery guy.

"Don't judge," he said before walking out of the door.

"Okay then," I said more to myself before turning my attention back to the wailing bride. "Roberta, there are a million things in this world that are red and white. If we don't get the flower situation straightened, I will personally go to every craft store I can find and get you something to make red and white centerpieces with. There's only going to be what—twenty guests and the wedding is still hours away. It's going to be fine. I promise."

"Okay, here's the deal. The bride and groom are wearing white. The Matron of Honor and I are wearing red gowns. The male attendants are wearing red vests and red ties with their white tuxedos. You freaking tell me how yellow flowers *aren't* going to stick out like a sore thumb?" Connie yelled into her phone. "That's right. There's no way around it! So, what are you going to do to make this right?" She listened into the phone for a while. "That's unacceptable. We're done. Your delivery guy will be returning shortly with the stuff you sent. Just know this—in case you haven't figured it out, I have a *very* big mouth and I know a whole lot of people. Goodbye." She hung up the phone and looked at me with squinted eyes.

"What? I didn't do anything," I said.

"Change of plans. Sure it's early November, but who says you can't have a Christmas themed wedding in November? Do you trust me, Roberta?"

She stopped sniveling long enough to answer, "Uh huh."

"A Christmas Winter Wonderland coming up. Em, I need you to run to town and get every candy cane, snowflake, poinsettia, holly bush, or Santa themed decoration you can find. Don't question or argue, just go."

"Damn, bossy much?" I asked.

She pointed to the door. I shook my head, grabbed my purse, and out the door I went. I presumed she was going to start Roberta's hair and makeup. Better to have Roberta stuck with her tyranny than me! I rode to several stores and collected what I thought would be nice decorations then made the trip home. I'd barely crossed the threshold when Connie came running down the stairs two at a time.

"She's up there with her hair in curlers. Give me bags," she said.

I unloaded everything into the foyer and she rapidly took inventory of my purchases. "Give me thirty minutes. You go upstairs and help her with her makeup. If you hear a male voice, it's just Bert. I asked him to come over and help me with a few things. By the way, we'll be raiding Celeste's Christmas stash."

"Okay. Do what you need to do," I said, happy not to be recruited into the decorating detail. I walked into my room and found Roberta anxiously chewing her nails as she sat at my vanity. She wore a thick, white terrycloth robe and her blonde hair was piled high in row after row of curlers. It looked as though nerves had gotten the best of her.

"My scars are showing really bad today," she said sadly.

"I don't even notice them from here. Let me see. You're probably just being self-conscious about them," I softy said. She got enough barking from Connie. I figured she could use a little calm, cool, and collected. She anxiously ran her hand across her forehead several times before she finally rested her hands in her lap. Very, very faint was the remainder of the word *SLUT*. "You have no makeup on, first of all. Second, that doctor did an amazing job, Roberta. Everything is flat and faint. I'll bet in a few months you won't even be able to tell it was ever there."

"Are you just saying that to make me feel better?"

I shook my head and she smiled.

"Thanks, Emily."

"You're welcome. Connie said I should help you with your makeup. Are you okay with that?" I asked.

"Sure. I either go to heavy or too light. I'm still finding

it difficult to find the middle ground."

"Believe me—Connie will let me know if I get it wrong. Don't you fret about it being imperfect. Just relax and I'll see what I can do."

"She really is quite bossy," Roberta commented.

"Yeah, but she sure does get things done, doesn't she? All I had to do was show up for my wedding."

"It is nice to have someone else handling everything for me. You know my first marriage wasn't anything to brag about. This one really means something to me," she said as I spread moisturizer over her face.

"You really love him, don't you?" I asked.

"I do. I know we make an odd pair, but I've never felt more comfortable or appreciated."

"Alphonse is a good guy. He kinda has to grow on you, but it's nice to have him on your side."

"Exactly," she said, closing her eyes so I could put on her eye makeup.

"I guess it doesn't hurt that he's so well-endowed, either," I said with an exaggerated whisper.

She opened her eyes to look at me. "I wouldn't know. We still haven't…"

"I thought Kinky Connie had given you some tips…"

"We didn't get to try them. He was attacked and I was tortured the night we were going to finally be intimate."

"Oh, Roberta. The circumstances surrounding it are horrible, but how sweet! Your wedding night is going to be your first time together. That's so romantic."

"It's not just our first time together; it's Alphonse's first time *ever*," she confided.

"I guess I knew he was a virgin, but I never really thought much about it—if that makes sense. Everything is going to be fine. You shouldn't be nervous. He loves you,

you're a beautiful woman, and you have the experience to help him with his—transition."

"That's the thing. I really don't. I dressed like a slut and I acted like a slut, but Em, I haven't been with a man since my first husband. I was nineteen then and I'm thirty-two now. It's been thirteen years."

"What about the time you spent at T-Jacks? I thought that the women out there were paid to be there to… you know."

"Some did, but not me. I only agreed to participate in the dancing. I'd bounce around for them topless, but nothing more."

"What about Donovan Guidry. Weren't you his high-priced girlfriend?"

"I was arm candy. Donovan was more interested in being with those rough and tough women. You know? The really thick ones that are so androgynous that you have a hard time determining whether they're male or female."

My eyes widened and my jaw dropped. "But he acted like he was the biggest ladies man in the parish! He's such a pig!"

"It's because he hates most women. He's got this real fetish for fat chicks, though. I haven't figured that one out. What it all boils down to is I was hired to show my face with him while wearing super-tight dresses. That's it. I was just there to help him maintain a certain image."

"I had no idea. We really need to sit down one day so you can fill me in on everything."

"Nah, there's not much to tell. It's all pretty boring and I don't come out looking so good in most of it."

"Says you!" I said with a smile. "I think you've done okay for yourself despite your circumstances."

"Thanks, Emily. That means a lot coming from you."

I gave her a quick hug. We were just finishing up her make up when Connie came into the room.

"You did a great job, Em. You are absolutely glowing, Roberta. Gorgeous!" Connie said.

Roberta and I let out collective sighs of relief.

"You two come with me!" Connie insisted.

Knowing it did no good to argue with Connie, we noisily followed her down the main staircase and into the parlor. When she threw open the door, Roberta and I let out simultaneous gasps.

The room was darkened, and directly in front of us, clear lights were threaded through a white lattice archway that was adorned with mixed evergreen and holly. The white, wooden chairs for the guests were arranged four to a side and extended back six rows. In the middle was a long, white runner that was lined with beautiful, potted poinsettias. Directly behind the large archway, a fire roared in the fireplace, the flames making the glittery snowflakes that twirled from strands of garland sparkle. Beautifully flocked Christmas trees were standing at various points around the room, and the table centerpieces were now candles floating in clear vases of various sizes that were filled with red-tinted water. The centerpieces sat atop mirrored bases which served to intensify the glow coming from the orange-colored flames. Connie had single-handedly transformed the room into a sparkling winter wonderland.

"Oh, Connie! I want to cry," Roberta squealed.

"This is outrageous! How did you do all of this so quickly!" I exclaimed, still trying to take in everything. "Forget nursing! You seriously need to consider a career as a wedding consultant."

"Aww, I'm just glad to help. It makes me feel all accomplished to know you guys are happy with everything.

But enough with the gawking, let's finish getting dressed. The show starts in an hour and a half. I want us completely done up and ready to go in forty-five minutes."

A much more relaxed trio ascended the staircase. We could now finish up the last minute details. After everyone was dressed and ready to go, Connie decided to give Roberta some more X-rated bedroom advice. Roberta was glowing bright red, but Connie proceeded like she was teaching a formal class. It didn't bother her, or me, in the least. Actually, I found it quite entertaining. *Have I been spending too much time with Connie? Oh, no! No, no, no, no, no! It's official. She's corrupted me!*

Everyone froze when a faint rap sounded at the door. I picked up the edge of the long, red satin gown I was wearing and went to answer it.

"Hey, I just wanted to let you know that we're taking the groom to the…" Holden stopped mid-sentence once I stepped out into the hall to be with him. "Baby, you just took my breath away. I'm…I'm…" He swallowed hard.

"Well, I'm speechless." I couldn't help but smile.

He wasn't the only one stunned. The white fabric of the tux made his tanned skin look even more radiant than usual and the cut of the jacket served to accentuate his broad shoulders and tapered waist. His blue eyes beamed with happiness and all I could think about was kissing those full, pouty lips of his. But instead of pulling him to me, I reached up to straighten his tie. "You aren't looking half bad yourself, Sheriff Dautry. What did you want to let us know?" I playfully asked.

"I don't remember. It can't be that important. Let's go downstairs to the pantry."

I laughed knowing that I wasn't the only one fighting impure thoughts. "No! We have a wedding to get ready for.

Where's the groom?"

"Oh, yeah. That's what I was coming to tell you. Bert and I have him in the guesthouse, but he's convinced Roberta's going to leave him at the altar."

"Well, put his mind at ease. I heard straight from the horse's mouth that she's more than ready to do this."

"Good. Maybe I can get him to calm down. Will you save a dance for me, Angel Lips?" he asked.

"Of course. I'll save most of my dances for you," I said flirtatiously before I shooed him back to the guesthouse.

"Roberta, your groom has arrived in one piece. Are you ready to get this show on the road?" I asked when I walked back into the room.

"I've never been more ready for anything in my whole life," she said with the sincerest of smiles.

~.~.~.~.~

We quietly gathered in the foyer, eagerly awaiting the cue to start the procession. Connie was first to walk down the aisle, and was met by Bert, who escorted her to the archway where they each took their designated spots. Then it was my turn. Soft string music piped through the speakers. Holden met me halfway, and like Bert and Connie, we walked arm and arm the rest of the way to the altar. The guests smiled warmly at us as we made our way down the stunning, poinsettia-lined path. Everything about that moment was dreamlike and surreal.

The soft music stopped and an extremely sweaty and pale Alphonse took his spot near the Justice of the Peace. The back doors opened and Roberta, who was beaming with radiance, slowly walked up the aisle escorted by Jerry from the Gas and More. Up until that point, everything was absolutely spot-on perfect. Then the event shifted into a typical Green Bayou blowout. As soon as Roberta took her spot next to Alphonse, he took one look at her in her long, flowing gown and down he went like a boxer with a glass jaw. "You owe me ten bucks," Connie leaned over to say to me as we watched Bert and Holden stoop down to wake him up.

"I know!" I snapped. "You'll get your money later. Dammit! I thought for sure he'd puke."

The guests who had gathered around to see what was going on took their seats again once Holden and Bert got Alphonse back on his feet. The ceremony continued—for about three minutes. Out he went again. This became such a pattern that one of the elderly gentlemen seated up front pushed his chair to the altar. The crowd roared when he said, "I don't know about y'all, but I'm ready for some cake. This thing will never end if he's left to do it on his own two feet!"

So, we all watched as Roberta and a seated Alphonse proceeded to tie the knot. Unfortunately, most of the guests couldn't hear the ceremony thanks to a cousin of Alphonse's who joyfully sobbed at a ridiculously annoying level. In addition to her obnoxious sniveling, nearly every word was interrupted by her cries of, "So beautiful!" or "How lovely!" I was very proud of my friend for not yelling at her to, "Shut the hell up!" The amount of willpower it took to restrain her outburst was evident by her flaring nostrils and her cracked bouquet holder.

Finally, Roberta leaned down to plant a very soft and touching kiss on Alphonse's lips once the Justice of the Peace said they should. Because Alphonse was still completely jelly-legged, Bert and Holden each grabbed an arm and hoisted him upright. Connie and I gasped as soon as he stood, and the Justice of the Peace, with a tremendous look of horror on his face, took three large steps backwards, then darted for the doors without even announcing the newly married couple. Connie and I dashed over before the full audience could get a gander at what was going on in Alphonse's pants.

"Hold this in front of you," Connie said, shoving her bouquet into Alphonse's hands.

"Huh?" he asked, his head bobbing all over the place.

"Is he coherent?" I whispered.

"Am I married?" he asked with a silly smile.

"Did you two give him something?" I directed at Bert and Holden. "Why is he goofier than normal?"

"Goofy's a dog, isn't he? No the other one's the dog. What in the hell is Goofy?" Alphonse asked. I could only imagine what was going through the guests' minds as we continued with our huddle near the archway.

"Well, he was so nervous he kept puking, so we gave him something your mom had left behind in the medicine cabinet," Holden answered.

"He puked before he passed out, you owe *me* the ten bucks," I said to Connie.

"Don't forget about the blue pill I took," Alphonse slurred while trying to waggle his eyebrows.

"What blue... No. No, no, no! Alphonse, what the hell? Why would you...? Oh, never mind!" Connie fussed. "It does no good to discuss this. He's flippin' fried."

"What are we going to do?" Roberta asked. "Maybe we shouldn't walk down the aisle and instead, have the guest take their seats in the reception area until we can get him straightened out?"

"Nah, he'll be okay to get down the aisle," Connie said confidently. "You keep that thing right there, Alphonse. You guys got him this way, so you can walk him down that aisle! Afterwards, we'll distract everyone with the food and booze. This wedding can still be salvaged. Now, everyone put on a big, ole smile and get ready to do this." She took the spot that had been vacated by the Justice of the Peace and announced to the congregation, "I now present to you, Mr. and Mrs. Alphonse Rivet!"

A chorus of applause erupted and I could only imagine how it looked from their point of view to see Alphonse girding his loins with a fluffy bouquet, while Roberta's arm laced through one of his to help steer him in the right direction. Bert and Holden each hiked up one side of his waistband and essentially puppeted him down the aisle.

Once they were well on their way, Connie extended her hand out to me. "Shall we?"

"We shall, my dear," I said, taking her hand so we could follow the rest of wedding party down the aisle.

With the jitters of the actual ceremony gone, logically, the reception should be a much smoother event. Wrong! One of Alphonse's family members got the *brilliant* idea to give him some hard liquor to perk him up. Problem was, with the pills still affecting him, the alcohol exacerbated everything.

With the help of the guys, he made it through the introductions, but it became obvious from the way that Roberta was struggling to hold him up, the alcohol had well kicked in during their first dance.

"What did you do?" I quietly asked, pulling Holden to the side.

"I didn't do anything! This one's on someone else," he answered, palms out in surrender.

Roberta desperately looked around the room for someone to help her pick up the now snoring mass in the middle of the dance floor. I went over to see if I could help, giving a good, solid pat to his cheek a few times before he began to stir. "Alphonse, you need to get up so we can get some coffee in you."

Once again, we managed to get him upright and propped on a kitchen stool while Roberta and Connie tried their best to salvage the evening. The guests seemed happy enough snacking on the delicious food and enjoying the music piping throughout the room. Three over-sized mugs of coffee later, Alphonse was able to stand on his own two feet without collapsing, so off we went into the parlor to continue with the celebration. And then the coffee kicked in...

Never in my life had I witnessed such an event. We all knew the exact moment the caffeine dumped into Alphonse's bloodstream. Everyone was all smiles as Roberta and Alphonse, one hand on the other's, carefully cut into and fed each other the first piece of wedding cake. I was just about to turn to Connie to congratulate her on a job well done when all of a sudden, Alphonse's eyes bugged out of his head. At first, I worried that he might be choking, but seconds afterwards he got the familiar silly-looking grin on his face. He whipped off his tuxedo jacket and practically dragged Roberta onto the dance floor.

"DJ, play me something with a beat!" Alphonse yelled, tossing aside his bowtie so he could send buttons sailing across the room as he ripped off his shirt. In a white, tank top undershirt and his white tuxedo trousers, Alphonse threw his hands in the air as he slowly stalked his way around a shocked Roberta. "Let's do this, y'all!"

The music started and Alphonse began wriggling his hips and thrusting his pelvis in a way that sent gasps echoing throughout the room. Connie rushed up to me when Alphonse jumped on top of one of the guest tables, threaded a napkin between his legs, and began to rapidly slide it back and forth to the beat of the music. "Should I dig through your mom's medicine cabinet for another sedative?"

"No!" I yelled. "No one is allowed to give Alphonse anything else!"

"Are you sure?" she asked, pointing to the table that was now devoid of guests because Alphonse was running in place on top of it.

"Oh, dear Lord! I'm going to take care of this. Connie, you try to get this thing back on track while I handle the pain in the ass up there."

She called everyone's attention to Roberta, announcing that she'd be tossing the bouquet shortly. I took the opportunity to, as discretely as possible, pull Alphonse from the table and shove him out the back doors and into the yard.

"I want to dance!" he said, jerking around spastically. I instantly regretted gripping his shoulders when his sweat saturated my palms.

"Stop dancing. Alphonse... Alphonse...Stop it!" The tone in my voice was harsh and he suddenly stopped thrashing about. His leg, however, continued to quiver and bounce around.

"I gotta move! I gotta go!" He looked like a little kid trying to hold it while desperate for a bathroom. Something had to give.

"Run!" I yelled. Alphonse looked at me like I was nuts.

"Run! Run laps around the backyard and don't you stop until I tell you to stop! Go now!"

"Huh?" he questioned.

"Dammit! You better take off right now before I give you a reason to run!" I said with the same tone that had gotten results before.

He was off like a shot and headed towards the bayou, but before I could shout my warning, I heard the splash.

"Oh, come on!" I fussed, headed to the bayou to assess

the damage. A sputtering Alphonse popped up from the edge of the bank, his breath leaving a misty trail in the frigid air. He shivered violently.

"Dude, when I said don't stop running, I meant *around* the yard! Did you really think I meant don't stop running until something made you stop!"

"I...I ...I dddddon't fffffeel like I hhhhhhhavvvvveeee to rrrrrruuun anymore," he proclaimed.

"Well, hallelujah for that! What are we going to do about this, though?" I pointed to his dripping body. "I think you have two options. A robe or some of my clothes because I can promise there's no way you'd fit into anything of Holden's."

"I dddddon't care. Cccccooolllldd!"

"Follow me up the back staircase," I said, holding the door open for him. I brought him up to my room and desperately searched for anything remotely gender neutral. I didn't have much luck. I managed to pull together a pair of black slacks and a plain t-shirt. The problem was the pants were loose in the hips and thighs and the shirt was fitted, so it looked extra-tight and rested high on his waist. All he needed was a brightly colored, sequined headscarf and sash combo to look like he was an extra from "Riverdance". I tossed him a pair of black socks so it would be less obvious that he was barefoot, not that it probably mattered all that much in the grand scheme of things, then I ushered him downstairs.

Needless to say, the wedding pictures from the rest of the night were the topic of conversation in the following weeks, right along with the ceremony, the reception, and the wedding night—but I'll spare you that story!

15

A few weeks after the wedding fiasco, it was time for us to celebrate Thanksgiving. To everyone's delight, it was much less eventful than the previous year! My parents didn't come in for the holiday; instead they enjoyed an authentic celebration somewhere along the Eastern seaboard. We did, however, host Jackson, Chuck, Bridget, and Samantha, as well as Bert, Connie, Andre, Alphonse, and Roberta. Samantha refused to go into the back yard (Who could blame her?) and I swear I caught Andre giving her the stink eye quite a few times that afternoon. Regardless, a good time was had by all and later that evening, Luciana joined Holden, Kimberly, and I for a more intimate dinner. We invited Connie and Bert to stay, but Connie quickly declined the offer. She still hadn't gotten over her run-in with Dick. I found it amusing because for as long as I'd known Connie, that one visit to Luciana's was the only time I'd ever seen her flush with embarrassment.

"I do wish you'd come by to see me. Everything is set with Kimberly's nanny, so you can simply relax when you visit," Luciana commented before raising her wine glass to her lips.

"Mother, a nanny is entirely unnecessary."

"Nonsense, she'll come in most handy so you and

Emily will be free to roam the grounds or relax at the pool while feeling confident that Kimberly is in the best of hands."

"I still think it's unnecessary. We are quite capable of taking care of our own daughter," Holden remarked.

"In regards to the nanny situation, I think otherwise," she said sternly.

"Did you have a certain time in mind for us to visit?" I interrupted, trying to relieve some of the tension in the room.

She stopped giving Holden an icy stare to look at me. "I'd be happy to have you anytime."

"Thank you," I said, hoping the conversation was over.

"What about this weekend? Please pack a bag and be prepared to stay. I'll have the chef prepare a spectacular feast and I'll make sure everything is ready for the baby," she said excitedly.

"So soon? Do you have anything going on this weekend?" I asked Holden.

"No, I do not," Holden said curtly.

"Excellent! I'll make all of the preparations. We'll have such a good time! I can't wait to spend some time with my beautiful granddaughter."

"And your son and his wife?" Holden asked.

"Well, that's just a given," she said indignantly.

"Have another glass of wine," I said to Holden as I filled it nearly to the brim.

"I think I'd prefer a beer." When Holden tossed his napkin aside to head to the kitchen, I excused myself and followed him. We left a confused Luciana sitting at the table alone.

"We'll only be a minute," I said apologetically.

"Of course," Luciana said, snapping her fingers and

pointing to her empty glass. Dick reached for the bottle to top it off.

"What's wrong, baby?" I asked, rubbing Holden's shoulders as he stood in the doorway of the opened refrigerator.

He shut the doors then pointed to the pantry. "We don't need 'supersonic hearing' to report back to my mother on this," he explained.

"I sometimes forget he has that gift," I said, taking a seat on top of the buffet while Holden shut the door. "What's up with the attitude?"

"Honestly, I don't know. Something's been bothering me about all of this. Maybe it's bringing back bad memories from my childhood. You know that I was raised that way?"

"What do you mean?" I asked.

"Some people think that life is grand for those who grow up with money. Sometimes it is, but it wasn't for me. I guess she struck a nerve when she started talking about hiring a nanny to watch Kimberly. I barely knew my father and my mother only popped in when she needed a monkey to perform for my grandfather. Hours and hours of piano lessons, violin lessons, foreign language classes—all spent not to better myself, but to for her to show off what a well-rounded and talented son she had."

"Awww, sweetie. I'm sorry. Come here." He reached out to hug me and as I held the embrace, my fingers lightly toyed with the hair at the nape of his neck. "I don't think that a visit a few times a year will be too horrible. As far as making Kimberly a little trophy grandchild, we're her parents. If we don't want her to take piano lessons, she won't. We have full veto power over anything your mother suggests."

"You're right. I need to let go of the past so I can keep focused on the future," he said.

I kissed him. "That sounds like very good advice, Mr. Dautry."

"You know what else sounds good?"

I jumped from the buffet and headed to the door. "Don't even start with your innuendos! Let's finish this evening up and then you can do more than talk about it. You can show me."

"You make me so glad I picked you."

"You picked me? I believe it was I who picked you!"

"You were a lost puppy before you met me," he said, pulling me into his arms.

"You were an ass when I met you," I countered.

"But you fell for me."

"Yes, I did. I fell hard," I said, lifting my lips to his.

~.~.~.~.~

"I don't suppose I could get you guys to come with us?" I asked Connie over the phone as I finished packing our bags.

"Not no, but hell no. First of all, we weren't invited. I'm not about to make the faux pas of simply showing up. Second, you aren't getting me within a hundred feet of Dick. I'm telling you, he wants me."

I laughed. "So what if he does? He knows you're married to a huge, meat-eater of a husband. If that doesn't say 'hands off' I don't know what does."

"Now you're making fun of me?"

"You deserve it. You should've left that man's junk a mystery."

"I blame you for this."

"Me? How is this my fault?"

"You know how curious I am. You shouldn't have told

me about the whole nickname thing."

"You ever hear the phrase, 'curiosity killed the cat'?"

"That's a stupid phrase. Just how exactly would curiosity kill it? And why a cat? Why not a dog or a bird? Was there a sudden abundance of dead cats sometime in the past that prompted a warning?"

"Connie, you're making my brain hurt. I'll call you when we get back."

"Have fun and be sure to maintain your distance."

"No worries. He wants you, not me," I said with a giggle.

"You're going to try to instigate when you get there! You are aren't you? I can hear it in your voice. This isn't funny!"

"I'll give Dick your regards. Goodbye, Connie!"

"Emily! Don't you dare..." I disconnected the call. *Good! Let her stew in it for a while. It's well deserved payback for all of the ribbing I have to take from her.*

Holden came into the room to gather the bags and load them into the SUV. "I didn't put the portable crib and the rest of Kimberly's usual travel essentials in there. I have a strong suspicion that my mother's provided everything she will need."

"Did I forget to tell you about the nursery?"

Holden let out a sigh and mumbled, "Always going overboard. Let's get going so we can get this weekend over with. I still don't know why you agreed to it."

"Because she's making an effort to be a better person and we should reward that. She's only been snide or rude four times this month." I laughed.

"Only four times? That *is* a record. I'll get our daughter and meet you in the car."

"Okay. I won't be long. I just want to make sure

everything is locked up before we leave."

He leaned in for a kiss. "I love you for keeping me in line."

I smiled broadly. "You'd better love me, Holden Dautry!"

"With all my heart, Sugar Plum."

~.~.~.~.~.~

Surprisingly, the first day we spent at Luciana's was actually quite relaxing—she made sure of that. She called in a team of professionals who brought the spa to us. There were massages near the pool, manicures, pedicures, facials, wraps, and later that evening—a private screening of a new movie I'd been dying to see. I was really starting to enjoy having a mother-in-law with more money than all of Canada. The fact that she was being gracious and accommodating made things even better.

I never once had to worry about Kimberly. The nanny Luciana had hired was a dream come true. Her recommendations were quite impressive, as were her stellar credentials. She was highly educated, medically trained, and probably the sweetest person I'd ever met. She doted over Kimberly and saw to her every need, so I found it easy to relax. Of course, when things go that smoothly, it's inevitable that the something unpleasant will be waiting around the corner. The drama started late in the evening of our second night there.

The night began enjoyable enough. Kimberly was fast asleep in the nursery and Luciana, Holden, and I were discussing some of the fonder memories of his childhood until we were interrupted by the ringing of his cell phone. Luciana and I looked on curiously as he muttered a long string of "uh huhs" with the occasional, "I see" tossed in.

"Must be work," I whispered to Luciana. The confused look left her face and she nodded knowingly. Holden disconnected from the call, excitement shined in his eyes.

"That was Jackson. Donovan Guidry says he's ready to talk. But he'll only do it now."

"That's good news," I said. "Do you need to be there?"

"I do, but here's the thing. He refuses to talk to anyone but you."

"Me? Why me?"

"I don't know, but you can bet that you're not going to be there alone."

"We can discuss that on the way there. I'll call Connie to see if she'll mind keeping the baby."

"Why burden Connie? Let Kimberly stay here," Luciana volunteered. "She's already fast asleep and Rebecca's in the room with her should she wake. There's no place where she'll be better protected. I have top-notch security." She flicked her hand towards Dick. "And, surely you'll be back by morning. It makes no sense to do all kinds of unnecessary shuffling, as well as the extra travel for an interview that might last an hour or so at the longest."

I looked at Holden for his approval and once he nodded, I agreed. "Thank you. We appreciate your help. You have our numbers if there are any issues or concerns. Please don't hesitate to call if you need."

"Dear Emily, please don't worry so much. She's going to be fine. You have my word. Would you like for me to summon a driver?"

"No thank you, Mother. We'll manage just fine," Holden said, rising from the sofa.

"Be safe and we'll see you in the morning." She gave Holden a kiss on the cheek, then me an arm-length, double cheek fake kiss. "Dick, please bring their car around."

"Yes, Mrs. Dautry," he said, disappearing before we could protest.

We met Dick on the front steps and then began the drive to Morgan City.

"You know, I could get used to this whole twenty-four/seven valet thing. I said it before, but now more than ever, I can see how it could be easy to settle into this lifestyle," I remarked.

"But think of all the things you'd have to give up to maintain it," Holden said.

"Oh, baby. It was just a random comment. I love our life and I don't want it to change." I reached for his hand and gave it a solid squeeze.

"Good! You scared me for a minute. I thought I was going to have to start forking out money for a live-in masseuse named Dolph or something."

"Would you do that for me?" I asked.

"I'd do anything for you, Emily. You know that. I'll run an ad in the paper tomorrow. Masseuse named Dolph wanted. Must be over seventy-five years old and pass a background check."

I laughed loudly. "Over seventy-five?"

"Can't take any chances," he replied.

We spent the rest of the ride to Morgan City discussing Donovan's sudden change of heart. Holden didn't want me in the room alone with Donovan, but if he was shackled and we were in an interview room where we could be watched, I didn't see a problem. He turned into MCPD's parking lot somewhere around ten-thirty that evening and we found Jackson anxiously pacing up and down. He shook

Holden's hand and then offered me a quick hug.

"Before we go in, tell me how your mom is doing," I requested.

"She's doing really well. I hired a sitter to stay with her. She's very caring and compassionate."

"I'm glad to hear that," I said.

"Thank you. About Donovan—if he does what he says he's going to do, this could be huge. There's no telling what will come from this. He says he's ready to spill his secrets."

"Did he say why he wants to divulge these secrets to me?" I asked.

"He said that he grew fond of you when Brad held you captive. He wanted me to get a prosthetic pregnancy belly for you to wear when he talked to you. Obviously, I refused."

"He's one sick bastard!" Holden snapped. "No way are you going in there by yourself!"

"Would you please calm down, Holden? Jackson, what kind of security precautions will there be?"

"The max. He'll be shackled, cuffed, and I'll have staff right outside the door should he so much as sneeze wrong. You and I will be watching via two-way mirror from the room next door and if he says anything to upset her or she's ready to call it quits, that's it. It's over."

Holden considered what Jackson said, then nodded his head in agreement. "If you feel threatened or you decide you don't want to do this, speak up. We've got enough on him to keep him locked up for a long time. Anything else he confesses is just lagniappe."

"If it gets too intense, I promise I'll end it."

"Ready?" Jackson asked.

I nodded and walked through the thick metal door

he held open. "Let's do this," I muttered under my breath.

They put me in the interrogation room first. Before I took my seat next to the two-way mirror, I checked the bleak, harshly lit room to assure there were no potential weapons or means of escape that may have been missed. I ran my hands under the table, inspected the two chairs in the room, and even gave the walls a quick onceover. Nothing stood out. I took my seat and shifted to one side so Jackson and Holden could have an unobstructed view of Donovan. I turned and offered a quick wave to the mirror to let Jackson and Holden know that I was still ready to do this. I needed to be mentally prepared for whatever might come out of Donovan's mouth, so I quietly meditated until I heard the rustling of metal chains against the concrete floor. He was coming. Slow and steady breaths helped keep me calm as the clanging got louder and louder. The noise stopped outside the doorway. I swallowed hard in an effort to push down the fear.

He looked much the same as the last time I saw him. Still short, fat, and disgusting. It was reassuring for me to know that I held all of the control this time. In fact, the more I pondered that point, the more confident I felt.

The two jailers who escorted him into the room worked diligently to secure his arms to the chair and to double check the integrity of the restraints that held him. Once they were sure that everything was in place, they left the room and stood outside the door.

"So nice to see you again, Miss Boudreaux. Oops, excuse me—Mrs. Dautry. No doubt your husband is nearby. Behind the glass, I'm sure?" he asked, staring blankly into the mirror. His face suddenly lit up. "Yes, behind the glass. Good evening, Sheriff Dautry. Who else do we have back there?"

I knew that he was bluffing. There was no way he could see anything besides the view of himself. "I don't think that matters much. What did you want to talk about?" I asked, getting straight to the point.

"It matters greatly. How nice for you. The two men who were so anxious to make an honest woman out of you, joining forces to put the bad guy away." He cocked back in his seat as far as the chains would allow. "See, here's the rub. One of them had to lose. It hurts really bad to lose—isn't that right, Chief Sonnier?" he said loudly as he looked past me.

"That has no bearing on this conversation. Let's move this along, Donovan. If all you wanted to do was torment Holden and Jackson, you could've done that without dragging me down here."

"True, true. So, what do you want to know?" he asked, finally looking my way.

"Everything," I answered.

"I know a lot, but I hardly know *everything*. Perhaps I should start with a story?"

I shook my head and rolled my eyes. "As long as it explains your actions, you can say whatever you want to," I said brusquely.

"Awww, you should be excited. It's a good one. I promise."

"So just tell the damn story," I snapped.

He laughed. "Give me a minute. I'm trying to think of a good place to start."

I sighed loudly.

"I know! Once upon a time, there was this super successful lawyer who had a slight gambling problem. He needed big money, untraceable money to support his habit. You see, when you start your career as a public defender, you learn all kinds of neat ways to become a better criminal. Then when you become DA, you get to decide who you're going to prosecute and who you aren't. You win friends and eliminate enemies. It was the perfect position to find new recruits. I knew who'd crack easy, and who'd take one for the team."

"Recruits for what?"

"My drug business. Big money with fairly little effort on my part. It's any gamblers dream."

"How many people did you end up recruiting?"

"You'd never believe me."

"Try me."

"By the time I was really established—hundreds," he said with pride. "All neatly organized and willing to follow my every command. Good little soldiers, they were. Don't get me wrong. I started out small. Way small. Then my supplier took notice of the good job I was doing and passed that information on to his boss. Before long, because I could make charges come and go, I was bumped up the ranks and put on the big guy's payroll. I made my way clean to the top."

"How long have you been working for this 'big guy'?"

"I should rephrase. 'Big guy' isn't an accurate term for this genius." He leaned in as close as his restraints would allow. "You think you can just pop into a position like that overnight? It's a game that's been running since before Prohibition."

"What? Are you trying to tell me that one person's been running the biggest drug ring in Louisiana since the 1920's?"

"I didn't say that."

"Sounds like that's what you're trying to say." I said

with a laugh. "Are you so remarkable a person that they would trust *you* to know their secret and no one else? I think you're trying to push the blame elsewhere hoping you'll get a deal. Am I close?"

His eyes squinted and his voice lowered. "You don't know shit."

"Then fill me in. No more of your bullshit stories. Tell me how you hooked up with Brad."

"After that intervening husband of yours locked me up... By the way, well-played to use the whore to get me, Sheriff. ...I bunked next door to the sick bastard, Dautrieve. You know he had to have some serious issues for *me* to call him sick," Donovan commented. "That son of a bitch would lie in his cot at night describing all the things he wanted to do once he got his hands on you."

"Yeah, yeah. I've heard all of that before. Brad's dead and gone."

"But, do you know who made him dead?"

"No, but I assume it has something to do with the Richardsons'."

"That's the bad thing about horny lovers. They'll go anywhere to get a quick piece of ass. They unfortunately wandered into the wrong place at the wrong time."

"Did Colin kill Brad?"

"What! I don't know what story you heard, but honey, that dude only wishes he'd killed Brad. He walked in on Brad trying to do his wife. He did try to get him off of her, but Brad cold-cocked him and that doctor dude was out like a light! Doctor dude didn't get shot until *after* Brad was dead. Dautrieve was getting to be way too much of a liability—too much deviant sex on the brain, so it was decided that he should be disposed of."

I felt sick to my stomach, but tried not to let

Donovan see that he'd upset me.

"So tell me the rest of what happened that night. Was it you who killed Brad?"

"No, those orders came from high up. Here's the deal. After your wedding, we were supposed to off you, so we hid out in the boat shed with the intention of rushing you and the Sheriff as you left that night. Everything was set and ready to go until we got a surprise visit from the boss's right hand man. We were told to disregard the plan and wait for new instructions. As we were talking it out, we were surprised by the chick and Brad volunteered to look after her. Well, he took her into a corner to do his thing and once Brad started in with the knife, the boss's guy had enough. Everything after that happened real fast. The Richardson guy walked in, made a grab for Brad, got knocked the hell out, and the rest you know. Except for the part when the boss's man got so mad that he snapped Brad's neck before he could even manage to get his pants up and then right after that, he popped a round into the doc. These people don't play."

"Why the sudden change of plans? Why am I still here?"

"Oh sweetheart, it's adorable how dense you are. You seriously haven't figured all of this out yet?"

"Obviously not. I'm still talking to you, aren't I? What's the name of the guy who killed Brad?"

Donovan slowly leaned back in his chair; hollow laughter rang throughout the room.

"How did you know we were in Morgan City? Did you have anything to do with the mysterious pictures that popped up in the newspaper?" I angrily asked.

"The ones of you with the mayor? Like I give a shit who you're screwing! No, that wasn't my handiwork, babycakes. And as for knowing where you were, a little birdie told me. Tweet. Tweet." His sardonic laughter rang out once again.

"If you're going to keep toying with me, I'm leaving."

"You're free to leave if you want to. I've done my job. Enough time's gone by."

"What are you talking about?" I asked, flipping around to anxiously look into the mirror before once again giving Donovan my attention. "Enough time for what?" That sinking feeling was hitting like a ton of bricks.

"The time the boss needed to get your daughter."

This time when I turned to face the mirror, desperation and horror covered my now pallid face. Holden and Jackson entered the room before Donovan could get another word out. Holden picked up Donovan by the front of his jumpsuit, lifted him chair and all, and slammed him roughly against the wall.

"What in the hell are you talking about?" he demanded.

Once Holden set the chair back on the ground, Donovan laughed and sank back into his seat. "You're the biggest fool of them all, dumbass! I did what I was supposed to do. I'm done. Finished. Not saying another word. You just as well take me back to my cell now."

"Tell me about my daughter," I pleaded, practically coming across the table. Holden had his cell phone out, repeatedly trying to reach Luciana.

"Mother, if you get this message, call me back immediately!" he said into the phone.

Donovan bent forward and used his fingers to make the sign that he was buttoning his lips, locking them, and then throwing away the key.

"Emily. Holden. I'll deal with this. Go check on

Kimberly. Be careful though. You don't know for sure that anything's wrong. It might be a set up for an ambush. We all know he likes to play games," Jackson said. "I'll call immediately with any news. I expect you to do the same."

"We will," Holden said, taking my hand and dragging me from the room.

"Hey, Emily!" Donovan shouted. I gripped the doorframe to stop Holden. Deep down inside, I prayed that Donovan had had a change of heart and was going to tell me this was all just one of his sick jokes.

"What?" I breathlessly asked.

"I'm going to die. No matter how this went, I knew that I was a dead man. The details of how I was going to die depended on whether I fulfilled this last request or not. If I did it right, a quick death. If I didn't—a slow, torturous one was guaranteed. I'm good at giving torture, not receiving it. Sorry about your baby. You were the hottest pregnant bitch I ever saw. If only you knew how many times I pleasured myself to your image. Thank you for getting me off." He stopped talking to look away and I knew he was mentally reliving it right then. I wanted to vomit. "I really like you, but I did what I had to do. Oh Holden, I have a message for you, too."

Holden had remained relatively silent in the doorway, except for breathing heavily and letting the occasional growl escape as Donovan ranted. "Quit playing games. Unless you're going to give me something solid, we're out of here."

"What I have to say will be really quick," Donovan said, suddenly turning very serious. "Fuck you!" He leaned his head back, laughter spilling from his wide open mouth. He shrugged his shoulders and looked as though he was wiping his mouth on his sleeve. He leaned forward one last time as he dipped his face to his forearms. His face dripped globs of dark red blood and the metal from a razor blade glinted from between his teeth. Copious amounts of the crimson fluid spilled steadily onto the floor, yet Donovan laughed through clenched teeth.

"Get the medic in here!" Jackson yelled into the hall before he gripped Donovan's head to get him to spit out the blade. Instead, Donovan swallowed hard. "Go you two! Go now! I've got this."

It took a long time for me to get my breathing under control and even longer for the trembling to stop. Holden concentrated hard on the road, cruising one hundred and twenty in the straight-aways, but it felt as though we were barely moving. I needed to keep busy, so I continued to try to reach Luciana.

"Shouldn't at least one of the bajillion people on your mother's staff answer the damn phone?" I shouted. I angrily tossed the phone down so I could grip my throbbing forehead.

"Hang in there, Em. We're almost there. Get my gun out of the center console for me, okay?"

I reached in, pushing aside his badge and pulled out the holstered weapon. He set it in his lap then quickly chanced a glance my way. "I'm not going to let anything happen to our baby. You have my word, Emily. We still don't know that anything's wrong. That sick bastard loves to play games and you know as well as I do how massive that mansion is. Hell, it wouldn't surprise me if she forbids the staff to answer the phones after a certain time. And don't forget that it's practically a fortress."

I tried to muster a smile, but a sob escaped instead. "I can't go through another loss—another crisis."

"I can't hold you right now. Baby, please don't cry.

We're here. I'm not going to make you stay outside, even though I think you should. Look at me and listen closely. No matter what, I want you to stay behind me. Do you understand?"

I quickly nodded. All was eerily quiet as we carefully inched our way to the massive, reinforced front doors. Holden punched in a code on the panel near the door and the magnetic lock clicked open. We slid into the house, gently closing the door behind us and listened carefully for any sign of movement. Nothing.

Holden led me through the foyer then through several other rooms. Finally, we made it to the nursery. He gently cracked the door and peered inside, but it was pitch black. He flipped on the light and it took every ounce of willpower to keep from screaming out when I saw Rebecca's lifeless, dilated eyes fixed on me. I rushed to the crib, relieved that I didn't find Kimberly dead in there. It was empty. We took off up the stairs to Luciana's room.

"Wait here," Holden whispered.

"No way," I answered, shaking my head for emphasis.

Knowing that it was no use to argue, he slowly opened the door. Faint moonlight streamed in from the massive row of windows, enough to see the thick puddles of congealed liquid on the floor. A pair of feet stuck out from the edge of the bed. My breath caught. We carefully edged closer to the unmoving body. Closer—a satin hem from a robe. Closer—a thin, female figure. Closer—long, dark hair spilled out all around. Closer—massive amounts of blood collected under her prone body.

Holden stooped down and touched the shoulder of the victim. "Mother?" he softly whispered. No response. He took a deep breath then moved to slowly turn the body.

He let out a garbled swear as he let it go. The body thumped against the floor. "It's not her. It's one of the housekeepers."

The silence was cut by the faint hum of something familiar. I listened hard trying to place it, but my brain refused to cooperate. It was definitely coming from outside and it was getting louder by the second. A super-bright light shined through the bedroom windows, temporarily blinding us.

"It's a helicopter," I said, jetting toward the door. Holden caught up and pulled me behind him. We slipped and slid across the marble floors of the upper level until we made it to the carpeted stairs. I ran like the wind.

We burst out of the back doors just in time to see the helicopter dip down below the tree line in the far corner near the cement wall. Holden and I were in a full run headed towards the whirling blades of the machine. Past the pool, past the guest house, through the garden... My lungs were on fire, but I wasn't about to stop. I willed my legs to move faster, and just as I got to an area where I could see the helicopter clearly, it began to hover overhead.

"No!" I screamed, dropping to my knees. "No! Our baby! Where's our baby!"

Holden continued toward the helicopter pointing his gun at the pilot.

"Don't do it, son," a voice said over the helicopter's loud speaker. "You don't want to risk hurting the baby. She's better off with me and you know it. This is for the best."

The spotlight shut off, the helicopter climbed higher, and Holden and I were left in the dark...alone. Without Kimberly. Without our baby. My cries tore through the night only to be matched by Holden's own heartbroken pleas.

"How could she? How could she take our baby! Kimberly! Bring my daughter back!" He sank to the ground next to me and wrapped his arms around my shoulders. Together we sobbed in the dank night air. After the initial shock of it wore off and our tears had been shed, we got angry—very angry.

"I swear to God, I'm going to find her Emily! And when I do, I'm going to kill her with my own two hands! It won't be a fast death either! She will pay for this, Emily. I swear I'm going to make her pay," Holden vowed as he held my damp, puffy face in his hands.

"Not if I kill her first," I said, emotionally exhausted.

"Let's go. Okay?" he asked, helping me to stand so he could pull my shivering body into his arms.

"Find our baby, Holden. Please, find our baby" I pleaded.

"I will. It's hard to think clearly right now, but I'm going to get her back," he confided, stepping away from me so he could pace to clear his head. He started to rattle off a list of things to do. "Call Bert. Get him out here with some detectives. I'll call Jackson. I'll have him use every resource he's got to get something rolling. After that, I'm going to put in some calls to a few people I know who might be of help. I've got this, Emily."

"I know you do, baby. I know you're going to do everything you can to get her back." I dug the cell phone from my pocket and dialed the number, trying desperately to shake the breathless, kicked in the gut feeling.

"Bert? It's Emily. I'm sorry to call so late, but Holden and I need you. Can you meet us at Luciana's mansion right away?" That's what I wanted to say, but what actually came out was pure gibberish. Bert passed the phone to Connie who was able to piece together enough of my rambling to relay the message.

I made my call. Now I just needed to wait. Torturous, mind-numbing, heartbreaking waiting. *Oh, my sweet Kimberly. Please be okay.*

<u>The Green Bayou Series</u>

Going Home: A Green Bayou Novel Book One

Awakenings: A Green Bayou Novel Book Two

Déjà Vu: A Green Bayou Novel Book Three

Unforeseen: A Green Bayou Novel Book Four

Deceived: A Green Bayou Novel Book Five

Vengeance: A Green Bayou Novel Book Six
(Coming Soon)

ABOUT THE AUTHOR

Rhonda Dennis lives in South Louisiana with her husband, Doyle and her son, Sean. She is currently working on the next book in the Green Bayou series. Rhonda would love to hear from you. Visit her website for more information. www.rhondadennis.net

Or write to her at:

Rhonda Dennis
P.O. Box 2148
Patterson, LA 70392

To like me, follow me, or leave a review:

Facebook: The Green Bayou Novels
Twitter: @Greenbayoubooks
Goodreads Author
WordPress Blog: Green Bayou Novels